paper books

Sarah Gertrude Millin

God's Stepchildren

Introduced by Tony Voss

AD. DONKER / PUBLISHER

AD. DONKER (PTY) LTD
A subsidiary of Donker Holdings (Pty) Ltd
P O Box 41021
Craighall
2024

First published 1924
First paperbook edition 1986

ISBN 0 86852 074 8

Printed and bound by Creda Press (Pty) Ltd, Cape Town

CONTENTS

PREFACE

God's Stepchildren, Sarah Gertrude Millin's fifth novel, was first published by Constable's in 1924, when the author was thirty-six years old.[1] But it was its publication, in a revised and trimmed version, in the United States some months later, which established Millin as a celebrity and confirmed her as a novelist. For thirty years Millin was South Africa's leading literary figure, the confidante of aristocrats and politicians.

At least since the time of Thomas Pringle (1789– 1836), miscegenation has been a recurring theme of South African English writing: Millin had touched on the theme in her earliest novels (and was to return to it later). Her obsessive treatment of the generations of descendants of the Reverend Andrew Flood in *God's Stepchildren* was suggested by a reviewer of her previous novel, *Adam's Rest*:

The slightly 'Coloured' present a village problem to which we have no analogy in England. Miss [*sic*] Millin treats it so sympathetically and without prejudice, that we hope she will return to the subject some day at greater length.[2]

But, as her biographer points out, Millin's treatment was neither sympathetic nor without prejudice. While she appears to accept the individual pathos (rather than tragedy) of the person of mixed blood, she sees miscegenation itself as socially foolish and disastrous; *evil*: different races or 'bloods' are, in and of themselves, superior or inferior — the mixing or contamination of bloods is indulged in by inferior individuals, and the strain of dark (weak, evil) blood never disappears from the 'stock'.

In an essay on 'Race-Mixture and Native Policy in South Africa', published in 1934, Professor R.F.A. Hoernlé attempted to answer the question 'What is the "philosophy" . . . which lies beneath the accepted South African attitude against race-mixture?':

We can, I think, recognise three elements within it, which may be conveniently distinguished as:

a) the ideal of race purity;
b) the ideal of race dominance;
c) the ideal of maintenance of white civilisation and culture . . .

The argument . . . assumes that there are distinct human 'races', or, better, 'stocks'; that these stocks can be graded as superior and inferior; that the measure of such superiority and inferiority is white civilisation, which must be regarded as the 'highest' so far created by any human stock and the starting point for all further advance.

In short, the basis of culture is biological, it varies with the innate qualities of different human stocks. Culture is a function of race.[3]

In terms of South Africa, as Millin understood it, this means that weak and misguided white men have mated with idle and sensual brown women. *God's Stepchildren* returns again and again to these ideas. The 'pure' white contributors to the generations of the Floods are weak and decadent, and are presented by Millin with undisguised revulsion: the Reverend Andrew Flood (pp. 21–2) and Mr Lindsell (p. 120). Other races are referred to in terms of stereotype

8

and caricature: 'the grotesque development which was the Hottentot ideal of beauty . . .' (p. 47), 'a bowlegged Indian' (p. 199). The bottom of the hierarchy of races is with 'the aboriginal' (p. 127), near 'to the African earth' (p. 128). In *God's Stepchildren*, the latest of the Flood line is Barry Lindsell. Millin makes Barry's experience in the First World War a test of his 'whiteness'. Is he a real 'white man'?

It was not till the end of 1915 that Barry crossed over to France. He was back within three months. Shell shock. In the middle of 1916 he went out again. And in even a shorter time than before he was once more in England. Shell shock. He knew it now. It was no use. He couldn't stand it. His spirit would not uphold his cringing flesh. His flesh shrivelled back upon his fainting spirit. He had tried telling himself to be white, he had besought God for strength — nothing helped. They might give it any name they liked. Barry suffered from fear. (p. 282)

Millin's racial views, late flowerings of nineteenth-century rationalism and Social Darwinism, which have lost all touch with the 'noble savage' were expressed more consciously and dealt with more honestly, in *The South Africans*, first published in 1926. In addition she there expressed views that were part of what J.H. Hofmeyr called in 1927 'the vogue of Spenglerism'.[4] Millin repeated with approval the words of Anthony Trollope in 1877: 'South Africa is a country of black men — and not of white men. It has been so; it is so; and it will be so.'[5] And she concluded *The South Africans* with an echo of her earlier novel: 'There shall be no brotherhood between black and white. At best, perhaps, a step-brotherhood. No more.' (pp. 323—4)

The violence of Millin's racial views is tempered or

9

disguised in *God's Stepchildren* in that some are ascribed to individual characters, some to the general South African public, while still others are expressed by the oracular, knowing, authorial voice. The narrative form of the novel is chronicle, in which each generation is focused on one member of the line of Andrew Flood, coming down inexorably to the person of Barry Lindsell, who, in a symbolic gesture, renounces wife and child and returns to the mission field of his ancestor among the brown people, exactly a century after the Reverend Andrew Flood himself. Barry, in the argument of the novel, is a tragic (pathetic?) figure: weak and impure, he is yet noble (if foolish) in accepting his 'sin'(p. 326) and making his dramatic (if futile) sacrifice.

The authority which Millin's narrative claims for itself is at least partly based on this chronicle's framework in a version of South African history. Significant moments in the Flood generations are located with reference to crucial socio-political events: the Boer emigration of the 1830s and 1840s (p. 89), Adam Kok's trek (p. 103), the discovery of diamonds (p. 108), the rinderpest (p. 310), the wars of 1899—1902 (p. 255) and 1914—18 (p. 281).[6] But the novel has little genuine feel for either historical circumstance or historical perspective. There is no conviction, authenticity or actuality in the picture of the social, economic or cultural life of any group — Hottentots, farmers, Griquas — until we reach the parochial life of Edith in the Cape Town suburb of Gardens in the last chapters of the novel. Edith is the figure closest to the author: it is Edith who acknowledges, at a revealing moment, the quasi-divine authority of the omniscient narrator. Edith has forced Barry to

10

acknowledge his 'blood' to his young wife, Nora:

She could not understand herself. Now, suddenly, she thought of Nora's pretty affectionateness; she remembered how Barry had run to her, in his frightened childhood, as to a saviour. The tears started to her pale old eyes. 'Oh God, why am I like that?' she cried in her heart. 'What is this twistedness in me that won't let me be good? Why do I have to make suffering for others, even if it causes me to suffer myself?'

It struck her all at once with an irony that dried the tears in her eyes that God would be able to answer that question. He, too, had created suffering for which He must suffer. (p. 291)

As an interesting contemporary review expressed it: 'Even Barry, himself, might have . . . [achieved and held] an unquestioned place in white society . . . but for Edith's interference'.[7]

Millin's disposition of this narratorial omniscience is another element on which the novel relies for conviction. This is often deployed in a melodramatic way: 'He had recently heard a tremendous sermon preached about the essential equality of all human beings, whatever their colour, in the eyes of their Creator. It was, throughout Britain, the creed of the moment.' (p. 24) 'In the end, however, they listened to him with yawning indifference, and, in the night, as if he had never spoken, they danced again.' (p. 43)

From the perspective of 1986, then, *God's Stepchildren* seems a prejudiced, ignorant and vulgar piece of work. Yet, when first published, in 1924, it was well received critically and, especially in the United States, popularly. Although not at first popular in her home country — only with the publication of *The South Africans* in 1926 did Millin become a household name in South Africa — *God's Stepchildren* gave her authority. In the 1950s the novel was re-

11

published in a South African/Rhodesian edition, with a new preface, and went through more than one printing. And Millin's ideas on race, which threaten to alienate the contemporary reader, are not, in the words of J.M. Coetzee, 'a hotchpotch of colonial prejudices but the reflection of respectable scientific and historical thought, only barely out of date in her time'.

In order to understand this novel's original and, to some extent, continued popularity one has to re-imagine the context in which it first appeared.

The novel's obsession with race, filtered as it is through a variously detached narrator, was open to a variety of interpretations. Millin herself said that her title was ironic rather than sentimental,[8] but it is easy enough to read *God's Stepchildren* as a vindication of white supremacy and racial segregation. The '20s was a decade of widespread concern with race and 'blood' in Europe and America. The rise of 'black' culture, of jazz and the influence of African art on European and American forms, led to a counter-assertion of white (Aryan?) culture. In the United States in the '20s membership of the Ku-Klux-Klan rose to four million: a prohibition-congressman claimed 'We are making the last stand of the great white race'.[9] In Europe the '20s was the decade of the initial rise of fascism and national socialism.

In South Africa, a chronically race-haunted polity, the '20s were notable: the decade opened with the African miners' strike in 1920, continued with the Bulhoek massacre in 1921 and the white miners' strike and Rand Revolt in 1922. It was the decade of Clements Kadalie and the ICU. In 1927 were passed both the Colour Bar Act (which forbade blacks 'the use of machinery and robbed them of the opportunity for any economic advancement')[10] and Tielman Roos's Immorality Act 'which made extra-marital relations between Europeans and Africans an offence. It did not prohibit marriage between the races (this being in any case extremely rare) and it did not affect illicit relations between Coloureds and Europeans.'[11]

In 1930, Dr A.B. Xuma summed up the South African situation:

Throughout our country today, there seems to be a spirit of excitement, of fear, of unrest, and of uncertainty. Everywhere our European community seems to have a nightmare of the rising black masses encroaching upon their position of privilege . . .[12]

On the English South African literary front *God's Stepchildren* (which appeared in the same year as *The Flaming Terrapin*) shared the '20s with *Voorslag*, Stephen Black and *Turbott Wolfe*. William Plomer's novel deals as explicitly and as programatically with miscegenation as does Millin's, but the temptation to categorise Plomer as a liberal and Millin as a conservative has obscured their similarities. *Turbott Wolfe* shares *God's Stepchildren*'s strange combination of fascination and revulsion with race and sex.[13] Even Professor Hoernlé, in the essay of 1934 referred to earlier, although he dissects and refutes the South African philosophy against race-mixture, allows that, in order for debate to continue, racial intermarriage should be forbidden. This reservation reflected the views not only of liberal whites but also of certain black leaders:

. . . I do not suggest for a moment that there should be INTER-MIXTURE OF THE RACES in any shape or form. I should be the last to advocate inter-marriage between the races. I love my race and its colour, and I am just as proud of it as the European is of his. And when I say the African is determined to keep the purity of his race, if only he could secure the assistance of the State to protect his women-folk against the low-class white men, I am voicing the feeling of every sensible and intelligent African.[14]

Millin's particular treatment of miscegenation, her personal racism, was perhaps influenced by her personal circumstances. Although not religiously active, she had a strong sense of her own racial identity, and her attitude to other peoples may have been conditioned by the exclusiveness and formality of orthodox Jewish social life. In South Africa the Liebsons were *parvenus*, brought here on the wave of the diaspora that rose in Tsarist Russia in the late nineteenth century. This too may have contributed to the author's defensiveness about her own racial place in South Africa.

The limitation of *God's Stepchildren* and of Millin's politico-racial views generally lies in the espousal of 'race' as a God-given irreducible determinant: miscegenation is to be feared because its process and issue would make necessary the acceptance of class (rather than race or culture) as a category of social judgement and action.[15] In South Africa in 1986 (when the repeal of the Immorality Act precedes the repeal of the Group Areas Act), we can only take *God's Stepchildren* seriously in a historical context and as a warning, and as a possible index of how little progress we have made. As has been recently and sensationally reported, and as George Findlay wrote in 1936:

'. . . among the 1,9 million Europeans there are today at least 733 000 coloured people "passing".' (p. 44)

In 1926, two years after *God's Stepchildren* had first appeared, Olive Schreiner's life-work novel *From Man to Man* was posthumously published. That work too deals, in part, with miscegenation. The heroine's husband fathers a daughter, named, with significant historical allusion, Saartje, with a coloured housemaid. The heroine (Schreiner's spokeswoman) does not reject the daughter; rather she takes the child into her re-constituted family. It is a gesture which Sarah Gertrude Millin was incapable of imagining.

Tony Voss
University of Natal
Durban

Notes

1 There is a biography of Millin by Martin Rubin, *Sarah Gertrude Millin: a South African Life* (Johannesburg: Ad. Donker, 1977). See also J.P.L. Snyman, *The Works of Sarah Gertrude Millin* (Johannesburg, 1955). W. D. Maxwell-Mahon's entry in the *DSAB* (vol. IV) is a judicious 'brief life'.

2 Quoted in Rubin, p. 78, from Millin's autobiography *The Night is Long* (Faber, 1941). The notice appeared in the *Westminster Gazette*.

3 In *Western Civilization and the Natives of South Africa*, ed. I. Schapera, (Routledge, 1934), pp. 269—280: pp. 269—70. For a comprehensive and subtle account of Millin's racial ideas and their relation to the thought of her time see J.M. Coetzee, 'Blood, Flaw, Taint, Degeneration: the Case of Sarah Gertrude Millin', *English Studies in Africa*, vol. 23 (1980), pp. 41—58. Coetzee describes the Millin of the '20s as a 'cautious liberal'; Nadine Gordimer's review of Rubin's

biography was headlined 'A Brilliant Bigot' (*Rand Daily Mail*).

4 Jan H. Hofmeyr, *The Open Horizon: Speeches and Addresses . . . 1924–1929* (Johannesburg? n.d.). The phrase comes from 'Nationalism and Internationalism' an address delivered to the Pretoria Rotary Club, 27 February 1927, p. 55.

5 Millin, *The South Africans*, 1926 (reprint London: Constable, 1937), pp. 3–4.

6 See Michael Wade, 'Myth, Truth and the South African Reality in the Fiction of Sarah Gertrude Millin', *Journal of Southern African Studies*, 1 (1974), pp. 100–112.

7 Mrs R.F.A. Hoernlé, anthropologist and wife of the Professor, in the *Rand Daily Mail* of 31 May 1924. She admired the book and seems to share some of Millin's general racial ideas, but hers is a more obviously liberal humanitarian attitude. She describes Millin as pursuing '. . . the thread of . . . tragedy through four generations, painting with sure swift strokes, a vivid picture of how life after life is broken in the struggle to escape from the taint of colour and achieve a place among white folks.' Yet Mrs Hoernlé observed that the real interest of the incidents 'lies in their impact on individuals'. This tension between the group emphasis of social (or racial) theory and the individual emphasis of the novel as fiction is also noted by Coetzee. Mrs Hoernlé is critical of Millin's history, anthropology and implicit aversion to 'the coloured people'.

8 *The Night is Long*, p. 149.

9 Oscar Handlin, *The American People, the History of a Society* (Harmondsworth, 1963), pp. 369–370. In a review of three US novels, 'Literary Hope for America: the Vigour of the Younger Writers' (*Rand Daily Mail*, 30 September 1925), Millin wrote: 'The world has lately been laughing at America over the Dayton trial. But together with Fundamentalism, the Ku-Klux-Klan, Ellis Island and Jazz Music, there are other aspects of hundred per cent Americanism.'
Of the three novels reviewed, Millin praises particularly *Birthright* by T.S. Stribling, the story of a Harvard-educated negro who returns to the South 'to labour among his people', but in the end, in Millin's account, he 'succumbs to his destiny', to 'the weakness within him'. The possible parallels with *God's Stepchildren* are interesting.

10 Clements Kadalie, 'Open Letter to Blackpool', *The New Leader*, 30 September 1927; repeated in Karis, Thomas and Gwendolen M. Carter, eds., *From Protest to Challenge: a Documentary History of African Politics in South Africa*, 4 vols (Stanford: Hoover Institution Press, 1978), vol. 1, p. 329.

11 Edward Roux, *Time Longer than Rope* (Madison: University of Wisconsin Press, 1966), p. 377.

12 'Bridging the Gap between Black and White in South Africa', address to the Conference of European and Bantu Christian Student Associations at Fort Hare, 27 June — 3 July 1930: in Karis and Carter, vol. 1, p. 219.

13 *Turbott Wolfe* appeared in the same year as D.H. Lawrence's *The Plumed Serpent*.

14 R.V. Selope Thema, 'The Race Problem', *The Guardian*, September 1922: Karis and Carter, vol. 1, pp. 213—214.

15 'Genetic considerations are emphasised only when they imperil the chances of environmental inheritance . . .' George Findlay, *Miscegenation: a Study of the Biological Sources of the Inheritance of the South African European Population* (Pretoria, 1936), p. 12.

Findlay's pamphlet is an admirably sober account of its topic, stressing clearly that the blood aversion of public opinion to miscegenation has social rather than metaphysical or any other causes. The progeny of primary miscegenation, in Findlay's account, finds that 'the traits that come to him via the germ cell, appearances and so forth, determine his opportunities in many ways, but his failure to inherit a consistent and definite tradition is the important factor. He is indeed a clanless, classless being of indeterminable potentialities.' (pp. 9—10)

BOOK I
THE ANCESTOR

CHAPTER I

1

COMING to the Cape in the year 1821 to spread the Word among the Hottentots, the Reverend Andrew Flood met on board ship a girl whom, it was vouchsafed to him, the Lord had destined to be the partner of his life and labours. Her name was Mary, and she had dark blue eyes, set deeply under delicate brows, and her eyelids were the eyelids of a Madonna.

Yet when the Rev. Andrew spoke to her of his holy aspirations as a preliminary to offering her a share in them, her response was a little vague; and, whatever he might do, he never seemed to be able to clear away this vagueness from their intercourse.

He finally parted from her in Cape Town under the impression—both worrying and comforting—that she did not know what was in his heart.

But, of course, she knew.

2

The truth was that Mary Keeble did not find the Rev. Andrew Flood so attractive that she wanted to spend her life with him labouring among unclad savages.

He was a tall, bony man, with hollow blue eyes, wistful and yet fervent; his teeth projected slightly, so

21

that he had difficulty in closing his mouth; and his chin, strained with the effort of assisting his lips to meet, was pricked with little holes. The bones of his long face were prominent, and they seemed to move visibly when he became agitated, as happened very often. His skin was naturally pale, but it was almost always flushed with embarrassed ardour. He had long nervous hands and long feet. He was clean shaven; and, already, at the age of twenty-eight, his light brown hair was thinning upwards in a point on each side of his high, narrow forehead, in the shape of a capital M. He wore a black coat with tails, tight trousers strapped under his instep, and a white tie. . . .

He was not a clever man, and he knew people did not consider him clever; but he believed that was because they did not understand the essential mystery of his being. He often felt that if they could see the wonderful things that went on in his mind, while his speech so lamentably failed him, they would be touched and surprised and impressed. He was anxious to touch and surprise and impress people.

Always at night, before he went to sleep, he had the habit of rehearsing between himself and some person or other, who happened at the moment particularly to interest him, conversations that never afterwards took place. In these conversations he displayed a kind of sorrowful wit, and made confidences which showed him in a noble and pathetic light. His auditor never seemed to reply, but only listened with a growing sympathy. The Rev. Andrew would go on breeding sentences, saying things and saying things, showing himself now in this light, now in that light; the silent auditor would begin to fade away; the same sentences would come round again and again; the Rev. Andrew would find himself either falling asleep comforted by his illusions, or, on the contrary, lying fiercely awake throbbing with unsolved and insoluble miseries.

3

He had a certain quality of imagination. He yearned towards nobility of thought and deed. He felt it would be glorious to give the boots from his feet to a beggar, and walk barefoot; to suffer a great misunderstanding in silence; to pray in fasting isolation.

Yet, when it came to the point, he could not even summon the initiative to go up to a beggar in the street and speak to him, let alone offer him the boots from his feet; as for misunderstandings, he no sooner felt himself misunderstood than he burnt to explain and explain; and, so far from fasting in isolation, he had never yet dared to resist the stern call of his mother to her punctual meal-times:

"Andrew!"

"Yes, mother?"

"Andrew! ... Andrew! ... How often must I call you?"

"Yes, mother. Just coming."

Impossible to tell her that he had determined to fast!

4

But he had suddenly, within a month of being ordained, offered himself to a mission society that was sending emissaries to savage Africa.

He had departed in a glow of exaltation.

He saw himself burnt out with religion and sacrifice, worn but triumphant, leading souls to God. Leading the souls of his poor black brothers to God! His brothers!

He had recently heard a tremendous sermon preached about the essential equality of all human beings, whatever their colour, in the eyes of their Creator.

It was, throughout Britain, the creed of the moment.

CHAPTER II

I

HE fell in love with Mary Keeble as soon as he saw her. She was coming out to Cape Town with her uncle, a doctor. She was leaning over the ship's rail, gazing vaguely into distance. She was wearing a white muslin dress, cut low in the neck, with ruchings and flouncings on the skirt, short puffed-out sleeves, and a fichu across the shoulders. Her feet were shod in sandals laced above the ankle. Her fair hair was dressed high on her head. She had been sea-sick for a fortnight (it had not been smooth sailing in the little three-masted, five-hundred-ton vessel) and was looking wan—like a little white flower, the Rev. Andrew traditionally told himself, as he walked up and down past her. Up and down for nearly another week without finding any means of approach, without knowing more about her than her name, though at night he inevitably rehearsed, long and mournfully, heroic speeches to her. He wished she knew why he was coming to the Cape. He wished it so desperately that one day he suddenly walked over and stood beside her, and said in a husky whisper:

"Miss Keeble!"

She turned towards him, a faint smile in her deep-set eyes.

"You are the Rev. Mr. Flood," she responded.

She knew about him! His fervent eyes glowed, his face reddened, and his hands trembled.

"Yes."

B

25

"Is this your first voyage to the Cape?" she encouraged him.

"Yes."

He struggled unavailingly to say something more.

"Shall we sit down?" Mary suggested.

He stalked across the deck beside her. They seated themselves, and he clasped his bony knees with his thin hands, and rocked himself backwards and forwards.

"You have heard," he said at last, "about my mission?"

"No. Tell me."

"To the Hottentots."

"To the Hottentots?"

He nodded his head with sombre pride.

"Only one white man has been among that tribe before me. He died a few months ago. I am taking his place."

"Where is it?"

He stood up unexpectedly and went away.

Presently he returned carrying a linen-backed roll. It was a map. He sat down again, opened it, and showed her Cape Town. He moved his bony, slightly crooked forefinger up the coast line till it rested on the mouth of a river. "The Orange River," he said. "They also call it the Black River, or, in the native language, the Nu Gariep." He traced the river to a tributary. "The Yellow River—the Gij Gariep. Somewhere about here I shall be."

"What is the place called?"

"Canaan."

"And is it a land of milk and honey?" she smiled.

"I cannot say. I know nothing more than I have told you. I only know——" he stopped; his heart was beating so violently that he could not breathe.

26

She looked at him, waiting.

"I only know that God needs me there," he whispered.

The tears started to his eyes as he finished speaking. He was thrilled with exaltation, in a mood when a man might go smiling to the stake.

"I hope that your mission will be successful," she said after a moment.

"It will be," he answered with sudden fierce confidence. "It will be."

2

Every day after that during the next nine weeks—the dammed flood having burst its restraints—he spoke to her either about himself or his mission. Sometimes she was sorry for him; and sometimes she even thought he was heroic, but, in the end, she could not bear to listen to him, and whenever she saw him approaching her she would look round in helpless desperation for some means of escape. By the time when, nearly three months after they had left England, they at last found themselves facing Table Mountain with its white table-cloth of clouds, she really hated him. And yet, so obsessed was he that, even at the very moment of disembarkation, he was still urging himself on her attention. He had no time to see the Hottentots (brothers to those distant, more savage people to whom he had come to minister) who were swarming around them. But as he pressed forward to help her into the carriage that had come to meet her his throat tightened. "Perhaps," he whispered. "Perhaps——"

The Hottentot slave who was driving the carriage flicked his whip at the team of horses.

"We shall meet again," said Mary Keeble impatiently, and turned to ask her uncle some question about her baggage.

The Rev. Andrew stood beside his boxes, staring after the departing vehicle.

3

The missionary who had come to meet him found the Rev. Andrew a quiet and abstracted companion as he sat beside him in the carriage pointing out the features of the town, and asking him questions about affairs at home and the voyage out. Enormous Dutchmen, in blue cloth jackets and trousers and tall hats, passed them in the street, each followed by a small Hottentot slave holding an umbrella over his master's head; and the Rev. Andrew looked at the curious procession with vague eyes. He had never before to-day seen a Hottentot, and his life was to be spent among Hottentots in future, and yet he could discover in himself no interest in these little yellow, monkey-like people, with their triangular faces (Mongolian in type), and peppercorned heads, whose little keen black eyes good-humouredly, and yet mischievously, regarded him as he passed down the street—the main street of Cape Town, the Heeren-gracht, the Gentlemen's Walk.

His companion mentioned the names of the owners of the houses on each side of them—tall, flat-faced, flat-roofed white houses, with open sun stoeps in front, on which stout Dutch vrouws, in white muslins, sat drinking coffee with their cavaliers.

"You will want to rest in Cape Town awhile" he said at last, "before making the journey North. You seem fatigued."

"Fatigued?" repeated the Rev. Andrew. "Fatigued? Yes. I must be. Yes."

28

His face was, indeed, quite white.

The other looked at him curiously.

"But you are otherwise well?" he asked. "Canaan is a desolate place, as you have doubtless been informed. There is not, within a hundred miles, another station, or another white man."

"So I have heard," the Rev. Andrew answered indifferently. "But, thank you, my health is satisfactory."

There was a little silence. Then the Rev. Andrew remarked, his eyes straight before him on the horses' heads:

"Was my predecessor a married man?"

"He was an old man. A widower. He had a grown-up family in England."

"But do any of the missionaries take their wives with them to these outlying stations?"

"Not frequently." The Cape Town missionary looked at the Rev. Andrew's bony profile with the projecting teeth, over which the lips hardly met.

"But you are not married yourself," he commented.

The Rev. Andrew shook his head.

"Nor betrothed?"

The Rev. Andrew shook his head again.

"I was—merely wondering," he answered.

4

He saw Mary Keeble once more before he left Cape Town. He sat in the corner of a large drawing-room, impatiently silent, while a Mary he hardly recognized, a gay and animated Mary that had never before been revealed to him, made pretty badinage with several red and blue coated young men belonging to His Majesty's services. Now and then she would come over to him, offering refreshment, asking him if she might not present somebody, conversing determinedly, but hurriedly, and he would morosely refuse all her kindnesses; and, presently, as if having dispensed a tedious duty, she would return with renewed eagerness to her more congenial companions. He stayed there in his corner for over an hour, speaking to no one; but at last he rose in his usual awkward manner, and, drawing Mary to the door, held out his hand in farewell.

"I have to leave Cape Town soon," he told her, keeping her hand desperately in his. "I may never return."

He stood gazing at her with his lost-looking blue eyes.

"I must see you again," he said then in a voice louder than he knew, so that Mary blushed in sudden discomfort. "But alone. There is something I have to tell you. When can I come?"

Mary considered, hesitating. She pitied the Rev. Andrew Flood, but she was utterly wearied of him.

"I am very seldom alone here," she answered at last.

"I ask you to be—for my sake," he insisted.

She glanced involuntarily from her position at the door to her friends waiting curiously for her.

"I shall let you know," she answered hurriedly. . . .

The Rev. Andrew Flood never again saw Mary Keeble. He received no message from her before he left; and when, in despair, he called, she was not at home.

CHAPTER III

I

LIKE an endless dream it seemed to the Rev. Andrew Flood, that long journey on a waggon drawn by sixteen oxen, with a little Hottentot interpreter, and two other Hottentots who acted as driver and leader to the oxen, that journey which he took across the desolate veld.

It was the month of December—the hottest summertime. The sun poured down a flood of heat and light; the earth lay burning beneath it, swamped in fire; the air danced and quivered as to the music of a thousand cicadas. The oxen moved slowly along, unheeding, apparently, the long whip of the driver. The Rev. Andrew Flood sat under the hood of his waggon in his close black clothes, his long, tight, black trousers strapped under his instep, sweat pouring down his body, his skin red and prickly.

They seemed to be getting no further. But, gradually, as the days passed, mountains and hills and water and green vegetation and sudden patches of wild bright flowers and an occasional Boer farmhouse became things of memory; and they proceeded unvaryingly along a flat desert land, with hills retreating to the horizon as they advanced towards them, where the sun was fiercer than ever before, and the earth lay beneath it, dry under its whitened stubble, like a skeleton.

The three Hottentots, wearing their sheep-skins— their karosses—to protect them against the sun, as in winter they wore them in defence against the cold, only turning then the hairy side inwards; with the little skin pouches round their necks (they kept in those pouches their knives, pipes, tobacco, charms, and the drug called *dagga*); with their feet bare and insensitive to the burning earth as they would be to coals of fire even—the little, wizened-faced Hottentots danced along their native soil—their Karroo, as, for its dryness, they significantly called it—happy.

The Rev. Andrew, in his stuffy black clericals, sat, smouldering towards exhaustion, in the waggon.

At dusk they outspanned. Then the Rev. Andrew would descend and stiffly walk up and down to stretch his legs; the oxen would wander about among the stubble searching for food; and the Hottentots would make coffee. They would put three stones together in the shape of a triangle; they would fill the little enclosure thus made with dry twigs from the withered-looking Karroo bushes that were the only growth of the land; and sit squatting on their haunches waiting for the water to boil. Then when it had boiled and they had put the coffee in, they would plunge a burning twig into the kettle, as they had seen their Boer masters do, to settle the coffee grounds.

The interpreter, whose civilized language was a mixture of Dutch and English (he habitually called the missionary "Mijnheer") and whose name had been given him by his original Dutch owner, was also the Rev. Andrew's personal attendant; and he would bring him the coffee.

"Mijnheer!"

The Rev. Andrew would lift his aching head.

"Will Mijnheer take coffee?"

"Thank you, Titus."

He would sit down on a box, and eat the game the

32

Hottentots themselves shot, perhaps some dried fruit, a biscuit, a little preserve . . .

And so the days, the weeks, passed; and gradually a sense of peace began to steal into his heart. He awoke to interest in his Hottentot companions, asked them questions about their language and customs and beliefs, even accepted the advice of Titus to go without his coat.

In the evenings that were cool, he would wander about in the neighbourhood of the fires with which, for fear of wild animals, they surrounded their camp, looking at the stars, brighter and more numerous than he was accustomed to know them, making plans for the betterment of those savage souls entrusted to his care, sometimes even exalted by his sense of personal loss.

Occasionally he would see three figures crouching forward, their heads on the ground, a strange acrid smell floating in smoke on the air around them. He took it that they were smoking some native form of tobacco.

But next day they would go about dazed and stupid, and sometimes there would be sudden vicious quarrels.

The Rev. Andrew had not been warned about dagga-smoking.

2

After seven weeks' journeying by ox-waggon, along tracks that none but a Hottentot would have recognized, they arrived one day before a broad, swollen, brown river. Trees fringed it on either side, and great, shiny, black stones here and there edged it. Behind the trees rose a low range of hills, and the veld here (for there had been rain a few days ago) was a summer green, covered with shrubs and wild flowers—little scented white flowers that looked like jasmine but grew close to the ground; and others like shrunken yellow daffodils; and still others like violets and buttercups. There were bushes with small red stone-berries, sweet at first taste, but leaving a tight feeling on the tongue and a weight on the chest afterwards; and these the Hottentots gathered and ate, and also various roots, and pods filled with what looked like small green peas. . . .

"It is not far now," Titus told the missionary. "Tonight, when the sun goes down, we shall see Canaan."

And in truth, when the sun set, Titus raised his small, claw-like brown hand, and pointed.

"Canaan," he said.

"Where?" asked the Rev. Andrew.

"Mijnheer does not see?"

The Rev. Andrew shook his head, and the Hottentot smiled.

"The white people have not eyes like the Hottentots and Bushmen."

It was a circle of about thirty reed huts—huts looking like big hives—that finally met the Rev. Andrew's eyes. As they came nearer, he saw that the huts acted as a barrier for the cattle kraaled within the circle. These, then, were not utterly wild Hottentots.

But when the people emerged to welcome the arrival of the waggon, he noticed that they did not altogether resemble the Hottentots he had hitherto seen. They were taller, not so wizened and wrinkled and monkey-like as the Cape Colony Hottentots, but equally Mongolian in type. Although he had been told that these were a tribe called the Korannas, he had not before realized that there were different kinds of Hottentots.

34

He tried not to feel shocked and embarrassed as, following the presentation of the chief, women, laden with beads, their bodies (characteristically protuberant behind) reddened with ochre, their heads stiff with grease (as were those of the men, too), a small apron of cords suspended from their waists in front, and a larger apron of skin at the back, approached him in greeting.

One woman, however, wore some sort of European female garment. She advanced with self-conscious dignity. Titus introduced her.

"This is Cachas," he said, "the servant of Mijnheer that is dead." He pronounced her name with an initial click, and the "ch", too, was guttural. "If Mijnheer wishes, she will also be the servant of Mijnheer."

Cachas smiled enormously, made sounds signifying that she spoke English, and led him, swaying her tremendous hips, towards the biggest reed hut.

"Mijnheer's house," she said.

CHAPTER IV

I

THE Rev. Andrew had thought out his plan of spiritual campaign during that serener time that followed the first hard days of his long journey. He had assumed that his predecessor had at least brought his flock right up to the road that led to Christianity, if he had not actually conducted them far along it.

Now he asked Titus to call together the older men for what he described as a little talk.

They came obediently, and squatted down like baboons in a semi-circle before him. There was an expectant look on their faces. Now and then they would fire off a cannonade of clicks at one another, and laugh a little throaty laugh which made the missionary feel vaguely uneasy. There was a subtle note of mischievous—one might almost say malignant—amusement in that close chuckling of theirs.

The interpreter began. "This man," he said, "like the one who is dead, has come to instruct you in the things of God."

There was a short silence.

The Hottentots looked at one another with their little wicked black eyes, as children about to bait a weak teacher.

At last one spoke.

"Where," he demanded, "does this man, God, live?"

Titus translated. The Rev. Andrew Flood looked

at them bewildered. Did they, then, not know even this elementary fact? He put his surprise to them through Titus.

They shook their heads. "If we knew, we have forgotten," they said.

The Rev. Andrew Flood began haltingly to explain to them what God was, Titus translating sentence by sentence. It hindered his flow of thought, this constant interruption. But he went on determinedly, his eyes gathering fire of enthusiasm as he spoke. Presently he began to feel that he was interesting his audience. They were looking from him to Titus, nodding attentively every now and then. When he came to the end of his discourse he suggested that they might ask him questions about anything they had not understood.

There was a pause. Then the oldest man present found tongue.

"You say God wants us to pray all our lives?"

The Rev. Andrew Flood smiled at him encouragingly. "Yes."

"But that is very hard."

"It is not very hard. Those who pray sincerely will soon find that it is not hard at all. Ah! no, not hard, but beautiful. When first you tried to swim in that river you had to struggle to keep afloat. But afterwards, when you knew how, was it not a glorious thing to do? . . . So, prayer."

The Rev. Andrew was pleased with his simile, but he noticed that a smile of amusement spread over each face until it reached even Titus. He discovered afterwards that these Hottentots, whatever might have been the custom among other tribes, never bathed.

The old man was speaking again.

"But why cannot God be satisfied with two or three days' prayer? One might agree to that—it would not be too much trouble. Now you say we have to pray all our lives. What is there to tell God that could not be told in two or three days?"

The Rev. Andrew Flood tried to explain to the old Hottentot the uses of prayer. The old Hottentot regarded him attentively, but with that same look of raillery on his face.

When the missionary had finished explaining, he came forward with a new argument.

"I am an old man," he said. "All my years I have lived in the world without God. Will it help me to change now?"

This time the Rev. Andrew answered him readily.

"The older you are the sooner you will appear before the judgment seat, and the more necessary it is, therefore, that you should make your peace with God."

The old Hottentot was as quick. "Then, first, if that can be done at the end of life, why should the young trouble? And, second, if God wants me to change, and if, as you say, He can do everything, why does He not then change me? Why have you to come all this way to us and make talk about it?"

"But He it is who has sent me," the Rev. Andrew cried triumphantly, his face suddenly ablaze. "I am His instrument. I proclaim His Word. Hear and believe; fear the Lord; repent your sins; and pray that you may be saved."

He lifted up his voice in prayer. When he had finished, the interpreter said "Amen".

But the squatting Hottentots sat silent.

Then, as with a common accord, they rose up one by

one, formed little groups of two and three, and went back towards their huts.

Suddenly the Rev. Andrew Flood heard the sound of long, loud laughter.

2

It was as if that meeting had set the tone of the association between the Rev. Andrew Flood and his Koranna charges. Whenever he addressed them there was in the air that sense of mockery.

Nevertheless, he persevered. He had them build him a long, rectangular hut of mud and reeds, and there he held services and Sunday school, and taught them hymns.

They came quite readily. It was a new amusement, and, but for their smoking all day long, and a little occasional Bushman killing, they had little with which to occupy themselves.

And so they used to bring stones or the logs of trees, and sit there pretending to listen to him and good-humouredly lifting up their voices in song when he asked them to do so. Although they had quick ears and easily repeated after him the sacred tunes, it was strange how different—how quite savage and Hottentot-like—the music they made sounded, so that the Rev. Andrew himself could hardly recognize the familiar old hymns.

But, however they listened to him and sang after him, he got no further with them. They were always trying to—yes, to trip him, that was the word—to trip him, to catch him. It became a kind of game with them. They were, in the main, stupid and indolent, but they really made efforts to discompose their pastor. They would lie in the shade of a bush smoking, excogitating questions that they hoped he might not be able to answer, conspiring to make demands he could not gratify.

At first when they had approached him, coming with innocent voices to consult him on religious matters, he had eagerly welcomed them, feeling that his mission was being very significant. But afterwards, when he grew to recognize the quizzically impudent look that accompanied the polite manner, his heart used to tighten with a sense of ill-ease.

They would ask him such questions as why God had made them evil if he wanted them to be good. To which he would return the customary answer that not God, but Satan, had made them evil.

As if it had all been rehearsed beforehand (as, indeed, it had been with their last pastor), the next question would follow as to why, if God was all-powerful, He allowed Satan to make them evil.

And the Rev. Andrew, floundering a little, would give them some such reply as that Satan, the first sinner, having fallen without temptation, had been cast into Hell for ever, and there he sat now causing all this mischief.

"But if Satan," the oldest Hottentot, who was their leading dialectician, would say, "if Satan were not in Hell making us wicked, would we not all be good? ... Therefore would it not be more simple for God to forgive him than to let him so trouble us for ever? Is it just for God to do this thing to us?"

And even as the Rev. Andrew, his face red and worried, considered what he might say to this, they would triumphantly go away; and, inevitably, from the distance, there would come floating back towards him their loud, derisive laughter.

Even his medicine chest was not an unassailable asset. It is true that experience with the last missionary had proved to them the value of Christian pills and powders and potions for certain obvious illnesses; but when it came to the more mysterious diseases, they still had greater faith in the efficacy of their own witchcraft. The Korannas, indeed, were called the Toorvenaars, or Wizards—and, in addition, many of them had taken to wife the relics of the Bushmen they killed whenever they had the opportunity, and these too, had brought with them a great tradition of magic. They could, for instance, diagnose and cure love troubles. They knew that, under certain circumstances, severe fevers might be caused by an evil-intentioned person burying his finger-nail parings on the threshold of his victim's hut. They could smell out an enemy. If they felt inclined they might even produce rain.

The Rev. Andrew's medical knowledge paled into insignificance beside such powers; and, although his charges came to him for a headache or a stomach ache, they quite obviously did not trust him with anything requiring deeper or more subtle understanding.

4

Yet it was not till the moon entered upon its first quarter that the Rev. Andrew Flood realized to the full what lay before him. Then, having lain awake all night long, and night after night, to the piping of reeds and the wail of songs, which were very unlike the hymns he had tried to teach them, and were yet now and then reminiscent of them, since often the Hottentots found the hymns quite adaptable to their purposes, he rose
c

one night, his head aching with sleeplessness and the close heat of his reed-hut, and he went outside and made his way towards the sound of the music.

And there, suddenly, he came upon them, his spiritual flock, on an elevation, dancing under the moon.

He stood staring at them for a moment, and then, his heart beating as if in wild rhythm with the music, he returned to the hut.

He had never conceived so utter an abandonment of all restraints as he had just witnessed.

He did not attempt to close his eyes all night; but next morning, weary as he was, he asked Titus to bring the men before him. "I wish to see them at once," he said.

"They are all sleeping, Mijnheer," said Titus.

"Then wake them."

"But they are very tired. They will sleep till the sun goes down. They have danced all night."

"That is what I must speak to them about."

"About the dancing?"

"Yes, about the dancing."

"But, Mijnheer, it is the Hottentot custom. They believe that the stars are the eyes of the people who are dead, and that the moon is God, and when the new moon is in the sky they come to pray. And this singing and dancing——"

"I have told you to call them, Titus."

The Rev. Andrew's heart was tired and sore, but it had courage.

Titus went away, shaking his head. Presently he returned.

"Not one man will come, Mijnheer. The sleep is too heavy on them. Mijnheer forgets that it is now five nights they dance."

42

The Rev. Andrew's face darkened. "Then I will go to them myself. There shall be no more such dancing."

He never knew how near death he was that day.

In the end, however, they listened to him with yawning indifference, and, in the night, as if he had never spoken, they danced again.

CHAPTER V

I

HE sat under a tree by the side of the river reflecting on the futility of his existence. No other human being in the world, he thought, could be as desolate as he was.

His mind went back to the voyage out, and the hopes and expectations he had then of human love and spiritual achievement. He wondered what Mary was doing now, whether perhaps, after all, he had not made his feelings sufficiently clear to her. He had certainly never quite—never quite—made full explanation.

He visualized himself addressing a love speech to her, telling her about his lonely life. She would pity him if she knew how, solitarily, he was contending against such overwhelming forces of evil. . . .

When he got back to his hut, he sat down before the box which was his table, and began impulsively to write a letter. Once in every few months a runner came to them from the next mission station, a hundred miles or so to the south-west of Canaan, bringing letters and papers. He should take back a letter to Mary Keeble.

He wrote and wrote, altering, rejecting, improving. Almost every day he made a different attempt. This is the letter that Mary Keeble finally received:

"MY DEAR MISS KEEBLE,—God, who disposes of our destinies, has led my frail vessel to this most distant and most lonely post. I am, as you know, the last white man in my direction; and the thought of what has been, and of what might have been, is all that can lighten a loneliness which is, indeed, at the present

44

moment, made the heavier by what I can only designate as the antipathy of the poor black brethren in Christ who here surround me.

"In that loneliness, my mind turns to the past. I think of the time when, a poor, slow, dreaming boy, scorned by masters and fellow scholars, I kept my vision ever ahead on one unalterable beacon—the Star of Faith. I think of my misunderstood youth, my tormented manhood; of the time when I felt it was demanded of me to throw aside all worldly hopes and give my life to Christ; and of that more recent time when, it seemed again, God had relented in His sternness and had offered me some earthly compensation.

"Need I tell you, my dear Miss Keeble, what that compensation was? Need I recall to your mind those beautiful days and nights when we paced the deck side by side, and at last I knew I had found one to understand my lonely soul, and to whom I might reveal what was in that soul?

"And yet I fear now I did not reveal enough. I, who have boldly adventured to live among this savage horde, did not dare to make my meaning plain to the woman who awoke in my heart the knowledge of earthly joy. Let me make it plain at last. I ask you, my dear Miss Keeble, to be my wife. I cannot offer you the riches of sumptuous living, but I do offer you the riches of holy endeavour. Together we could effect that which I, alone, am finding well-nigh impossible. Even these poor benighted souls would be led towards holiness by the light in your eyes.

"The last occasion on which I saw you you were gay among the gay. But is it not more to bring one lost soul to the gates of Heaven than to dance in palaces? 'Lay not up for yourselves treasures upon earth, where moth and rust doth corrupt and where thieves break through and steal. But lay up for yourselves treasures in heaven, where neither moth nor rust doth corrupt, and where thieves do not break through nor steal.'

"I await the arrival of a runner that I may send this to you; but, even at the best, I fear it must be months before I hold your answer in my hands. Until then I shall pray that it may be God's will to direct your heart towards me,

"Your devoted servant,

"ANDREW FLOOD."

2

That brought back his first exaltation—the excitement of sending such a letter and waiting for a reply to it.

To make the time pass more quickly in the lengthening nights of approaching winter, he sat by candle light compiling a little rough dictionary of Hottentot and English words, and trying to translate the Bible into Hottentot.

Cachas, who cooked for him and tended the two cows for which he had given tobacco and beads in exchange; her daughter Silla, who assisted her in her domestic and pastoral duties; and Titus, the interpreter, lent him their often conflicting aid. He laboriously sucked his tongue against his palate in an effort to imitate them in producing the Hottentot click, at which Titus, as became his dignified position, would remain imperturbably silent, but Cachas and Silla, being only women, would laugh in hearty, though not ill-humoured, amusement.

Cachas and Silla were among the most civilized of the tribe. They had, indeed, been converted to Christianity by the last missionary, and Cachas, as the only woman wearing a European garment, had a unique social position. Cachas was thirty-six years old and a widow, for her husband had been killed in a Bushman cattle-raid; but while she was still strong and useful, she had her place in the community. When she became old and burdensome, however, it was not improbable that she would be dragged out on to the veld and left there to be devoured by wild animals. She told the missionary so herself. "What is the use of old people?" she said. "They only eat the others' food."

Silla did not, in the least, resemble her mother. With maturity she would no doubt achieve the grotesque development which was the Hottentot ideal of beauty. But for the present she was only seventeen, and slim, and daintily shaped, as were most of the other young girls, with a small head whose brown scalp was visible through the peppercorn hair, set on a splendid neck. Her face was the usual Hottentot face—triangular, with high cheek bones, bridgeless nose, little keen black eyes, a high mouth, and a small, pointed, retreating chin. But it had a quick and animated and not unattractively impudent look; and her eyebrows, more strongly marked than was usual, made her rather distinctive.

She had a queer little cheeky laugh, and did not hesitate to let it be heard when the Rev. Andrew made his futile efforts at reproducing the Hottentot click.

"No, Mijnheer," she would say. "No. That is wrong. Look!"

She would open her mouth and show him her red tongue achieving the correct effect.

3

The months passed and it was mid-winter. A runner had recently been, but he had brought no letter from

47

Mary Keeble. The Rev. Andrew's hand had shaken visibly as he received his post; he had unheedingly dropped two letters from his mother as he rapidly turned the bundle over in vain search; and then he had gone back to his hut and sat himself down on his bed in lost and bitter silence. It seemed to him for the moment that if he had not Mary to hope for he had nothing.

But he had got so into the habit of hanging his thoughts and expectations on her that imperceptibly the mood of despair passed, and he found himself again envisaging a future which held her. As ever, in the long, cold, winter nights, as he lay in the dark under his karosses of sheep-skin, he spent hours addressing her. Sometimes he pleaded with her; sometimes the talk was of love achieved; and sometimes he even discussed his problems with her in a spirit of happy domestic companionship.

He began to think that quite probably—in this uncertainty of postal communication—she had not even received his letter. Or she might have received it and answered it, and the letter destined to brighten his life was wandering about heaven knew where in dark Africa, lighting the desert.

The next time the runner went from Canaan he carried another letter from the Rev. Andrew Flood to Mary Keeble.

In the meanwhile, the Rev. Andrew struggled as before to bring the Hottentots to God.

4

He wondered if any man had ever had to contend against such forces of spiritual opposition as he. A few of the Hottentots had consented to become converted, but the Rev. Andrew had an uneasy feeling that their conversion was not genuine, that they expected to get something out of him for it, a little material consideration—in other words, a donation from those big packing-cases he had brought with him.

Yet so pathetically anxious was he to feel that his mission was not in vain that he welcomed even such scabby sheep to the fold.

The ancient dialectician, with his following, was still standing firmly against him. It appeared to be the amusement of his old age to lay traps for the missionary, as other old men join committees or go to law. But the Rev. Andrew had an obstinate courage that persisted in the belief that, sooner or later, he would get him, and thus the others. He would go on arguing patiently, but not very successfully.

And there he would sit, the ancient—he was nearly ninety years old—with his head of white peppercorns (though his face was as naturally innocent of hair as it had been in babyhood); his little black eyes sharp and shrewd in their bunched up setting of wrinkles; his gnarled, dirty, brown paw demonstrating—he would sit there and amiably taunt the white man.

"You say I will be better and happier if I become a Christian?"

"Yes. Yes. Oh, yes!"

"But the people in your land are Christians."

"Yes."

"And are they good and happy?"

The Rev. Andrew hesitated a moment, and then committed himself.

"Yes."

"And they do not do evil things, nor make wars?"

"No human being is perfect," the Rev. Andrew

qualified. "They are better than they would be were they not Christians."

The old man spat meditatively from between his teeth—a thin, well-projected stream.

"No man can be better than I am. I am too old to be bad now. I do not kill, I do not take the other man's wife. To be old and to be Christian, it is the same thing."

That triumphant discovery he now maintained in all future conversations with the Rev. Andrew. Until one day, bored with argument, he came along and laid down a final condition.

"There is a drought in the land," he said.

The Rev. Andrew admitted it.

"Your God has made the drought."

"He knows best."

"And if He chooses He can end it?"

"He can do all things."

The old man bunched up his wizened face and pointed his finger, that looked like a little brown twig, towards the river.

"Do you see that black rock rising from the river?" he said.

"Yes," said the missionary wearily.

"It stands strong against the wind, and the waters do not move it."

"Yes."

"Even so do I stand against your God; nor will I think of serving Him; no, nor of going a step to hear the word you preach unless He sends us rain. You say He wants me. Let Him show it by doing this thing I ask. You say He can do all things. Let Him make the rain we need."

It was a definite proposal—a challenge.

Now for rain!

On Christmas Day the Rev. Andrew Flood at last got his letter from Mary Keeble.

He had now been living for nearly a year among the Hottentots, and he felt exhausted, body and spirit. He could not sleep and he could not eat. He was quite emaciated, and his fervent blue eyes were haunted with lonely suffering. He wished sometimes that he might lie down and rest for ever.

And then, at other times, he would remember how all his young life he had aspired to sacrifice; how he had wanted to give the boots from his feet, to suffer misunderstanding in silence, to pray in fasting isolation. And his eyes would suddenly burn with spiritual ardour, and he would go gauntly in and out of the dirty, evil-smelling, vermin-infested reed huts in which the Hottentots lived, attending to their wants, battling for their souls.

This Christmas Day it was sultry with the promise of rain—rain, alas, too long deferred to save the soul of the old Hottentot who had quietly one day given up his heathen ghost—and the Rev. Andrew, in his low, rectangular, reed-and-mud church, through the incense of never washed Hottentots, was struggling against an inexplicable and increasing faintness to tell his congregation about the birth of Christ. He had not been well this last week. . . .

As he left the church, the runner came into sight. The Rev. Andrew leaned against the door, waiting, He stretched out an unsteady hand as the runner approached him.

On the very top of his bundle of envelopes there lay one addressed in a delicate feminine hand.

"MY DEAR MR. FLOOD" (it said)—"Sensible as I am of the honour which you have done me in asking me to be your wife, I fear that I cannot accept it. Even were the circumstances, of which I am about to inform you, otherwise, I should still feel that I am not naturally fitted to share so holy and arduous a life. But, indeed, I have to tell you that I am shortly to be married to Captain James Anstruther, whom you may have seen on the last occasion on which you visited me before going North.

"I hope——"

The letter blew to the ground. Cachas, conversing at the top of her voice with a group of friends, started suddenly running towards her master.

The Rev. Andrew Flood had fallen in a heap against his church door.

CHAPTER VI

I

THE Rev. Andrew Flood lay for six weeks on his bed.
For part of that time he was delirious, and when he was
not delirious he thought he was dying of a broken heart.

But, in fact, the Rev. Andrew had been suffering
from what, in these days, is called typhoid or enteric
fever. And, since it was destined to him to go on living,
he recovered from his sickness—despite the ministra-
tion of Cachas and Silla and Titus, which were not,
after all, very harmful, even although they secretly
included a little sorcery. And as, for the rest, he had
not been tempted to take anything but milk and water,
Nature had not, on the whole, been too greatly hindered
in her efforts on his behalf. . . .

And so one day, very thin and weak, he was led
outside by Cachas and Silla, and there, in the shade of
his reed hut, he lay on a pile of karosses and felt the
wish for life reviving within his heart.

A man might be happy merely in being alive and
able to do his chosen work. Ah! He would work, he
would work. He would save them yet.

He spoke to his attendants about his problems.

"What is it," he asked them, "that stands between
me and your people?"

"It is that you are different, Mijnheer," answered
Titus. "The folk" (he said it in Dutch—"the volk"),
"they think that God does not feel the same for a brown
man as for a white man."

"But I have told them, Titus, that we are all the same in the eyes of God."

"Yes, I know that, Mijnheer."

"Then——"

"But they do not believe it, Mijnheer."

"Why not?"

"Because, Mijnheer, they can see with their eyes we are not the same."

"It is the colour of the skin," put in Silla. "They say why did God give one man a white skin and another man a black skin if He did not wish to show them that they were different."

The Rev. Andrew Flood shook his head. "We are all God's children," he said.

"But is God Himself not white?" asked Cachas.

And, as the Rev. Andrew hesitated for a reply, she made a suggestion:

"Perhaps we brown people are His step-children," she said.

2

The Rev. Andrew Flood sought for means to prove his contention that the Hottentots were his equals in the sight of God. He made efforts to speak their language, visited them in their homes, and ate their food. He took the little monkey-like babies on his knees and played with them. He had a desperate feeling that only one thing remained to him in the world now—to succeed in his Christian mission.

He believed that he had come to the kernel of the matter. These people thought that the Christian God made distinctions between black and white. Not till he could convince them to the contrary would his preaching have any effect.

He had recently received a letter from Cape Town suggesting that, after a year's work under such conditions, and in view of his illness, he might find himself entitled to a rest. But he had refused the offer. He did not want holiday. He did not want rest. He only wanted to snatch these black souls from Hell, and thus to vindicate himself.

He was prepared for any sacrifice.

It was winter again. He had lived now for eighteen months among the Hottentots. They no longer offended his senses as they once had done. He had become used to them. He was himself hardly delicate in his person any more. He had given up shaving and wore a beard—it was less trouble. He did not, as in summer, bathe in the river. And it was an uncomfortable and chilly affair to have a bath in his reed hut, through which the cold air blew. The grease-spots on his clothes were sometimes washed over, but, in general, they showed brown with dust; and his stockings and shirts, which he had at one time clumsily mended himself, were full of holes.

He had only a small looking-glass, and had accustomed himself to the appearance of his haggard, bearded face, his bald forehead, from which even the narrow central point of hair had disappeared, his pained-looking, visionary eyes; but he had no conception how shabby and neglected and unwholesome the rest of him looked.

And yet he found a difficulty in winning over these heathen!

3

The Rev. Andrew Flood was sitting in the hut of Cachas. There was a fire of sticks and dung burning in the centre of the hut, which was full of smoke, so that every now and then the Rev. Andrew found himself coughing. On the right side—the men's side—sat Cachas' nephew, Harina. On the left side—the women's side—sat Cachas and Silla. Silla, her face shiny with grease and ochre, her hair glinting with blue mica powdered over the grease, was moulding an earthenware pot. From a stake in the ground hung the sheepskins they used for clothes, Silla's coquettishly ornamented with ostrich-shell beads. Supported on two poles hung a skin filled with milk. On the floor, on each side of the fireplace, lay some other skins, covering a depression in the ground a few inches deep. These were their beds. The men, women, and children ate and slept in the same hut.

So far had they become accustomed to the Rev. Andrew's presence that they were all—Harina and Cachas and Silla—smoking. He had come to the conclusion that to make them like himself he had to make himself like them.

But they realized none of his spiritual motives. They only knew that the white man was not so much better than themselves, as they had once supposed; and such little respect as they had originally had for him (in spite of their teasing) on account of his whiteness, they had gradually lost. They allowed themselves liberties with him which they had never allowed themselves with the old missionary who was dead. and Harina contradicted him, and Cachas scolded him in a mild maternal way, and Silla smiled at him with the impudent little manner which was naturally hers.

"Mijnheer," Cachas was saying, "must be feeling very lonely here."

The Rev. Andrew shook his head. "No, I am not

lonely," he smiled rather pathetically. "I have all my brown friends around me."

"But it is not good for a man to live by himself. Mijnheer should have a wife."

The Rev. Andrew's heart sprang forward as if it might rend itself from his body. He could not answer. She was another man's wife by this time, Mary Keeble.

"Does not Mijnheer," persisted Cachas, "believe that a man should marry?"

"Yes," he said slowly, his face very pale. "I believe that a man should marry."

"Then why——?"

"No woman will come to live here, Cachas," he said almost inaudibly.

"Then will Mijnheer remain without a wife as long as he lives?"

"I suppose so," he answered, feeling anew his desolation. "Yes, I suppose so."

"That is not good," commented Cachas.

"No, it is not good," endorsed Harina.

"It is not good," said Silla, looking up quickly from her earthenware pot to meet the Rev. Andrew's eyes.

4

The Rev. Andrew lay awake that night with those words ringing in his ears. "It is not good to remain without a wife . . . It is not good. . . . No, it is not good. . . ."

He remembered Silla's provocative glance.

Backwards and forwards the words ran in his mind, until it seemed to him that some outside force was saying them.

Yes, this was what God had meant him to do. For this Mary Keeble had been denied him. He had gone

D

around, the Rev. Andrew, for the last eighteen months, telling the Hottentots that, in the eyes of God, in his own eyes, there was no difference between black and white. And they had not believed him.

He would prove it to them!

CHAPTER VII

1

HE journeyed with Silla and Cachas and Harina by ox-waggon to the next mission station. It was called Kadesh, for when the Rev. Thomas Burtwell had pitched his tent there he had whispered to himself "a city in the uttermost of thy border". It was no longer that, but the name had remained.

Although the days were bright and clear it was very cold in the nights, and having made a fire, not only for warmth, but also to keep away possible wild animals, they hung skins down the back of the waggon and across the wheels, and all slept under it. The Rev. Andrew ate with them and slept with them, but he hardly spoke to them.

He was going to be married to Silla.

The journey took them nearly a week. They travelled slowly across the flat, yellow veld, with its bare thorn-trees, and now and then a meerkat flitted past, and now and then a springbok; but for the whole of the hundred miles they saw nothing else.

When, finally, they arrived at Kadesh, the Rev. Andrew told Silla and Cachas and Harina to remain in the waggon while he went before to meet his fellow-missionary.

2

Mr. Burtwell came out to greet the tall, thin, bearded figure in dirty black clericals. He held out a friendly hand. "This is a great pleasure," he welcomed him heartily, "to meet a brother-missionary. It must have been a weary journey. Are you on your way back to Cape Town?"

"No, I am not going further," said the Rev. Andrew.

"My wife will be happy to see a white face again," said Mr. Burtwell. "That is our home—that smaller of the two mud-houses. The other is our church. I understand you have not yet arrived at such heights of luxury."

The Rev. Andrew walked slowly beside his host.

"No, I live in the ordinary Hottentot hut," he answered in a dull voice.

"Ah, well, it is different when a man is alone," said Mr. Burtwell, "but when a woman has to be considered——"

He left his obvious conclusion unspoken, smiling at his companion.

The Rev. Andrew did not return the smile.

Instead he stopped still, his face now very red, now very white.

"That is the object of my journey," he said quickly.

"That?" questioned the other, puzzled.

"A woman. I mean a wife."

"Indeed?" Mr. Burtwell looked more puzzled still. "But I understood you to say you were not going any further than this?"

"No, I am not going any further. I have brought my—my intended wife with me."

The Rev. Thomas Burtwell looked at his fellow-missionary. He had heard through the last runner stories about a long sickness. Could it have been a— a *mental* sickness?

60

The Rev. Andrew was regarding him straightly with his painful, blue eyes.

"She is on that waggon," he said.

"Yes—yes," murmured the perturbed Mr. Burtwell.

"It has been a hard struggle," said the Rev. Andrew, with apparent inconsequence, "trying to win over the hearts of my—our—brown people to Christ. I have discovered at last the way to remove the obstacle."

"Indeed?"

"It is the difference in colour which stands between us. They cannot forget that fact."

"It has, naturally, always been a great problem."

"I have solved it," said the Rev. Andrew, his eyes burning.

He pointed to the waggon. "I have wiped away the distinction. My intended wife is—one of them."

Mr. Burtwell stared. "One of them!"

"A Hottentot woman," said the Rev. Andrew clearly.

Mr. Burtwell laid a gentle hand on his arm. So it had been a mental sickness then!

"You are over-tired," he said. "Let us get home. My wife will refresh you with a cup of tea brewed in the good English way."

"No! No!" cried the Rev. Andrew. "Have I not made myself plain enough? I have come to be married!"

Mr. Burtwell walked on quickly.

"To be married," repeated the Rev. Andrew. "I wish you to join us——" his strained voice broke suddenly. ". . . holy matrimony," he mumbled.

Mr. Burtwell stopped still. There was a short pause.

"You are not well," he said at last. "You do not appreciate what you are saying."

"I do appreciate what I am saying. I do, fully. I know my action will be misinterpreted. But I have prayed for light. I am prepared for the sacrifice. 'Blessed are ye, when men shall revile you and persecute you, and shall say all manner of evil against you falsely, for My sake. . . .' Mr. Burtwell, it is my duty."

3

The Rev. Mr. Burtwell had married them in the end. The Rev. Andrew had persisted to the point where he had maintained that it was more important for him to be altogether assimilated with the Hottentots than even to receive the benediction of the church on his union with Silla. He had vowed that if Mr. Burtwell did not perform the marriage ceremony over them he would return with Silla, and live with her in sin. "I will give up even my own soul to save theirs," he had cried.

They had argued and they had protested, and Mrs. Burtwell had wept and had begged him to think of his mother (she had almost even dared to mention his unborn children; still, to that she had not been able quite to bring herself). But he had remained as immovable as the black rock in the river with which the old Hottentot had once compared his own self.

And so, three days later, Silla, wearing for the first time, through the generosity of Mrs. Burtwell, European garments, stood in the mud church that had been built by Mr. Burtwell, and was joined in holy matrimony to the Rev. Andrew Flood.

BOOK II
MIXED BLOOD

PART I
THE FIRST GENERATION: DEBORAH
1824

CHAPTER I

I

So now Silla came to live with the Rev. Andrew Flood in his reed hut.

She was very proud, and when she walked she swayed her body from side to side on her hips out of sheer dignity.

She never spoke of her husband except as Mijnheer. She called him Mijnheer.

The Rev. Andrew tried to teach his wife to read and write and count. And at first it amused her to draw strokes this way and that, and to recognize similar strokes made, for her instruction, by the Rev. Andrew, and to put little stones in a row and count them. For a time she went about counting everything: huts, trees, bushes, oxen, people. But all this mental exercise began to weary her unaccustomed brain after a while, and, having learnt to sign her name, Silla Flood, she suddenly refused to continue her education any further. "I am learned enough now," she said.

On Sundays, however, she would go to church carrying demurely a Bible and a prayer book. And she would sit there with her eyes cast down with an instinctive self-conscious decorum, listening to the words of her husband.

Her numerous relations rallied around her in reflected triumph, and they all now came to church, and such of them as had not done it before at last allowed themselves to be baptized.

The Rev. Andrew, his voice a little tired, his tall frame beginning to stoop, accepted their conversion as the first-fruits of his sacrifice.

The people were all more friendly with him, too. He told himself that at last he had won them.

They despised him utterly, and his religion.

2

When Silla and the Rev. Andrew Flood had been married nearly a year their first child was born.

He had felt, when he heard of the child's coming, like Abraham when God had called upon him to sacrifice Isaac. "Take now thy son, thine only son Isaac, whom thou lovest . . . and offer him . . . for a burnt offering upon one of the mountains." He had sacrificed his coming child's white heritage—if not his body, the purity of his blood.

The analogy did not strike him further that, although Abraham had only been tried for the deed where he himself had accomplished it, the award in each case would be precisely the same: "I will multiply thy seed as the stars of the heaven, and as the sand which is upon the seashore."

The child was born, and he called him Isaac.

A year later another child was born—a girl.

When he had come to christen her the name of Mary had flashed through his mind.

But it was not for him to call a Hottentot child Mary. And he christened her after his mother, Deborah. He told himself, with a momentary bitterness, that his mother was responsible for him as he for Deborah, and he might quite as justifiably transmit her name as her blood.

With maternity Silla was beginning to develop the typical Hottentot figure. All the Hottentot matrons were stout to malformation, although their men remained slim and wiry till death. And Silla's youthful litheness had disappeared so completely that the recollection of it seemed like an impossible dream. She waddled when she walked, like an overfed goose. Her face had almost doubled in size, and all its youthful alertness was gone. She was fat—fat all over. Her years were exactly twenty.

She was extremely indolent, and whereas before Cachas had kept the reed hut in some sort of order, under Silla's management it was in a state of overt filth. They ate and slept in the same room—the Rev. Andrew and Silla and the two children; and in winter they even cooked there, though in summer culinary operations were transferred to three stones outside among which a fire was built, and over which stood a tripod pot.

Silla, as was the custom among the Hottentots, attended to the two cows the Rev. Andrew had always had, and their three calves, and milk was the principal food of the family.

It was practically Silla's only domestic activity. For the rest, she spent her time smoking tobacco of *dagga*. The latter left her in either a dazed or a vicious state. The children crawled about naked in summer, and in winter wore little skins. Their fuzzy brown hair stood away from their heads in golliwog fashion, and they were full of sores and vermin. They had yellow skins and brown eyes. Isaac was a very little darker than Deborah, but they were both almost mathematically half-bred in appearance; and they were commonly, and with simple literalness rather than malice, referred to by the tribe as the bastards. They played about, however, with the other little Hottentot children on a complete equality.

The Rev. Andrew could not bring himself to take a great interest in his offspring. He could not feel as if they actually belonged to him. The language they were learning to speak was Hottentot, with a few Dutch and English words here and there. They referred to their father as Mijnheer.

CHAPTER II

I

WHEN Deborah was three years old, there was another
baby, and he was sickly from birth. However the
Rev. Andrew, with the rather listless paternity that
was his only guide, struggled with him, it was useless.
The child wailed and wailed, and would not eat, and
would not sleep, and grew thinner and thinner.

The Rev. Andrew tried to dull his senses to the fine,
whimpering noise that beat against his ear-drums by
day and by night; prayed that he might learn uncom-
plainingly to bear his cross; and, when he forgot to
pray, wished that he might be lying at the bottom of
the brown river that flowed unheedingly past—at rest.

He knew, by this time, that, from no point of view,
had he acted wisely in marrying Silla. He had lost such
respect as had been the reward of his whiteness, and he
had not replaced it by that intimacy of closer association from which he had hoped so strongly for spiritual
results. The Hottentots did not regard him as a
brother. They regarded him as a fool.

Although a large number had, at some time or other,
in some way or other, allowed themselves to be pre-
vailed upon to accept Christianity, their religion was
of the vaguest. They came to church and stood up or
sat down with the grave and histrionically solemn
reverence of children playing games. They sang hymns
with the utmost enthusiasm, but they did not know the
meaning of what they sang, nor did they want to know.

A few of them had genuine religious instincts and really liked the idea of a God and a Saviour, and a Heaven and a Hell, and a reward and a punishment, but most of then came to church simply because, except dancing and hunting (either of men or of beasts), it was their one formal amusement.

Silla had never tired of taking her Bible and hymn-book and going to service every Sunday. She wore the cotton dress which was her official uniform as the pastor's wife, and which had been brought by waggon, with other things for the lonely outpost, from Cape Town. Her feet were bare to the burning sand, but she carried under her arm the shoes which she put on painfully just before entering the church; because, although she liked to show herself in shoes, she hated to have them hamper her walking. And she held her head up with an air of superiority, and swayed her huge hips from side to side, feeling like an actress before the footlights; conscious of eyes following her movements. She no longer pretended even to listen to her husband's religious exhortation.

2

But it was not until this illness of their youngest child that the Rev. Andrew thoroughly realized the completeness of his failure.

He came home one day from the Bible-class he held for adults as well as children and, as he approached his hut, he heard a noise which sounded like devils let loose. He stood still for a moment, and then, with his thin, unaccustomed legs, he started running towards the uproar. The flap, made of rushes, which hung over the entrance of the hut, and which Silla fastened down nightly with stones to shut out the only means (but for the draughts, which were accidental) of admitting air, was down now. But from within there came a crescendo of cries and howls, and the noise of a rattling that appalled his ears.

He struggled against the flap until it gave way from the top, and, panting, surveyed the scene that revealed itself to his eyes. The sick baby was lying corpse-like, and not even crying any more, on a skin on the ground, and over him was bending a half-breed Bushman, the son of a Bushwoman acquired in wifehood by a conquering Hottentot, and skilled in Bushman wizardry. He was sucking at the child's body, and every now and then, with a triumphant yell, he would exhibit a few goats' hairs or birds' feathers, or straws, which he had thus apparently, extracted from the patient, and which, of course, had been the root of all the trouble. To lend him their moral and spiritual assistance, there were several Bushwomen. One of these stood muttering—urgently, insistently—in a corner, her body now rigid, now violently shuddering. Two others were dancing and singing and groaning and yelling and clapping their hands, and still another was making a noise by shaking with each hand a pebble-filled calabash—a gourd—that, by comparison, reduced her friends' efforts to the position of a mere obligato.

There were also present a few of Silla's relations, who, belonging, as all the clan did, to the Koranna or Toorvenaar (wizard) branch of the Hottentots, had a little magical skill themselves. One of these was bounding about on the ground, leaping on all fours, in a kind of slow, regular march. He had the tail of an ox attached to a leather cord round his waist, and a pair of horns on his head, but he was otherwise naked. In a hole in the middle of the hut was a fire, and some-

71

times he kicked it, and sometimes he sprang over it. Harina was standing on a log, manipulating a knob-kerrie—a stout stick with a knob at the end. Silla herself was letting out periodically loud, trailing cries.

They were intoxicating themselves with wrought-up violent emotion, and now and then one would suddenly drop down momentarily exhausted and almost senseless.

The Rev. Andrew stood at the entrance of his hut, petrified with horror, until suddenly he felt his knees giving under him, and leaned against the side of the hut for support. If the magical operators in the hut were aware of his presence they gave no sign of it.

He found his voice at last. "Stop!" he called to them, using instinctively his own English word. "Stop! Stop!"

They took no notice of him. He could not tell whether they heard him or not. . . .

He forced himself among them, but Silla pushed him back. He struggled with her, against her mountainous frenzy, but he was no match for her. And Harina sprang from his perch and helped her to throw him out of the hut.

He stood there panting, his coat half off, his beard wild, blood trickling down his face, his blue eyes lost and agonized. He had not the strength left even to call upon his God.

CHAPTER III

I

THE baby died; and Silla and her friends blamed the
Rev. Andrew for the misfortune. At the very point
at which the bad spirits were about to be exorcised, he
had come and interfered, and while they were occupied
in ejecting him the spirits had taken their opportunity
of returning to the child's body and completing their
evil work.

However, now that the child was dead, they accepted
it stoically. They made a hole near the bank of the
river, and wrapping the body of the child in a skin,
buried it there, in the same attitude in which it had
lain in its mother's womb.

The Rev. Andrew was not allowed to approach.

And then Silla left him and went to live with Harina.

The two children, Isaac and Deborah, remained with
their father.

2

For nearly a week the Rev. Andrew wandered about
like a man from another world. And then, his face
whiter and thinner than ever, he took up again those
duties to which he had consecrated his life, and having
now sole charge of them, also the training of his
children.

They were, surprisingly enough, quiet and amiable
children by nature; and the girl, Deborah, was not
unintelligent, though the boy was slow. Now and then

E

73

there came to their father's mind the idea that he would go away and take them with him. But the very fact of their existence made it impossible for him to live in any civilized community. However the talk might be about black brethren, no one would suffer this practical manifestation of the principle.

The Rev. Andrew Flood and his coloured offspring! The sole result of his sacrifice. . . . He understood at last. . . .

Now a passionate desire to make his children such restitution as was still possible overcame him. He washed and cleaned and tended them; and, when they grew a little older, tried to teach them.

3

The next mission station, Kadesh, was by this time—by about the year 1830—the home of a flourishing community.

The Rev. Thomas Burtwell was a man of character and enterprise. He was not as militant as some of the other missionaries, and kept as clear as he could of tribal dissensions and conflict with the neighbouring Bushmen and the various Basuto tribes. Instead, he had taught his people to till the ground, and they planted mealies and pumpkins and even some quite delicate European vegetables; and grew fruit trees—peaches, apricots, pears, apples and quinces. The rainfall was not very dependable—sometimes it did not rain at all, and at other times it rained so much that their reed-and-mud houses were destroyed. In the summer, too, the river had a way of rising suddenly so that it overflowed its banks and lapped up their cultivated ground, and even sometimes forced them to move their huts; and then the water they had to drink was thick and brown and muddy; though, in the winter, on the other hand, there was almost no water at all in the river, so that the rocky bed of it lay open and naked. . . .

But it was wonderful how quickly things grew if they grew at all, and wherever a man sank a well he was almost sure to find water—dead to the taste, still, useful enough, as the vegetation around proved.

These people did some primitive manufacturing, too, made mats and karosses and earthenware and wooden vessels, and were learning the use of iron.

Then they had more communication in these days with the outer world; and when they came to church they decorously wore European clothing—it was, indeed, of the ugliest and shoddiest possible, and it covered bodies no cleaner than they ever had been; but it nevertheless marked a stage in civilization.

They were, besides, a very religious community, the Kadesh Korannas; and the Rev. Andrew Flood, comparing them with his flock, found his heart swelling with renewed bitterness as he thought of the vanity— the irony—of his sacrifice. He had lost everything to give them nothing.

The years passed, and he stayed on at Canaan, conscious of his failure, but unable, on account of his children, to go anywhere else.

There had been some vague discussion at missionary headquarters about removing him and his retrogressive influence, but no missionary who had a family was willing to go to what was still the furthest Northern post; in any case, the field was over large already, and finally, it was thought wiser, at the moment, not to add to the already existing unpopularity of the missionaries among the colonists by bringing any nearer civilized eyes the Rev. Andrew Flood's coloured family. The colonists were angry enough, as it was, about the missionary domination in South Africa which had culminated in the emancipation of their Hottentot slaves. Better not to give their animosity this weapon. Better to hide the Rev. Andrew Flood. Better to keep him where he was.

CHAPTER IV

I

By the time the Rev. Andrew Flood had been at
Canaan for fifteen years he was himself in many ways,
a savage. He was dirty and unkempt and wild looking;
he seldom read; he wrote to no one; he knew nothing
that was going on in the big world; and it embarrassed
him to meet a civilized person. If a travelling missionary chanced as far as Canaan he encountered so cold
a reception that he was only too anxious to leave again
as soon as he could. The Rev. Andrew hardly realized
his own existence.

One day his neighbour, the Rev. Thomas Burtwell,
came to pay him his annual visit. He stayed at Canaan
overnight. He tried to speak to his outlawed colleague
in his usual cheery way, but he found it impossible to
draw any response, and, finally, the two men sat there
together in the reed hut in utter silence.

It was not until the next morning, within half an
hour of his departure, that Mr. Burtwell could bring
himself to say what was on his mind.

"You are not considering moving from here at all?"
he asked.

The Rev. Andrew shook his head.

"But your children?"

"My children?" The Rev. Andrew's tones were
vague.

"Have you no other hopes for them?"

A smile flickered bitterly for a moment round the

Rev. Andrew's lips that never closed perfectly over his projecting teeth. "What hopes can I have?"

"Then you mean them to grow up here?"

"Where else?"

"And, eventually, one day when—we are in the Lord's hands—if something were to happen to you——"

The Rev. Andrew met the stammered suggestion in silence.

Mr. Burtwell was forced to directness.

"Are you content to think that these poor children may be left by themselves among savages?"

The Rev. Andrew forced his mind for a retort.

"They, too, are savages," he muttered at last.

"They need not be," the other countered quickly.

"But——"

"If you will give them a chance of civilization, they need not be."

"What do you want me to do?"

"Send them away."

"Away?"

"Yes."

"And—I?"

"Will you not give yourself a chance too?"

The Rev. Andrew's lost blue eyes sprang into life for a moment. Then they died again.

"There is no chance for me any more," he said.

It seemed useless, even to so optimistic a soul as the Rev. Thomas Burtwell, to dispute it. He wondered, indeed, how life maintained itself in that worn-out body before him.

"I wish I could do something for you," he murmured.

They sat looking at one another. The little girl,

Deborah, now twelve years old, came into the hut and stood gravely examining one of the few white men she had ever seen. Her hair stuck out bushily around her head, her scrap of a calico dress was torn and dirty, her feet were bare; but her face had the alert look her mother's had worn in youth, and her share of white blood gave it a deeper significance.

"Well, Deborah?" smiled Mr. Burtwell, to break the difficult silence.

She smiled shyly back.

"Come here," he suggested.

She approached.

"You are getting a big girl."

Her smile broadened.

"When you are quite big, what are you going to do?"

She shook her head. "I do not know, Mijnheer."

"Do you want to stay here always?"

She shook her head again. "No, Mijnheer."

"Would you not"—he patted her brown, grubby little hand, but his eyes were on the father—"Would you not like to leave this place and go to a real school?"

She followed his gaze. "I cannot tell what would Mijnheer—my father—what would he say about it," she answered with breathless eagerness.

"What *would* you say about it?" the missionary asked his colleague directly.

"I have not considered the matter at all," the Rev. Andrew answered lamely.

"Consider it now."

"I scarcely follow."

"I am suggesting that Deborah ought to go to school."

"How? What school is there to which she can go?"

"Mine," said Mr. Burtwell quickly. "It is a native school, but we—my wife and I and our assistant—will do the best we can. And, if she shows promise, she may, in due course, herself be trained to assist in the teaching. I think—it seems to me—it would not be such a bad idea."

"I have taught her occasionally," the Rev. Andrew put in with pathetic self-justification. "She can read and write and figure a little. She is not—unintelligent."

"Quite the contrary," Mr. Burtwell asserted heartily. "Oh, quite the contrary."

"But—where will she—where will she live?" stammered the Rev. Andrew.

"Why, with us."

"With you?" The Rev. Andrew's pale, haggard face flushed deeply. He looked from the white missionary to the brown child. "With you? I could not—could not allow it."

"Why not?"

"It would not be right. You know yourself."

The muscles of his face worked visibly as he tried to draw his trembling lips firmly together over his high teeth. His eyes reddened. "Not right," he repeated in a whisper. "Poor Deborah."

And for the first time in many years, he put his head down on his arms and wept.

Mr. Burtwell stood up beside him, his hand sympathetically on the other's shoulder.

"Let us try."

"If she could be of any assistance to Mrs. Burtwell in the house," mumbled the Rev. Andrew into his smothering arms. He had an undefined idea that only in a position of service would it be seemly for his daughter to remain in a white household.

Mr. Burtwell delayed his departure for another day.

When he returned to Kadesh, Deborah went with him.

CHAPTER V

I

IT had been a little difficult for Mrs. Burtwell to fit Deborah into the household. She had, indeed, protested strongly at first. "How am I to treat her?" she had demanded.

"You will know, my dear," her husband had answered amiably. "I trust your wisdom."

"My dear Thomas, it is easy to speak and to flatter. Am I to behave to her as to the native children?"

"Do we not behave to them all as to the children of God?"

"Then am I to make no difference between her and our own children?"

"No difference."

"Let her share a room with Arabella, for instance?"

"If necessary."

Mrs. Burtwell's square-built, freckled face set. "I have been an obedient wife to you always, Thomas," she said, "and I have tried to do my duty under difficult circumstances. But such a thing I will not agree to. Deborah is a little savage."

"She will not, under our roof, remain a little savage."

"And if John had been fifteen years old instead of six?"

"What do you suggest?"

"I suggest nothing. I say quite plainly that I understand human weakness, and I would not, in the days to come, like a son of ours to get interested in a half-caste woman. Now I thank God our three eldest children are girls. But, even so, I shall not accustom them to the idea that there is no distinction between black and white."

She flushed to the roots of her drawn-back, reddish hair as she spoke, but her pale blue eyes met her husband's firmly.

"Her father wished her to assist in the house," Mr. Burtwell murmured.

"If she does not hinder me, I shall be satisfied. But I am surprised to find a man so low sunk as Mr. Flood capable of making a proposal exhibiting some intelligence and good feeling."

"My dear Fanny," Mr. Burtwell protested.

"Don't dear Fanny me! Dear Fannying will help nothing now. The child is here, a perpetual burden on us, and I see trouble ahead. When it comes, I shall blame no one but you, Thomas. Dear Fanny!"

"How should there be trouble?" asked Mr. Burtwell.

"How should there not be?" retorted Mrs. Burtwell.

2

Deborah was, as her father had said, not unintelligent. She had, as most half-caste children have, a capacity for imitation. She copied the manners and habits—even the gestures and intonations—of Mrs. Burtwell.

She seemed to learn quickly, too, but only to a certain extent. Inevitably the point would be reached where a solid barrier of unreceptivity would hinder all further mental progress. And she would gaze blankly at Mr. Burtwell and shake her head and tell him she could not understand. And, however he might explain and explain, the blankness would not leave her face, and he

83

would realize that she spoke truthfully—she *could* not understand.

He had thought that a child with a white father might be different. He knew that the native children arrived at their full capacity very early. At the age of four or five they were far in advance of white children of the same age; but at fourteen or fifteen they would begin to falter, to lag behind, to remain stationary while their white competitors went ahead. It seemed to the missionary as if their minds were unlocked sooner, but also sooner locked again. He had a vague theory that it all had to do with the traditional hardness of their skulls.

But he had certainly hoped that Deborah might be more white than black in intellect. . . . He often wondered now in what way her white blood would manifest itself. . . .

The years passed.

3

At the age of sixteen, in the year 1841, Deborah Flood was a fully-developed young woman who had recently risen to the dignity of school assistant. Four years of constant oiling and plaiting and hard brushing had trained her outstanding fuzz of hair to lie flat against her head like a cap; her little brown eyes were bright and alert; there was a natural flush of colour on her high cheek bones; her figure was even more slim and erect and graceful than her mother's had been at the same age; and she had the same regal carriage of the head. She was by no means an ill-looking girl, and her manners were soft and complaisant.

Her position in the household had gradually adjusted itself, too. Although she was treated with an easy intimacy by the members of it, in the end, the very fact that her skin was a different colour had been enough to mark a sharp distinction between the other children and herself. She might learn with them, play with them, eat with them, live with them—but never could she belong to them.

It was not necessary to assert the fact even. Never, subconsciously, was the knowledge of it absent from any of their thoughts. Without defining it to herself, Deborah realized that there were certain limits beyond which she might not go in her intercourse with white children. And the young Burtwells, although they had lived all their lives among Hottentots, and had been trained to regard the brown people as equally, with themselves, the children of one Heavenly Father, never forgot that Deborah was not as they were. In deepest essentials they were secret from one another.

There was no use in deploring or resenting such a condition of affairs. This was her position in life, and Deborah accepted it.

But now the time had come for new cravings to occupy Deborah's heart. And, as naturally as any animal, Deborah looked about her for a mate.

4

Nearer Cape Town it would, of course, have been different. There the half-caste was an established factor. Farmers, like the Biblical patriarchs, had their official and their unofficial households; their white wives and their concubine slaves; their white heirs and the children of their bondwomen. And the offspring of Hagar were beginning to seed the wilderness; were uniting in marriage and tradition; were becoming a nation. They carried well-known European names. They called themselves proudly the Bastaards.

Since the beginning of the century they had spread themselves over Southern Africa like an opening fan; fighting, marauding, settling. But, although at various places along the river, now generally called the Vaal— the dun-coloured—River, there were camps of emigrant Griquas and Bastaards under various chiefs, each tribe lived independently. And at Kadesh there were as yet none of Deborah's kind.

And this being so, and Nature welling up strongly through Deborah's blood, her questing desire had led her towards one of her own pupils—a full-blooded young Hottentot, a great dancer under the moon, a magician with bow and arrow, a man with an alluring laugh and a provocative, insolent manner. Her heart beat when he approached her, her eyes swam, she found him irresistible; and when he said to her one day, "Meet me to-night," she agreed.

She met him secretly many times, and then one afternoon Mrs. Burtwell said to her:

"Deborah!"

"Yes, Mrs. Burtwell?"

"I want to speak to you."

"Yes, Mrs. Burtwell."

Deborah's voice was soft, her manner meek, but there was that in the expression of Mrs. Burtwell's face that warned her and steeled her to hostility.

"What is this I hear about you and 'Kon'gap?"

"I don't know, Mrs. Burtwell."

Mrs. Burtwell looked at Deborah in silence with her small, keen, blue eyes.

Deborah returned the gaze without flinching.

"Do not try to deceive me, Deborah," said Mrs. Burtwell at last.

Deborah did not answer.

"Tell me the truth, and we shall not be hard on you."

Still Deborah made no reply.

Mrs. Burtwell's face flushed with her effort to keep calm.

"Deborah," she said, in a voice a little quieter than usual for the control she put on it, "I know that you have been meeting 'Kon'gap. You were seen. Have you no explanation to give?"

Deborah opened her mouth, then closed it again.

"Nothing to say?"

Deborah shook her head with the slightest possible gesture.

Mrs. Burtwell waited a few moments longer. Then she rose from her chair.

"Go to your room," she dismissed her. "To-night Mr. Burtwell will speak to you."

5

It was not often Mr. Burtwell officially "spoke" to any one. He was a man so full of pleasant courtesy that people who did not know him well thought him, indeed, incapable of sternness. Nevertheless, his character was built on a foundation of granite principles. And, although those who gave him obedience and service told themselves that they did so to please him, it was only really because, for his rigid morality, they unconsciously feared him. Not for nothing had he been able to raise the savages of Kadesh into an almost civilized community.

"Deborah," he began directly, "I hear you have been meeting 'Kon'gap, and that you would give Mrs. Burtwell no explanation of it. Is that so?"

Deborah's eyes drooped. "Yes, Mr. Burtwell."

"It is true you have been meeting 'Kon'gap?"

"Yes, Mr. Burtwell."

"Why would you not admit it to Mrs. Burtwell?"

"I—I was a bad girl, Mijnheer."

Irresistibly the old respectful form of address, that had been established by the first little Hottentot interpreter at Canaan as a convention, supplanted the more ordinary one.

She raised her little dark eyes.

"Now tell me the whole truth."

"I—liked 'Kon'gap. I was lonely, Mijnheer."

Mr. Burtwell's stern face softened a little.

"But 'Kon'gap is a wild man, Deborah."

"Yes, I know that, Mijnheer, but I liked him."

"You are half-white, and you have lived with us for four years. Has that not made you different?"

"No, Mijnheer," she whispered. "I am wild, too."

The missionary remained silent for a moment. Then he said quietly:

"It is our work to drive that wildness out of you, Deborah. You will not meet 'Kon'gap again."

Her lips hardly moved. "No, Mijnheer."

"You understand that, then."

"Yes, Mijnheer."

He got up and looked at her with softened eyes. "I am sorry for you, my child," he said. "You have a heavy cross to bear. But it must be done. You will try?"

Her hands in her lap trembled. Her eyes moistened.

"I will try, Mijnheer."

CHAPTER VI

I

BUT Deborah's mood of repentance passed, and, as the weeks went by, she grew daily more silent and sullen.

She was not subjected to further temptation in connection with 'Kon'gap, for the next transport waggon that went southwards carried, through Mr. Burtwell's influence, 'Kon'gap on it, and for several months, at any rate, Deborah did not see him.

One of the manifestations of her new spirit was a deliberate neglect of her personal appearance, an overt indifference towards her small household and school duties, a habit of isolation. When she thought they did not see her she cast looks of conscious malevolence at the various members of the Burtwell family, and now and then her lips moved in soundless execrations.

It was not until the advent of the three waggons of emigrant farmers that Deborah allowed herself to return to normality.

2

On each of these waggons lived a whole family of white people, come northwards to look for land on which to settle. So they would journey, the farmers, into great unknown spaces, with their wives and

F

children, with their span of oxen and their horses, and their primitive agricultural implements and a few things—such as tobacco or beads—for barter. And when they came across a likely-looking bit of ground along the bank of a river, or beside a natural spring (which they called a *fontein*), they would outspan their oxen and they would say, "Vrouw, here we will settle". And they would call the place some such name as "Welgevonden" (well found), or "Weltevreden" (well contented), or after themselves, "Potgieters-fontein" or "Labuschagnes Rust". And they would do a little casual farming and a certain amount of shooting, both of wild animals and wild men. And they would raise a clan of enormous, illiterate sons and daughters. And the land would be theirs and their heirs' for ever. And they would rest at ease in their desolation, uncramped —sky above and earth below, and emptiness all around —at peace with life. . . .

Of the three families now arrived near Kadesh, two consisted of relations, of the name of Kleinhans, and the third was a family of van Wijks. And among these called Kleinhans there was an uncouth young giant of about twenty-two, with wild, fair hair falling over his forehead, with a great coarse laugh, and blue eyes unsteady in everything but the sighting with a gun, and he chose to be attracted by Deborah.

Hardly had his associates outspanned at the *fontein*, about ten miles from Kadesh, when there he was daily coming on horseback to the settlement, meeting Deborah after school, taking her out, his arm, after a time, openly about her waist, unashamed.

And even more readily than she had gone with 'Kon'gap, Deborah now went with Hans Kleinhans. She followed merely her natural impulses.

And when, after a few months, Mrs. Burtwell said in a worried voice to her husband:

"What now, Thomas? This time it is a white man," he found it difficult to give her an answer at first.

"Do you think it is better?" she demanded.

"It is better for her," said Mr. Burtwell. "But not for him."

"Then what will you do?"

"I must speak to the man."

"And if he is serious? The black blood will go further."

"I am to blame for bringing Deborah here," said Mr. Burtwell. . . .

Again Mrs. Burtwell spoke to the girl. Now Deborah answered ardently.

"You say black is not for me; you say white is not for me. What is for me, then?"

"The same as you are."

"The same as I am! Where are they?"

"They will be found one day. You are very young, Deborah."

"I am not very young. I am seventeen. It is my time. And I want this white man. I want him. You will not stop me."

"Deborah!"

"If you say so, I can go away from your house to-day."

Mrs. Burtwell did not answer for a moment. Then she said:

"Not to-day, Deborah. But I think soon. It is perhaps time you went back to your father."

"To-day," stormed Deborah. "I will go to Hans Kleinhans. To-day!"

She told Mr. Burtwell so when he came home in the evening.

"I am going away, Mr. Burtwell."

"Where?"

"Mrs. Burtwell——" she began to sob.

"Yes."

"She hates me, Mijnheer. She will not let me be happy."

"What has she done to you?"

"It is Hans Kleinhans, Mijnheer."

"I see. Yes. So you want to leave us, Deborah."

"I am going to Hans Kleinhans."

"Ah . . . Deborah," he added after a moment, "you cannot go to Hans Kleinhans."

"Why?"

"He will not have you. He does not want you. I spoke to him this very afternoon. He laughed at me. He said he would not think of marrying a brown *meisje* —a brown girl."

"Let him not marry me, then. He can have me. without marrying."

"That I would not allow," said Mr. Burtwell.

Deborah did not answer for a few moments. Then she spoke in a soft voice, but there was a look of almost malicious triumph in her little dark eyes:

"But he has had me," she said. "It is no use talking any more. The thing is finished. There is going to be a child!"

4

"When you brought her to us five years ago, Thomas, I told you there would be trouble," Mrs. Burtwell pointed out.

Mr. Burtwell made no reply.

"Now I am not listening to you any more. The next waggon that goes to Canaan takes Deborah back to her father. We have our own children to consider."

"I am sorry for the girl," said Mr. Burtwell.

"Sorry? She is an unprincipled savage."

"That is why I am sorry," said Mr. Burtwell.

PART II

THE SECOND GENERATION: KLEINHANS
1842

CHAPTER I

1

WHEN Deborah returned to Canaan she did not find her father in the hut. But Cachas was in the reed-enclosed yard bending over something that was cooking in a big three-legged iron pot. She was fatter than ever, and the grease on her face seemed to have come as much from within as from without.

She raised herself laboriously as Deborah walked into the yard, and looked at her. Then she said:

"It was a white man?"

Deborah nodded.

"That is bad."

She led Deborah into the hut.

"Your father is not here. He goes about on the veld. The trouble is with his head. Your mother Silla and Harina and their children went away a year ago. I hear they are with the Bastaards. Your brother Isaac has gone to live with our people. There is no more to tell. Sit."

2

The Rev. Andrew Flood returned to the hut next day. His face was the colour of dust. His long beard was matted. His clothes were ragged and dirty. His toes came out of his shoes.

He made a little humming noise on one note all the time. He looked at Deborah vaguely, as if he did not recognize her.

"I am back," said Deborah.

He drew puzzled brows together.

"They sent me back because I am going to have a child."

A faintly frightened look came into the Rev. Andrew's wandering blue eyes. Then suddenly his singing stopped, and he began to cry.

"It is no use crying," said Deborah. "The thing is done. It will be a white child."

"White?" said the Rev. Andrew.

"Yes, white."

"There can be no more white children," said the Rev. Andrew.

And he commenced his humming again.

3

There were letters lying around that the Rev. Andrew had not opened for nearly a year. Deborah, moving indolently about the hut, found them and read them.

"There is a letter," she told her father one day, "which says another missionary is coming to Canaan."

The Rev. Andrew mumbled something unintelligible.

"He will be the pastor instead of you."

"Ah, yes," said the Rev. Andrew, and went on humming.

"Then they will not send you any more money," Deborah pointed out.

Her father made no remark.

"And how will you live?"

Her father smiled faintly.

"Will you go away?"

"Go away?" said the Rev. Andrew. "Go away? Where to?"

He did not go away when the new pastor came. He remained in the hut, and Cachas and Deborah lived there with him. And when the Hottentots killed a sheep or shot some game with their bows and arrows they gave him some, and Cachas shared her milk with him, and he ate the roots she ate, and smoked the same tobacco she did, and he slept and lived in his clothes without ever removing them.

Deborah's son was born there, too. And she called him after his father, Kleinhans. He never had another name. Kleinhans stood to him for Christian name and it stood to him for surname, too. The Hottentots were at first a little amused at his lightness of colour, but they soon grew accustomed to it. He had a yellowish skin; frizzy, rusty-coloured hair, and grey-brown eyes. His nose was broad and his cheek-bones were high, but his ancestry—three-quarters white and one quarter Hottentot—was marked plainly on his face.

When he became bigger he played with the Hottentot children as one of them. He knew, of course, that his skin was a different colour from theirs, but it did not strike him as a fact of any importance.

Not till many years later, in Kokstad, where he became a prosperous man and a decorous church-goer, did he reap the benefits of his paler pigmentation. . . .

In the meantime, of course, many things had happened.

To begin with, a year after his birth, his grandfather, the Rev. Andrew Flood, had died. He had gone on getting thinner and thinner, and dirtier and dirtier, and more and more vague in his comprehension; and always and ceaselessly he made that little monotonous humming noise.

And then one day he had remained lying on the skins which had long ago replaced his broken bedstead and mattress, and he had not got up again.

No one knew what was the matter with him, and no one cared; and the missionary who had come to take his place was not even told of his sickness. And in due course he died. He did not make any illuminating reference to the hopes and mistakes of his life before his spirit left him. He did not see his far-off European home, or say distinctly the one word "Mother" or "Mary". Now and then he spoke a rapid, incoherent sentence—a long, continuous stream of words—which remained uninterpreted because it was not listened to; gradually he ceased his humming; his right knee began to quiver involuntarily; and when next Deborah looked at him, he was lying still. It was over.

And that night some Hottentots came and took his body away and buried it according to their own rites. They made a hole by the river and disposed his limbs as they had been in his mother's womb, and covered him with skins, and put the earth over him.

When the new pastor protested at their action they listened quite respectfully.

"Mijnheer is right," they admitted with gravity.

And afterwards they laughed.

But the new pastor was made of different stuff from the old, and they did not go on laughing at him for very long. He made them take the body out, and he put it as best he could into a box (though it was stiffly settled in its position by now), and he gave it Christian burial and planted a cross on the grave.

The Rev. Andrew Flood's was the first grave in what became the Canaan graveyard. And all the Hottentots who died were afterwards buried there, too, and crosses were erected over their earthly bodies to mark the ascent to Heaven of their converted souls.

CHAPTER II

I

BUT Deborah, with her son Kleinhans and her grandmother, old Cachas, had, before there were many bodies in the Canaan graveyard, gone away from Canaan. They had joined a party of Hottentots and trekked along the Vaal River until they met a group of Bastaards who were pursuing their leisurely way to the land of Adam Kok the Third. They went with them and settled there.

They found a community of Griquas and Hottentots and Bastaards in whose veins the blood of their own kind met the blood of white men and Bushmen and Kaffirs; and Adam Kok was their hereditary leader, the fifth of his line, and a maker of history. He had recently, by treaty, been recognized as a sovereign prince and an ally of the Queen of England. This short, stout, almost illiterate half-caste, with his brown, pock-marked face, his thick lips, woolly hair, and difficult little beard; this leader of shamefully born savages and fugitives and outlaws and emancipated slaves; this Kapteijn Adam Kok, as he chose to style himself, once ruled a great land in Africa, and when that was taken, led his people, Moses-like (but across mountains, not deserts) to a new home. The name of it was Nomansland, but it was changed to Griqualand East; and in Griqualand East they settled down to forget their old home which had been, and is now, Griqualand West. And they built a town and called it after their leader, Kokstad.

Cachas and Deborah and Kleinhans went with Adam Kok. By this time—by about the year 1860—Cachas was seventy-seven years old (but old age, under Adam Kok, was no longer a punishable offence), and Deborah was thirty-six, and Kleinhans was eighteen; and it was on that long and difficult trek that old Cachas died. On the crest of the Drakensberg Mountains, in a ravine at Ongeluks (Misfortune's) Nek, her bones remained to rest. She was not solitary in death. All around her lay the wreckage of those who had succumbed in the attack on the great mountains as, dragon-like, in accordance with their name, they stood guard over Nomansland—men and women and children, and horses and cattle, broken waggons and carts, and little homely possessions.

But Deborah and Kleinhans survived to settle with Adam Kok in his new national home.

3

They were given a piece of land, and there, with such cattle as remained to them after the trek (the natural increase of those far distant two that Cachas had tended at Canaan, and whose descendants she had driven before her when she went to join Adam Kok), they settled down to farm.

Heaven knows what germ in his distant white ancestry had quaintly chosen to establish itself in Kleinhans' character, but it happened that he was, by nature, a husbandman. In that community where work was universally despised, Kleinhans vigorously farmed his land; he wrought in wood and iron, he was sober, he was frugal, he was religious.

But he was something else. He was bitter with hate. He hated the people he lived among for the blood that was in them; he hated his mother for her fuzzy hair, her high cheek-bones, her thick lips, her yellow-brown skin; he hated his own flesh. . . .

But he did not hate the white man who had idly begotten him; nor the white man who, in the service of God, had betrayed his unborn descendants; nor all those other white men who had sown seeds of disaster in a clean land. Of these he was proud. It was the meek, dark bearers of shame whom he hated. He despised a man in proportion as he was brown. Just physical lightness or darkness was his only test.

And, indeed, it was, in general, the chief test in Kokstad. In that community of illegitimates, illegitimacy was no disgrace, and how a man arrived at lightness of skin did not matter. What mattered was simply his pigmentation, and he was respected just in so far as his white blood expressed itself visibly. If, as happened often enough, there were several members in a family of different shades of brown, they were socially graded according to whether they were lighter or darker.

It was even a thing of pride for a man to call himself a Bastaard, for that definitely assumed European blood; and, in fact, many people passed themselves off as Bastaards who were not entitled to the distinction at all.

Only the missionaries did not like the description: Bastaard. And it was they who had decided that the community should style itself the Griqua nation, after a tribe that had once, a hundred years ago, attached itself to the first Adam Kok, the founder of the line.

So that now, when people in Kokstad referred to

themselves as Bastaards, it was simply out of snobbish-
ness, for the real Bastaards were the descendants of the
followers of another half-caste chief, Barend Barends,
and a much more directly white clan.

4

Rather later than if he had been a pure white man,
Kleinhans' beard began to grow. It grew slowly, and
it was too curly, but it was a fair beard, much lighter
than the hair on his head—quite tawny-coloured.

Kleinhans treasured his beard. He oiled it and
brushed it, and all day long fingered it. It made him
feel whiter. As it grew it made him look more of a
European too. He trained his moustaches widely
across his face, and, in time, his beard grew to cover
all his throat.

"You look like Hans Kleinhans, your father,"
Deborah told him.

"Like a Boer?"

"Yes, like a Boer."

"If a person did not know, could he tell that—?"
He left his sentence unfinished.

"Yes, he could tell," said his mother, Deborah.

"But there are white men with the sunburn on their
faces as dark as I am."

"Yes, that is so," admitted Deborah.

"And still—?"

"And still it can be seen."

"It is because every one here is known to be a
Bastaard."

Deborah shook her head.

"It is not for that. It is the blood. You cannot
hide the blood."

Kleinhans felt he could hurt her for that statement.

G

105

But Deborah went on placidly.

"You should be thankful you are as white as you
are. My brother Isaac's children, I have heard, are
Hottentots."

She was thinking, however, of 'Kon'gap.

5

Deborah cut quite a social figure in Kokstad. She
had never married, but she called herself Mrs. Kleinhans.
No one so decorous in the whole of Kokstad as the
Deborah of these days. She went to church regularly,
she taught Sunday School, she entertained visiting
missionaries, she spoke only Dutch interspersed with
a little English, she wore a hat, she was on friendly
terms with Mrs. Kok, Adam Kok's wife. . . . That,
however, was not so great a privilege as it might sound.
Although Mrs. Kok had married two reigning Koks
(she had been the widow of Adam's elder brother and
predecessor, Abraham), she was really nothing but an
extremely stout, short, and dirty old Griqua woman,
who had borne three daughters to Abraham, a son to
God, and no children at all to Adam, so that the noble
line of Kok was about to end in Griqualand East. . . .

Deborah could not, in her heart, help despising Mrs.
Kok, but courtiers have before been known to minister
to royalties in spite of irony, and, after all, Adam Kok
was Adam Kok. . . .

Why, see him on gala days in his personally-designed
state-dress of blue and purple, with scarlet tassels, and
imitation gold chains—no nonsense about Adam Kok
then, even if his splendour did a little diminish at each
end with the black bowler on his head, and his rough
old veld-schoenen on his feet. All the year round Adam
Kok's subjects loved and respected him. But on days

when he dressed as befitted his station, they admired him, too.

6

He was deserving of their fealty. He had made a nation of them, had led them to a country of their own, had given them land, and made them laws. His white allies took advantage of him wherever they could, but they liked and respected him for all that. He was a wise and just ruler.

He had instituted a kind of government by parliament, where the proceedings were conducted in Dutch. Each of about half a dozen wards sent two deputies, and when parliament was assembled an ox was killed. The session lasted until the ox was eaten.

The finances of the country took the form of cattle, and horses, and sheep, and goats; and the treasury was, naturally, a kraal. (Adam Kok's own cattle were kraaled on the main street, opposite his "Palace".) Although the government had power to make treaties, wage wars, and execute criminals, its laws were kept in a fluid and uncertain state because the records were not regularly kept, and so no one was ever quite sure what the parliament had decided.

There was, however, a resident magistrate to administer justice. He was chosen for the position largely as he had no other means of livelihood, and he paid himself and his officials with the court fees and fines. Then, when it was felt he had made enough out of his job, he was put aside, and the next needy man on the list was given a turn on the bench.

It was crude, but it worked. And nothing would really have interfered with the prosperity of the Griqua nation if only the Griqua nation had not considered it beneath itself to work. Rather than do that, the Griquas sold the farms that had been assigned to them at threepence an acre, and their building plots for a pound or two, cash, an old suit—indeed, anything tangible.

Kleinhans bought, and later, when prices went up, sold to the white settlers who were beginning to invade Griqualand East.

By the time Kleinhans left Kokstad in the year 1871, he was a moderately prosperous man. But he left because he could no longer bear to be surrounded by nothing except brown and yellow faces. What was worse, the white settlers classed him with the other Griquas—him!

He was twenty-nine years old, and had never married. He was determined to have no woman but a white woman to wife.

He went, on the first discovery of diamonds, to the diamond fields. On these diggings might be found a great concourse of white men, the beginnings of a new civilization, a chance for every man to start level with his fellows. He would be a digger like all the diggers. He would be one of them.

He took his waggon and eighteen oxen and trekked to the diamond fields.

Just half a century before his grandfather, the Rev. Andrew Flood, had passed through those very parts.

Kleinhans left his mother, the Rev. Andrew Flood's daughter, behind him in Kokstad.

He wanted to be rid of her brown society, and begin altogether afresh.

CHAPTER III

I

HE outspanned beside a group of waggons on the outskirts of the diggings, and his oxen wandered off to browse on the veld. The sun had set in a cloudless glow. The hard and level country of the diamond fields—the blatant, sunlit country—lay now wide, mysterious, and alluring, around him. Between sky and earth were nothing but distant tents, hooded ox-waggons, and inhospitable camel-thorn trees. The earth was sandy and still hot underfoot.

Kleinhans' white blood felt a longing for its kind.

Now little fires began to be dotted about the veld. And the sound of big laughter, ending in falsetto notes, punctured the stillness. And the squatting forms of huge men and stout women, of lanky boys and slender girls, showed blackened by the night and reddened by fire. And the aromatic smell of coffee rose invitingly into the breathless air.

Kleinhans walked over to the nearest fire. They would take him, the amiable and hospitable Boers, for one of themselves—had not even his mother admitted that he looked like a Boer, and was he not actually, to the half of him, one? and they would see him now only by the light of the fire—and they would friendlily say to him: "Sit maar, kerel"... "Do sit down, old chap."

He spoke and heads among the group were raised. For the words were in their own tongue, but the voice was the voice of black men. Let him hear but the echo of it, and the South African will recognize that sombre note.

Kleinhans said good evening.

"Yes?" said the head of the family. "What do you want?"

Kleinhans hesitated. "It's a fine night," he murmured.

The Boer did not answer.

"The veld was good as I came up," persisted Kleinhans. "I have just outspanned. Are you here long?"

The Boer rose.

"Now what is this talk?" he asked.

They looked not so different as they stood there beside one another, the Boer and Kleinhans. But the blood of savages and sin ran in Kleinhans' veins. He backed a little.

"We are busy," said the Boer. "We are going to eat. If you have some talk with me—perhaps you wish to sell your beasts—you can come and see me in the morning."

He turned his back on Kleinhans and took his place again beside the fire. He made some humorous remark to the others, and laughter jumped along the air.

Kleinhans retreated to his waggon. He had heard the word "Bastaards".

Beside his waggon he arranged three stones, piled sticks upon them, and set fire to the sticks. Presently he made himself some coffee, drank it, and then lay down on his back, looking at the stars, smoking a solitary pipe, brooding.

A short distance away, his rein holder, a little Hottentot, who had just been making himself some

110

coffee, too, also lay watching the stars, smoking and brooding. His tobacco was very bad, and the smell of it rose acridly on the soft and lovely air.

Even as the Boer had not spoken to Kleinhans, Kleinhans did not speak to the little Hottentot.

2

Before five o'clock in the morning—for it was high summer time—the sun rose as cloudlessly as, the night before, it had set. And Kleinhans sat up between his karosses of jackal skin and looked about him. Shadow and dew still lay on the earth; the world, but for the little human eruptions immediately around him, stretched unbrokenly away to far, hill-topped horizons; here and there a yawning figure was bending persuasively over a newly-made fire.

Hope came dancing back into Kleinhans' heart. He sprang up; went to see his oxen; good humouredly gave his Hottentot a piece of roll tobacco to chew; returned for his breakfast of coffee and bread and biltong—the salted and dried strips of game.

Then he made himself as spruce as he knew how, and set off for the centre of diamond activity, the township of Du Toits Pan.

Other men were going in the same direction, but Kleinhans walked alone, a big burly man with a brownish skin, broad features, high cheek-bones, small grey-brown eyes, and a well-grown tawny beard and moustache. He followed the other walkers past holes, flanked by siftings, and swarming with men—some white, but mostly black, until they reached a square outlined by shops of corrugated iron, and off that square into a street, bright with talking and laughing men in front of cheerful drinking and eating-houses,

They were clad in dungaree trousers, and shirts open on their hairy chests, and they were most of them the sort of men of whom he had met only odd specimens before: Jews—he had seen a few traders, Englishmen—his pastor was an Englishman, there were several in Kokstad now, and some of the farmers recently come to Griqualand East were English too, and one or two solid, square, light-haired men—Germans perhaps, he had just heard the name. But yet they all looked different from the people he knew—gayer, harder, more reckless, adventurous. He could not describe it to himself—he only felt that he could not understand them.

He followed a laughing group into a bar, and stood for a moment unnoticed, just within the door. Presently the barman saw him. "Hullo," he said. "You there. What do you want?"

Kleinhans' thick voice came out hoarsely.

"Drink," he said.

"Who's your boss?" asked the barman.

Kleinhans' face darkened.

"I am my own boss."

"You want drink for yourself?"

"Yes."

"You do, eh?"

All the men were looking at Kleinhans now.

"Yes," he said.

The barman emerged from behind his counter. "D'you think this is a coloured bar? " he demanded. "You get out there. Come along now. Out you go. Your place is in the canteen next door."

He gave Kleinhans a little prod. The men began to laugh. Kleinhans found himself standing, bewildered, in the street.

After a time he gathered himself together, and began wandering vaguely about. Nervous now of white men, he spoke to one or two Kaffirs, but they could not follow him, nor he them; and so presently he found himself standing uncertainly outside a little corrugated iron shed, at the open window of which, before a deal table, sat a red-faced man writing on official-looking paper. It was he, thought Kleinhans, who probably gave people the *briefje*—the licence—to dig.

There were several other men in the room talking sometimes to him and sometimes to each other. One of them pointed out Kleinhans' hesitating figure to the red-faced man.

"Yes?" he demanded sharply of Kleinhans.

Kleinhans cleared his throat wordlessly.

"Well, what do you want?"

Kleinhans began to stammer explanations and inquiries.

"Come inside," ordered the red-faced man. "I don't follow you. Speak slower. Now what is it?"

"I want to dig," said Kleinhans at last, badly, in his difficult English.

The man who had first noticed him hovering about outside touched his arm. Kleinhans turned round towards him.

"Look here," said the man, "whatever your name is—"

Kleinhans stared at him, listened to his curt voice, with his heavy trembling hand, as his custom was, fingering his tawny beard—his uselessly fair beard.

"If it's a job you want, I can do with you. I need someone to look after my boys. A sort of boss boy. I'll give you five pounds a month and your mealie-meal."

113

A boss boy! Mealie-meal! Kleinhans' face darkened with indignant blood. Was that what they took him for? His temples were throbbing and his eyes dim. A boss boy! . . .

He began fumbling unsteadily at his waist. He took out a packet. The men watched him in curious silence. He opened it recklessly, passionately. Showed them the thick pile of the notes he had brought with him. "Vuilgoed!" he shouted, and his voice was only a rushing in his own ears. "Filth! . . . My grandfather was an English pastor, my father was a Boer farmer. I am as white as you are. Boss boy! Five pounds a month! Mealie-meal! Look at my money! I could spit you out and not know it. Mealie-meal!"

His would-be benefactor whistled. "Christ!" he said, eyeing the notes. "I say, you fellows, I wonder where he stole those."

"I.D.B.," said one of his companions.

As if at a prearranged signal, they seized Kleinhans and marched him, struggling and raving, down the street. He was weeping, too, by the time that, having harangued him and searched him, and found on him a letter from the Kokstad pastor, and a deed of sale of his farms, they let him go with his money grudgingly restored.

"You'd better be careful," they warned him. "It looks a bit fishy for a coloured fellow to have all that money."

He hurried back to his waggon as if pursued. All day he could not eat, but towards sunset he went to collect sticks to make a fire for coffee.

3

His day of tribulation was not yet over. It was, indeed, mounting to a climax. As he was picking up

114

his sticks a girl of about fifteen, whom he remembered as one of the group he had approached the previous evening, came towards him, weeping.

"Have you seen a goat?" she asked him in Dutch. "There is a goat missing from my flock."

"What sort of a goat?" inquired Kleinhans.

"A white goat—a ewe. My father will beat me if it is lost. It is our best milk goat."

Her tears flooded over, unrestrained.

"Come, then," said Kleinhans. "I am not such a bad one at following a spoor. A few months ago I was a big man in the farming world."

His humbled spirit exerted itself to rise again. He wandered along beside her, boasting. But it was true that he was not a bad one at following a spoor. That was the Hottentot blood in him. His eyes were still the physically observant eyes of the aboriginal.

He pointed out to her a newly-nibbled bush. "Did you go in this direction?" he asked her.

"No," she answered.

"But a goat did. Let us see what happens here."

Then his ear caught a sound. "Three riders on horseback are coming this way," he remarked.

They walked on, but an uneasiness began to spread itself over Kleinhans' spirit.

Now the horsemen came into distant view over a little rise.

"I think it is better you turn back," said Kleinhans.

"I must find the goat," the girl protested.

"Then go home, and I will search for it myself."

"I am afraid to go home. My father will be angry."

The horsemen were coming nearer. The heart of

Kleinhans was beating uneasily. He had learnt some lessons during the last twenty-four hours.

"Your father will be more angry still that you walk with me," he said.

His companion gazed uncertainly about her.

"Go," said Kleinhans. "That is your father on one of the horses."

She turned from him and began to walk back. Kleinhans went on, but every now and then he looked round at the steadily approaching horsemen. He saw them stop, say something to the girl, and then come along again in his direction. The girl was running now. And the impulse came on him to run, too. He restrained it, and tried to continue on his way indifferently.

They came up with him in a moment, the father and two younger men, sprang from their horses, and, with never a word, fell on him. He resisted, shouting breathless protests and explanations, and one of them hit him on the mouth. "Still!"

His struggling arms were held fast while a thong of ox-hide—a reim— was tied about him. Then the father of the girl took his whip and beat Kleinhans till he fainted; after which they loosened him, and the man who had hit him on the mouth gave him a kick for good measure. "That will teach you to speak to white girls," he said. "Verdomde Bastaard!"

The three men caught their horses where they were complacently feeding, mounted and rode off.

Kleinhans remained, unconscious, on the veld.

4

But not for long. Presently there came by two people on a Cape cart, a lean, sallow, white man and his Kaffir driver. They were leaving the diamond fields by night

116

to escape the heat of the day. As they thinly cut, with the light of the candles in their lamps, the clean and sweet air, the Kaffir stopped his horses, and pointed to a bundle on the veld.

"There is a man lying there," he said. "He does not move. He is drunk or sleeping or dead."

"Go and have a look," his master instructed him.

The Kaffir handed him the reins, took a lantern from under the seat, and went towards Kleinhans. He bent over the unconscious body, and returned, with a shaking of his head, to the white man waiting on the cart. "I don't understand this thing. It is not as we thought. There is no brandy in the man's breath, nor is he sleeping or dead. But there is blood on him, and he has been beaten."

"Is it a white man or a black man?"

"A Bastaard."

"Wait a bit. I'll go and see myself."

He took the lantern, the hollows of his face black in the light that met it, and made examination. Then he raised himself and stared into the darkness, pondering.

"Half-bottle," he called, addressing the native by his name.

"Yes, Baas?"

"Come here. You can leave the horses. They are quiet . . . I want to get to the farm," he went on. "If it means going back to Du Toits Pan on account of this man, and being troubled there, I am having nothing further to do with the whole business."

"No, Baas."

"But we cannot leave this man here like this."

"No, Baas."

"The thing to do, it seems, is to take him with us."

"Yes, Baas."

"Come along then. Let us carry him to the cart."

They deposited Kleinhans on the back seat of the cart, the white man complaining of his heaviness, and muttering the word "nuisance", and drove on.

CHAPTER IV

I

KLEINHANS found himself, after midnight, on a
mattress in a small room. The taste of brandy was on
his tongue, and his body was in pain. He saw, by the
light of a candle, the native, Half-bottle, in his dirty
cast-off European clothes. He was squatting on the
floor on his haunches, watching Kleinhans. The hot
room was heavy with the smell of him, that smell
which Europeans consider peculiar to Kaffirs, but
which is really a matter of dirt and neglect rather than
of Nature. . . .

Kleinhans looked at the native for some moments.
Then, with difficulty, he spoke.

"How do I come here?" he asked him in the Dutch
that was the common exchange between such as they.

"The Baas brought you. You were lying on the
veld."

"What place is this?"

"The Baas's farm."

"Is it far from Du Toits Pan?"

"Five hours with the cart."

"What is your Baas's name?"

"Baas Lindsell."

Kleinhans became silent again.

"The Baas has gone to bed now. He will see you in
the morning."

In the morning not only Mr. Lindsell, but also Mrs.
Lindsell, their two little daughters, dressed alike in

119

checked dresses, and the young Cape girl who attended to them, all came to see him. Kleinhans was destined to marry that Cape girl, but he was little interested in her now, and, indeed, for many months to come. At the moment his mind was divided between his rescuer and his waggon and oxen.

"Well?" said Mr. Lindsell.

He was a tall, stooping man of forty-five, with a lined and hollow face; dim, deep-set, greyish eyes, with wrinkled, lashless lids; a long, drooping, grey-brown moustache, and a few grey hairs brushed from the right side to the left across his bald head. He looked like the final effort of an exhausted, aristocratic family.

He had a strange, self-absorbed expression. He did not make a very attractive receptacle for gratitude, but Kleinhans was determined on worship. He began to thank him.

"Oh, all right, all right," said Mr. Lindsell impatiently. He had not slept much that night, and lack of sleep always annoyed him. It made him feel as if life were not holding him fast enough. The one concern of Mr. Lindsell's existence was to continue that existence as long as possible.

2

Just to live, that was all Adam Lindsell wanted. That was why, although a rich man, he was spending his days here on this Cape Colony farm. . . . It was the healthiest place in the world, he considered. That was why he was careful of his rest and his digestion. That was why he took precaution against colds. And that was why he habitually sat with the fingers of his right hand curled over the inside of his left wrist, feeling his pulse. He was not a vicious man; he had no objection to doing any one a kindness that involved no extraordinary effort on his part; but he had such a horror of death and dissolution that he hardly ever thought of anything else.

It was a feeling that had been left with him after an attack of pneumonia when he was quite a young man. He had nearly died of it, had had to take the utmost care of himself afterwards; and the habit of worrying about his health had not only remained, but had grown with the years into an obsession.

It was as if he were fighting over his own body with Fate. He flattered himself that he neither felt nor looked older than he had done fifteen years ago. He put aside the fact of his baldness and greyness. "A family failing," he said; and, as for his wrinkles, those came, he maintained, from the glare of the African sun. And, sometimes, to prove to himself that he was, indeed, as young as ever, he would make athletic experiments, only to discontinue them suddenly when he remembered that, after all, undue exertion might not be good for him. But then he would point out to himself how many quite young men had strained their hearts by reckless athleticism. "It's not a question of years at all," he would comfort his anxious mind. "No man ought to put any unnecessary strain on himself. There's such a thing as *wearing* oneself out."

His wife's association with him was one long uneasiness to her. She had married him in England ten years before, thinking that she was doing well for herself, since she was a poor clergyman's daughter, nearly thirty, with neither occupation nor interests in life, and he was a wealthy man, cultivated, and of good family, about to go farming in South Africa. That was why—because, on account of his health, he was leaving

H

121

for loneliness in Africa—he had married at all. He wanted a buxom companion, and his choice had fallen on this Caroline Bickerton because she was tall and sturdy and red-cheeked, and looked as if nothing in the world could disturb her even temper.

But he was wrong. Babies on a lonely farm in Africa soon exhausted her vitality; she lost her colour together with her complacency; she developed a permanently anxious look in her brown eyes, and a habit of perpetual complaint.

Mr. Lindsell had an annoyed feeling that she had cheated him. It was a point with him never to get angry if he could avoid it, but he had gradually fallen into the habit of speaking to her in a manner of tired sarcasm, and she went about her wifely duties feeling that, at any moment, she would sit down and burst into tears.

What was worse, Mr. Lindsell's sarcastic manner was even extending to the children, now that they were getting older, and sometimes his wife felt despairingly that she could not bear it any longer, and that one day she would take a child by each hand and walk out of the house, never to return. But she was a helpless woman, with no economic or spiritual energy, and so there she remained on year after year, letting things happen as they would.

The two little girls, Edith and May, were nine and seven years old respectively. They both had pale eyes like their father, and, unlike him, lanky brown hair; they each showed gaps where their first teeth had fallen out; they were always quarrelling, and as soon as he could face the exhaustion of a severe dispute with their mother, Mr. Lindsell intended to send them to boarding school.

In the meantime, Mrs. Lindsell was clinging to their company, and teaching them herself; and Lena Smith, the pretty little coloured girl, was acting as a kind of mother's help.

3

Mr. Lindsell wondered what he was going to do with this tawny-bearded, brown fellow he had rescued. He might turn out a nuisance with his contused and quivering body. He had taken him and carried him home because it was, under the circumstances, the easiest thing to do. But that was the worst of impulses. They trailed their inconvenient and persistent effects after them.

The two children and the girl, Lena, stood at the door, looking at Kleinhans.

Mrs. Lindsell asked him his name, and he told her. "How did it happen?" she enquired further.

Kleinhans did not answer. Where was he to begin with this nightmare story. And he felt so exhausted.

"He may have done something dreadful, and been punished for it," Mrs. Lindsell whispered to her husband.

"Quite possibly," he replied.

"Do you think we're safe to have him here?"

Mr. Lindsell was asking himself the same question, but it irritated him that his wife should suggest that he had taken all that trouble over an undeserving case.

"No," he said. "Of course, I regard him as a dangerous character. That is why I brought him."

Mrs. Lindsell faded into her customary injured silence.

"I have a waggon and eighteen oxen and things on the waggon outside Du Toits Pan," said Kleinhans.

"Your own?"

Kleinhans fumbled, as before, in Du Toits Pan, at his waist, and took out the same packet. He handed it, without a word, to Mr. Lindsell.

"And what is all this?" asked Mr. Lindsell.

"Will Mijnheer kindly keep it for me?" said Kleinhans in the same way as he would have addressed his pastor. "There are papers in the packet which will explain. Mijnheer will see from them that I am not a good-for-nothing. . . . But now it is the thought of my waggon and oxen that troubles me."

He relapsed into weary silence, while Mr. Lindsell looked at the credentials he had offered.

"Will you leave them there until you can go back?" he asked Kleinhans.

"I am not going back," said Kleinhans. "I am finished with cities. I spent in Du Toits Pan one night and one day. It is enough for my whole life. I am a man that was meant for the land."

He closed his eyes.

He was thinking of the vainglorious hopes with which he had left Kokstad. He had cherished them all his adult life, and lost them for ever in one day.

PART III

THE THIRD GENERATION: ELMIRA
1872

CHAPTER I

I

HE remained where he was. It appeared that Mr.
Lindsell had long wanted such a man as Kleinhans to
help him on his farm. It was a farm twenty thousand
acres in extent; and, having sent for his waggon and
oxen, Kleinhans built himself a house of unburnt brick
and corrugated iron about half a mile away from the
Lindsell homestead, and bought cattle which Mr.
Lindsell allowed him to run on the farm, and helped the
Englishman with his own stock, getting, in return, a
small share of the profits.

And within a year he was married to Lena Smith.

She was quite a different type of half-caste from
Kleinhans himself. She was a light-coloured Cape girl.
Her father had been a German—his name Schmidt
anglicized into Smith—and her mother a coloured
woman, with a little Malay blood in her and a little
St. Helena blood, and the usual incursion of white blood.

Lena herself showed in her delicacy of feature and
clear yellowish skin her ancestral superiority over
Kleinhans. For all she had the straight, coarse, black
hair and shadowed black eyes of the Cape girl, and
Kleinhans' hair and eyes were light in colour, it was
quite obvious that she was further removed from the
aboriginal than he was. The Hottentot blood in him
expressed itself in his heavy, triangular-shaped face and
wide nose; but she had the thin little nose, the well-cut
mouth and the oval cheek-line of her Malay grand-

mother, her German blood showed in her paler skin, and her voice, too, was light and gentle where that of Kleinhans was heavy with nearness to the African earth. It is doubtful whether she would have married Kleinhans had he not been, for her standards, an exceedingly prosperous man; but having done so, she made him a meek and amiable wife.

And Kleinhans, except in moments of sudden recurrent bitterness, learnt to forget, in his successful domesticity and happy husbandry, that he had once intended to marry a pure white girl, and that he had been beaten almost to death for merely speaking to one.

2

Their eldest child, a daughter, was born within the first year of their marriage—in the year 1872, and they called her after Lena's mother, Elmira.

She looked at birth like a typical European baby. Deborah, who had come over from Kokstad for the event, shook her head at her in proud amazement.

"Such a white child I have never seen before," she said. And she would hold her in her arms and rock her to sleep to the same tune with which old Cachas had lulled her when she had been a baby in Canaan: "My mother is here, my mother is here, mother's darling," the Hottentot words meant.

And as she sang the little tune she saw again the river at Canaan—they called it the Vaal River now; and she saw her father, the Rev. Andrew Flood, wandering around like an ejected spirit, with his lost-looking blue eyes and his lips which would not close over his big teeth; and she saw her guardian, her grandmother Cachas, her face all bunched up with wrinkles, bending her fat body over a three-legged Kaffir-pot; and she saw her mother Silla, and the man she had gone to live with, Harina, and their many little brown children; and she saw her brother, Isaac, who had returned to his mother's people; and she saw the Hottentots of Canaan dancing naked under the moon. . . . She herself had not participated in their lunar festivals, but she had gone with the other Hottentot children dancing down to the river to the sound of their singing, a line of little girls with vessels on their heads for water, swaying their hips to the rhythm of the song they were making—some little tune or other endlessly repeated—their voices ringing out loud and wild on the high notes. And they did all sorts of things with their songs—sang them this way or that, improvising parts, throwing them from one to another like a ball. . . .

But these things were past for her and hers. How different life was these days; how one tried to be just like the white people. . . . how one was *getting* white.

She looked at the child she was nursing. Who would say its grandmother's mother had been a pure-blooded Hottentot? Or who, she was sure, looking at Isaac's grandchildren (he must have many grandchildren—his grandchildren did not come only through one channel as hers did—and Kleinhans had married late at that), yes, who could suppose that Isaac's grandchildren had had an English great-grandfather, a learned man, a predikant, like Mijnheer, the pastor at Kokstad? . . .

She remembered how the good missionaries who had taken charge of her, Mr. and Mrs. Burtwell had been distressed on account of her adventure with Hans

Kleinhans. Well, as the result of that adventure here she was sitting with a grandchild on her lap who looked like the grandchild of a white woman, and what harm had it done her? . . . Thank heaven, though, it had not been the Hottentot, 'Kon'gap. How easily it might have been! She wondered now what it was that had attracted her about 'Kon'gap. But she could no longer even remember what he looked like, so that was a useless question to put herself. . . . Why, she was not very clear about Hans Kleinhans himself, who had walked about at Kadesh with his arm openly about her waist, and had laughed at the idea of marrying a brown *meisje*. To-day, no doubt, he was the father of big and blonde and sturdy Boers, and sat peacefully on his farmhouse stoep, drinking his perpetual coffee, careless of the fact that here was another family descended from him, trailing its illicit way down the slopes of time. . . .

Little Elmira yawned a big baby yawn.

"A la!" said Deborah, on a rising inflection, and began again, but more softly now, to hum her little tune.

3

They had wondered at the homestead, Mr. and Mrs. Lindsell (for the girls were now at boarding school) what the baby would look like. It was really quite amusing—as interesting as a gamble—to watch the results of these half-caste marriages. . . . One had a feeling that they might turn out to be anything.

And yet, generally, they were just what one might have expected, as if an accountant had balanced debits and credits. Still there was always the *chance* of some peculiar variation, and that kept one's curiosity alive.

Mrs. Kleinhans, their Lena Smith that used to be, came over with the baby and sat in the kitchen while the Kaffir girl went to call Mrs. Lindsell, who was in the dining room with her husband. The post had just come in bringing unsatisfactory reports of the girls' progress at school. For this Mr. Lindsell (not altogether unjustly, since the girls were naturally intelligent) was blaming his wife's teaching, and there was discord in the air.

"Lena has brought the child for Missus to see," the Kaffir girl announced.

Mrs. Lindsell rose.

"No, sit down, Caroline," said Mr. Lindsell. "Let Lena bring the baby in. I should like to see it too."

The Kaffir girl returned to deliver the message to Lena, and Lena came rather shyly into the dining room, and stood uncertainly at the door.

"Take a chair, Lena," said Mr. Lindsell.

His wife threw him an amazed look. Coloured people were not customarily asked to seat themselves in the presence of white people. But she went over to Lena, and a little awkwardly examined and praised the baby. She was thinking how white it was, but that she did not mention. It seemed, somehow, indelicate to discuss a baby's whiteness with its not white mother. Besides, she had a queer feeling that she would not like to give Lena the satisfaction.

But Mr. Lindsell had no such qualms. "Why, she's whiter than our own children were," he said. "And prettier, too. She doesn't look as if she'd been boiled."

It seemed to have been deliberately said to hurt Mrs. Lindsell, and she felt her heart rising in her, and the blood flooding her sun-dried cheeks. Mr. Lindsell had always been annoyed with her because the girls had not been boys; and because, being girls, they were not at least sturdy and attractive girls. They had

131

brains of a kind, but he felt their physical deficiency to be an insult against his own virility, and it sometimes seemed to his brooding wife that he almost hated them.

"No, she wouldn't look as if she had been boiled," she answered. "It's generally fair children who look that way."

Lena's pretty dark face flushed a little, more, perhaps, at the tone of unaccountable enmity, than at the words. She half rose to go.

"No, stay and have tea," suggested Mr. Lindsell with perversity.

Lena looked uncertainly from one to the other with her soft, shadowed brown eyes.

"Mrs. Kleinhans, Kleinhans' mother, is expecting me at home," she murmured.

"Yes, perhaps you had better not keep her waiting," said Mrs. Lindsell, her voice unsteady with angry emotion, hardly able to contain herself until Lena should go that she might open up on her husband her flood of bitterness.

"Come again, Lena," said Mr. Lindsell, as the girl stood up. "And bring the baby. I want to see how she gets on."

Mrs. Lindsell held herself in until the door had shut after Lena. Then she turned her red and furious face on her husband.

"There will be no coming here again to exhibit the baby. . . ." she said.

Mr. Lindsell smiled.

". . . that comparisons may be made between coloured children and mine. That their own father should shame them—and me—and himself—by preferring coloured children to them! . . . I tell you, Adam——"

132

Her voice broke and she began to cry.

Mr. Lindsell felt that he had gone too far. He told himself that he had been annoyed by those bad reports, but that he was not really the man wantonly to give any one pain. It was only that he got irritated.

"Oh, come, Caroline," he said. "Don't do that."

At his gentler tone, Mrs. Lindsell's tears ran faster still. "You're driving me mad," she sobbed. "I can't bear it any longer. Everything I do is wrong—everything. Why didn't you teach them yourself if you weren't satisfied with the way I taught them? I did my best, but I never even got a word of sympathy. You took no interest. You——"

"I said three years ago that they should be sent away to school."

"When they were only babies. But what difference did that make to you? You couldn't bear the sound of their little childish arguments; or the way they cried when they fell and hurt their poor little knees; or if they sniffed when they had colds. You never had the feelings of a father for them. My poor babies! Oh, God, why did I ever marry an unnatural man like you!"

Nothing could have hurt Mr. Lindsell more than that last reproach. Manhood *in excelsis* was the craving of his life.

He laughed a little hard laugh—not even now would he allow himself to be angry. There was nothing, he knew, so exhausting to his vitality as anger; and his father had died of apoplexy. But there was a throbbing at the top of his head.

"You married me, my dear," he explained, "because you never had the opportunity to marry any one else."

Mrs. Lindsell's body was shaking now.

"And I wish I had died instead," she retorted in a strangled voice.

4

And so it was over a year before they saw Elmira again. Deborah had by that time returned to Kokstad. She missed, on the farm, the social life to which she was accustomed.

Mr. and Mrs. Lindsell were sitting on their stoep. Life, of course, had continued as usual after their quarrel. They bore with one another. Mr. Lindsell was reading, and Mrs. Lindsell was darning, and the young native girl who was in charge of Elmira, had come for a chat with the Lindsell's kitchenmaid. They were squatting on the ground under a blue gum tree facing the stoep, and Elmira was toddling about near them.

She was a strong and beautiful child, with an olive skin, delicate little features, large golden-brown eyes, shadowed beneath as her mother's were, and straight golden-brown hair. All that Mrs. Lindsell noticed was the olive skin.

"What did I tell you, Adam?" she turned on her husband triumphantly.

"I can't remember, I'm sure," said Mr. Lindsell, with his little ironic smile. "You tell me so many things."

"When you said she didn't look as if she had been boiled like our own babies——"

"Oh, yes."

"And I answered that that was because she wasn't going to be a fair child."

"Well?"

134

"She's turned out a little coloured girl, after all."

There was a great satisfaction—the revenge of insulted and brooding motherhood—in her voice.

Mr. Lindsell smiled again. "Possibly," he said, and remained silently regarding the child for nearly a minute. "Nevertheless," he added then, "she is quite the most beautiful child I have ever seen."

His tone admitted of no argument in the matter. But Mrs. Lindsell felt that she must say something further.

"I think it's an impertinence for Lena to keep a nursemaid," she cried, her voice charged with bourgeois indignation.

"Why—if she can afford it?" commented Mr. Lindsell. "Kleinhans is a well-to-do man."

"Yes. Because you choose to have a Hottentot for a partner. All the farmers round about despise you for it."

"And envy me my prosperity. My dear Caroline, you should be the last person to cavil at any means I take for increasing my wealth. Our daughters will need to have a rich father."

With that same little smile on his pale lips, he returned to his paper.

The lanky and increasing plainness of Edith and May was a continual source of aggravation to him.

CHAPTER II

I

By the time Elmira was eight years old, Edith and May were nineteen and seventeen respectively, and were finished with school. Now they were back at the farm, and complaining all day long of boredom.

Lindsell's farm was not a very beautiful place. There were a few tall old blue-gum trees near the homestead, and some vines, and peach trees, and apricot trees. And Mrs. Lindsell had made half-hearted attempts at a flower garden too; but the dry heat killed everything except the most hardy of plants, the Kaffir "boys" grumbled at having to draw well-water merely for flowers, and the unfortunate garden was always in a state of dying off and having to be re-made. As often as not the poor beds contained nothing but some sand surrounded by a border of stones. And Mr. Lindsell had lately been suggesting that his wife had better give up trying to grow flowers and put down some neat gravel round the house instead.

Outside the stone wall of the house, the farm stretched away in an interminable yellow-brownness, quite level, and varied only by patches of short grass, greyish-green shrubs, and an occasional thorny tree. There were two windmills on the farm, a large dam and a small one, and some sheds. And here Mr. Lindsell's cattle and sheep ran and throve. And it was very hot and bright.

But, then, evening came, and the stars sprang alight,

and a little delicate breeze drove away the heat of daytime, and little scents of wild flowers, growing close to
the earth that one hardly ever saw, began faintly to
assert themselves, and the world looked so big and
mysterious—and yet friendly and safe—because the
unbroken sky reached down on all sides to the horizon
like the walls of a great protecting tent . . . and so at
night one felt a little sad, but also a little happy, and
not, as in the daytime, only hot and weary with the
monotonous heat.

The house itself was comfortable, but not beautiful.
It was made of brick and whitewashed, with a corrugated iron roof, and on three sides the roof was extended,
supported on wooden poles, to make a verandah. The
house inside had large, airy rooms, full of all kinds of
odds and ends of furniture. Only the beds, and Mr.
Lindsell's easy-chair were really good. "One spends
a third of one's life in bed," Mr. Lindsell always
maintained, "and one might as well be comfortable
there. A good horsehair mattress is worth its weight
in gold."

And so Edith and May did a little sewing and fancy
work, read such books as came their way, made a cake
now and then, went for an occasional ride, and spent
the long, hot hours dreaming that romance would one
day appear to them in some mysterious fashion.

It was the year 1880. Women, if they did not marry,
did nothing else. Poor Mrs. Lindsell looked at her
daughters with unhappy eyes, and suggested to her
husband that she would take them to England to visit
her relations. They might have a chance there.

It seemed to Mr. Lindsell a good idea. It worried
even him sometimes to see them eating their lonely
hearts out.

I

137

"Arrange for a housekeeper to look after me," he said. "And you can go as soon as you like."

2

They went, and Mr. Lindsell, unexpectedly missing his wife, who, in spite of her nagging and grumbling, had grown to understand him and how to attend to his wants, felt extraordinarily lonely and depressed. He was now nearly fifty-five, but had hardly changed since the time he had rescued Kleinhans ten years before. He was, perhaps, a little thinner, a little sallower, a little more hollow-eyed and hollow-voiced—almost quite bald; but the general impression he made was just the same. He had looked like a wandering spirit then, and he looked like a wandering spirit now. They said, the folk around, that he was like those strips of dried meat—game or beef—that the Dutch people called biltong . . . like biltong they said he was, desiccated; and he would probably, they added, prove as persistent. Indeed, there were people who remembered him looking almost exactly the same for more than twenty years; and, what with the care he took of himself, and his blood that was so poor, that the very disease germs scorned to inhabit it, there seemed to be no reason why he should not last on like that indefinitely.

He was, however, human enough to hate his solitude; and so on those walks which, as long as any one could remember, he always took, weather permitting, between sundown and dark, he now formed the habit of dropping in at Kleinhans' house and having a little chat. First it was about farming matters, but afterwards it really was about nothing in particular, so that, essentially, it was quite an ordinary social call. And for this even the Kaffirs despised him. A white man to visit a Bastaard! It offended their whole code of behaviour.

But much Mr. Lindsell cared what any one thought. He did as he pleased, and there the world ended.

At first when he had come to see them, the whole Kleinhans family had felt a discomfort amounting to positive unhappiness. There were now five little Kleinhanses, and everything seemed to go wrong with them precisely when Mr. Lindsell appeared. Then they would fall and shriek at their hurts; then they would quarrel and abuse one another; then they would happen just to have untidied their mother's precious sitting-room. It signified Lena's claim to importance, that sitting-room. Long ago, in Cape Town, she had admired sitting-rooms like that, but had never dreamt that she herself would ever be affluent enough to be able to have one.

Her sitting-room was full of furniture and ornaments —paper fans pinned against the walls, pink and white grasses, ostrich egg shells and things like that—and it always had a peculiar, stuffy smell. But she would awkwardly insist on Mr. Lindsell's sitting down on some rickety chair, and she would hurry out in perturbation to make him the coffee (which was the customary beverage), and bring in the preserves—the Dutch *konfijts*—that, from her service in his home, she knew he liked.

Still after a time, they all got used to his visits, and the children no longer distressfully obtruded themselves, and Lena and Kleinhans allowed him to sit, as he preferred, on their little dung-smeared stoep, and they learnt to talk quite freely.

And one day, sitting there like that and looking at

the five children, he asked them what they intended to do about the children's education.

"Elmira is now eight," he pointed out, "and Hans (Kleinhans had proudly called his eldest son after the white father who had left Kleinhans himself without a name) Hans is nearly seven. Are they not to have any schooling?"

"But what can we do, Mijnheer?" said Kleinhans. ... He was, probably, the only person in the world who loved Mr. Lindsell, and he still—speaking in a combination of English and Dutch, because he did not know English very well, and Mr. Lindsell had never troubled to learn to speak Dutch, though he understood it—called him "Mijnheer" in respectful gratitude for his rescue. ... "What can we do? It is very hard for people like us. There is the mission school for black children, but I do not wish my children to go there. And to send them to a town to a white school— Mijnheer, a white school would not take them."

"Elmira might pass for a white child," said Mr. Lindsell.

"But Hans—takes after my mother's people," confessed Kleinhans.

And it was true. Hans was darker than either of his parents.

"Yes, that is so," admitted Mr. Lindsell.

He did not know why he took so much interest in this coloured family. Boredom, perhaps, or his natural perversity, he thought, almost amused at himself. "But it's a pity for Elmira. She is a beautiful child."

"Yes, she is, Mijnheer. And what then? The school people have but to see her father and mother, even if they notice nothing about herself, and the whole

thing"—he spread out his hands in a gesture of fatality
—"is finished."

"If they see her father and mother," repeated Mr.
Lindsell. "Yes. But if they do not?"

"What does Mijnheer mean?"

"If, for instance, I were to take her to the school?"

Kleinhans and Lena looked at him in dumb be-
wilderment.

He smiled at them. "We shall see."

3

And that was how Elmira got her education. By
the time Mrs. Lindsell and the girls had returned,
matrimonially unsuccessful from England, she was
already a boarder at a convent in the nearest town to
Lindsell's farm. If the nuns suspected anything—
well, they only suspected. Mr. Lindsell's basilisk eyes
between their wrinkled lids admitted of no arguments.
They took Elmira.

And until she was twelve she stayed there. A few of
the other girls had whispered to one another at first
that Elmira Kleinhans was darkish, but as she became
a part of the convent constitution they ceased to discuss her, and so, presently, she was freely accepted as
one of themselves.

Nevertheless, she could not feel really safe. It was
as if she were leading a double life, in the manner of a
criminal. At school she was one thing; and at home,
when she came there twice a year for the holidays, she
was another. And although, at school, as time went
on, she actually got to the stage of putting on a few
little airs and of looking down on other children for this
or that—although she even went to the length of joining
in the universal condemnation of one little girl because

her father was in prison, another little girl because her father was a butcher, and a few more little girls because they were Jewish—there was always at her heart a frightened pain. If she saw two children smiling about something she did not know, her blood would congeal with suspicion. "They are talking about me. They have found out!" If fathers and mothers were discussed, a high artificial note would come into her voice as, without actually telling lies, she would still convey wrong meanings.

"What does your father do, Elmira?"

"He's a farmer."

"Was that your father who brought you here the first day you came?"

"No."

"Silly, that must have been her grandfather. It was, wasn't it, Elmira?"

"No. That was an old friend of father's."

"Have you got some brothers and sisters?"

"Yes."

"Aren't they coming to school, too?"

"You mean here?"

"Yes."

"But the one next to me is a boy, and he couldn't come to a convent."

"Is he going to boarding-school then?"

"Perhaps he will, one day."

"What is he like, Elmira?"

"Like me."

"Dark too?"

"I'm not very dark." (The blood was burning her cheeks now.)

"Oh, of course, you are. Elmira is dark, isn't she?"

"Perhaps she's Spanish," suggested a fiction-reading

elder girl. "Her name might be. Is Elmira a Spanish name?"

"I think so," said Elmira, and for good and all, adopted a Spanish ancestry.

Sometimes the girls spoke about coloured people.

"My father says he hates them worse than the real black people."

"Why?"

"Because, whatever they are, they aren't pure, he says. I heard him tell mother that he couldn't stand mongrels. He says they've got all the bad of both sides. What would you do if you found out you had coloured blood in you, Elmira, with that dark skin and all? I'd drown myself or something, wouldn't you?"

They were very romantic on the question. There was something excitingly illicit in the idea of these strange begettings of mixed colours—the subject was always in the air, they liked to talk about it.

4

But even as she dreaded being at school, she dreaded still more being at home. She was ashamed of her father and mother, she hated her brothers and sisters. There was always at the back of her mind the thought: "If the girls knew!" She kept herself apart from them. She had different manners, different standards, different hopes and ideas. She felt herself to be white. She felt them to be coloured. She would not associate with them.

Her father and mother idolized her as Abraham and Sarah idolized Isaac, as if she were miracle-born. And so, to them, indeed, she was. None of the other children approached her light colouring

All through the holidays, Lena, prepared to neglect

anything else for the purpose, would sit and sew for her daughter, making her the sort of clothes she said her friends were wearing. Kleinhans bought her a pony and taught her to ride. Every time she came home there was something new for her: a lamb, a baby calf, a little bracelet, a watch.

They spoilt her, and she took this spoiling as her due.

But her sisters and brothers jealously disliked her.

"You think you're a bloody Englishman," sneered Hans. "But you're a Bastaard just like us."

"I'm not," said Elmira.

"You've got the same father and mother."

"But all the same I'm not."

"You can say you're not, but you are. You can't come and tell us lies about it like you tell the people at school."

"I don't tell them lies."

"Yes, you do. They wouldn't keep you if they knew you were a blacky."

"But I'm not one."

Her voice would be charged with tears.

"And I say you are. You're the same as the rest of us."

"I'm not the same as the rest of you."

Hans' anger would break out now.

"Don't you keep you grand with me, Mrs. Blacky Elmira. Don't you——"

Elmira would run from him, weeping aloud, and he would follow, angrily taunting her, his bare, ragamuffin legs flashing brown in the sun; his unshod feet comfortable to the hot, stony earth.

"Mrs. Blacky Elmira. Mrs. Blacky Elmira."

It was his curious habit always to use the married title when he sneered at her. . . .

She would look forward eagerly to returning to school.

5

But four years saw the end of it. Then a misfortune happened. Elmira caught scarlet fever. There she lay in the sick-room with two other girls who also had scarlet fever, and it seemed to the good nuns that she was going to die. They sent urgent messages to Mr. and Mrs. Kleinhans to come to their daughter. Never before had Mr. and Mrs. Kleinhans done so. Hitherto, at holiday time, Elmira had simply been seen into the train, and from the nearest railway siding to Lindsell's farm she had been fetched by Cape cart for the twenty-mile trip. Once or twice Mr. Lindsell, if he chanced to be in town, had called on the nuns in his capacity as a great friend of the girl's parents. The nuns knew that a Mr. Kleinhans existed who paid his daughter's accounts very regularly, and that was all they knew.

But now, in the crisis, they recognized it as their duty to send for them.

They came, Kleinhans and Lena. They knew their coming to be the deathblow of their child's reputation. "But what difference is it now?" wept Lena, in the Dutch Taal which was their colloquial tongue. "What does it matter when she is going to die that we are brown and she is white?"

"No, ma, you mustn't say the word 'death'," protested Kleinhans, fingering, with his brown farm-worn hand, his tawny beard, still without a white hair. "It is unlucky."

"Unlucky," cried Lena. "Unlucky! But we are unlucky people. We are unlucky to be born, and still more unlucky was Elmira to be born ... that

145

now, when she is dying, her father and mother have to trouble their heads about shaming her with the colour of their skins."

"If she does not die," said Kleinhans, "it will be bad for her that the nuns should see us."

"Then you say we should stay at home, and let her die alone among strangers!"

Kleinhans shook his head. "No, I don't say that."

"We must go," said Lena, "whatever comes of it."

"Yes, that is so," agreed Kleinhans. "We must go."

6

They stood outside the convent door, a big burly man with a tint of red in his face, and fairish hair on his head and lips and chin, whose ready-made clothes were even bigger than he was, whose hands, with their broken finger nails, were almost as black, from sun and work, as the hands of a native; and beside him his wife, Lena, lighter and more delicately fashioned than he was, with pathetic dark eyes, and a small lined face, and a body, drained by children, that had grown ever thinner with the years.

They knocked, and a maid came to the door.

"Yes?" she said, in the sharp voice she always used to coloured people.

"We have a letter from the nuns," said Kleinhans "to come."

"What name?"

"Kleinhans. Mr. and Mrs. Kleinhans."

"Mr. and Mrs. who?"

"Mr. and Mrs. Kleinhans."

The maid stood staring at them.

"It is our daughter who is sick."

"Your daughter?"

"Elmira."

"Is Elmira Kleinhans your daughter?"

Shame and pride struggled conflictingly in their hearts.

"Yes."

"Wait a bit."

She left them standing there with the door half open, and went to fetch some one.

After a few minutes, during which Kleinhans and Lena remained, with pale, tight faces, silently waiting, a nun—it was the Mother Superior—came towards them.

"Will you come in?" she said, and showed them into her study.

They followed her, not knowing what to say. They had hastened to see their dying child, and here were these unhappy preliminaries.

"You are Mr. and Mrs. Kleinhans?" she addressed them.

Kleinhans nodded. One great rough hand was trembling on his heavy knee, the other was at his beard.

"Elmira's father and mother?"

"How is my child?" cried Lena, her usually thin voice harsh and breathless.

"She is better to-day."

"Thank God," said Lena, and as she said it the thought fell on both of them that, if the nun was right, they had come unnecessarily to destroy their daughter's happiness.

The Mother Superior kept her wise old eyes steadfastly on them. There was a little mysterious smile on her lips.

"Do you wish to see her?" she asked, and rose, leading the way.

Outside the sick ward Lena suddenly clutched her husband's hand.

"Wait a moment," said the Mother Superior before entering. "I shall tell Elmira her father and mother are here."

She returned to them very soon.

"Come in."

They walked towards their child with glazed eyes. At the bedside Lena suddenly fell on her knees, her arms over the bed, and began to cry. Kleinhans plucked at her sleeve. "Don't, ma, don't. You upset her."

Lena tried to control herself. Elmira looked at her parents with hollow eyes. She was wishing that she might die. Her heart was bitter with shame and misery. She looked at the white faces of the nun and her two friends in the room, and back again to her mother's brown arms flung across her bed. "Why did you come?" she said.

The Mother Superior turned away, and walked over to one of the other girls. She had suddenly realized to the full the tragedy of the little group.

"We should not have come," said Kleinhans heavily. "No. Not even if——"

"They told us you were dying," said Lena. "Oh, my child, are you angry with us?"

Elmira looked away. Anger was too small a word to express her feeling.

"I shall have to leave this place," she said. "It is all finished now."

And it was. As soon as Elmira reached convalescence she was returned to the farm. And, in due course, a letter followed regretting that the nuns could not further keep her. "We have no complaint to make against Elmira, and we have all loved the dear child;

but we think it wiser, in order to avoid unpleasantness with our other pupils and their parents, that Elmira should not come back to us."

Mr. Lindsell shrugged his shoulders over the letter. "Well, it's unfortunate, but there is no one to blame," he said.

CHAPTER III

I

BACK at the farm, Elmira wandered about like a little ghost. Her high-handed pride was gone—as if she had committed a crime and been found out; but the fact did not make her life with the family more easy. Only now, instead of protesting her whiteness, she isolated herself in sullen resentment against fate. She practised none of the manners the nuns had taught her. She hardly spoke to her brothers and sisters; she would not eat; her big, golden-brown eyes were old with pain; she grew, within the next few months, into a tall, pale, thin girl.

Even Mrs. Lindsell was sorry for her. And Mr. Lindsell once more spoke to Kleinhans.

"This sort of thing can't go on, you know, Kleinhans," he said. "The child is eating her heart out."

"It is our fault," returned Kleinhans. "We should not have wanted to see her. If she had to die, we should have let her die white. I might have remembered my own day on the Diamond Fields."

"But that is over now," said Mr. Lindsell.

"Then what can we do?" said Kleinhans.

"There are other boarding schools."

Kleinhans shook his head.

"The news of such a thing goes from one to the other."

"She can be sent far away."

"I am afraid now."

"As far as Cape Town. My own daughters went to boarding school in Cape Town. I can write to the very same school. What do you lose by trying?"

2

And so, at thirteen, Elmira was sent to school at Cape Town. Her brothers and sisters (there were seven in the family by this time) who were brown, had never had any schooling at all, and the older ones could just sign their names and make figures.

But now Elmira was provided with prettier little clothes than ever, and before going away she became quite friendly with her family. She laughed and played with them as if she really cared for them. And, indeed, she was so happy with renewed hopes and expectations that she loved everybody. She gave her mother an occasional kiss, and her father an occasional hug. No one had ever known her so affectionate before. And, even if they dimly felt that all this joy was rooted in her satisfaction at once more leaving them, they could, nevertheless, not withstand her charm and condescension.

She was golden and pretty again by the time she arrived at Cape Town.

3

And she was more sophisticated now. She began to realize that certain colours made her look fairer. She arranged her golden-brown hair noticeably about her face instead of, as hitherto, ineffectively drawing it back from her rather high and round forehead (which, except her neck, was the brownest part of her body), and she even, now and then, used a little powder.

Her manners were very pretty, too, she spent pocket-money lavishly, and she found herself soon quite popular.

She was not as clever at her schoolwork as she had promised to be when a child. It was as if her brain, running a race against the brains of white children, was very quick at starting but soon tired and lagged behind, so that the time came when it fell altogether out of the running. At sixteen Elmira had ceased to make any mental advance, and was really, in all essentials, a mature young woman. She gave an effect of being much older than any of her contemporaries, too. They realized it themselves, and rendered her school girl homage.

At home her brothers and sisters, at last recognizing the distance between themselves and her, also treated her with an almost formal respect.

Elmira, in her happiness, looked neither behind nor before her, but took what the day offered.

4

It offered, among other things, the admiration of young men—the brothers or boy friends of her schoolfellows. And it was owing to the too serious devotion of one of them that she finally left school. He was twenty-two, the only son of a very rich Cape Town merchant. And he talked firmly of marrying her. His young sister, who was a day scholar, brought Elmira to the house and Mrs. Krell looked at her with the defensive suspicion and hostility of the mother about to be robbed of her young. Who was this Elmira with the surname of Kleinhans, this interloper in the nest, this girl of whom her Henry thought to the exclusion of everything and everyone else, even his mother? Her heart was filled with a sense of impending loss. He was

152

her firstborn, she had loved him for longer than he had breathed, she had tended him and brooded over him and hoped for him. But she had pictured him always and inevitably as her son, nothing but her son. And, suddenly he had thrown her over. He wanted no more of her—no more of any of them. In the darkness of night she sobbed to her husband: "He notices us so little now that if we were to paint our faces black he would not be aware of it."

"Poor little sweetheart, what nonsense you talk," her husband comforted her. "And even if it is true, wasn't I the same with you once? Haven't we been happy? Don't let us grudge Henry what we had."

"I never sympathized with your mother enough," Mrs. Krell whispered. "She seemed to give you to me so gladly and ungrudgingly. But now I know how she felt."

"It happens in every generation," said Mr. Krell. "Over and over again you lose your children and get them back in some other form. You lose your baby, and you find a little naughty boy; your little boy and there comes a big-voiced, argumentative youth; the youth, and you have a man who frightens you by his manhood."

"And then it is the last time," said Mrs. Krell. "Then he doesn't come back again."

"But he reproduces himself in his children for you."

"But never mine—only mine—again! I don't want to share him, and have the least part at that!"

Her husband thought of his mother. She had been dead many years, and seldom came to his mind now.

"Be satisfied with the least part," he said. "I was wrong when I said a moment ago that you get them

K

153

back. My mother, I see now, was left with nothing. Most mothers are left with nothing."

5

But a curious expression his wife had used came back to his mind unexpectedly. "If we were to paint our faces black he would not be aware of it."

It made him think how fair all the Krells were. They would be a greatly contrasted couple, Henry and Elmira —if anything ever came of it, he so fair and she so dark. They were both very young, of course, Henry only twenty-two, the girl not yet seventeen; but the Krells were a young marrying family. Pretty girl, Elmira, with that all-over golden colouring of hers. . . . Kleinhans! Who were the Kleinhanses? He knew of no good Kleinhanses. Where did the family belong? He must make enquiries before the thing went any further. Elmira Kleinhans. Queer combination of a name. Her dark, interesting face stood clear before him.

6

He asked Mary, his daughter, about her friend.

"She comes from near Griqualand West, dad. From the same place as some girls called Lindsell who went to our school years ago."

"Lindsell?" said Mr. Krell. "Lindsell? Why, I knew a man Lindsell. Adam his Christian name was."

"The place Elmira comes from is called after him, 'Lindsell's Farm'."

"And do her people live there?"

"I think so. She doesn't talk about them very much."

"Has she any brothers or sisters?"

"Yes, she has. Younger than herself."

"And where do they go to school?"

"I don't know. At the farm, I suppose."

"And what does her father do—Mr. Kleinhans?"

"I think she told me once he was a farmer. Oh, yes, she said he was a partner of Mr. Lindsell."

"Well, that doesn't seem so bad," said Mr. Krell, half musing.

"What doesn't?" asked Mary.

"Oh, nothing," murmured Mr. Krell.

But he talked paternally and watchfully to Elmira, and he wrote a letter recalling himself to Mr. Lindsell's memory.

CHAPTER IV

I

DURING the last year Elmira was at boarding-school in Cape Town there had been changes in the Lindsell family. Just that year ago Mrs. Lindsell had died suddenly. She had felt, she said, rather bilious, and had gone to lie down. That was in the evening. Next morning she was a little better; but then, just as she was getting up, that queer biliousness—not quite the ordinary sort of thing—had come back. She had felt, too, a pain near the shoulder.

"Adam," she had called, her voice a little faint.

"Yes?" he answered from the bath-room next door.

"What are you doing?"

"Shaving."

"Come here, Adam."

There was an unaccustomed, frightened-sounding note in her voice that caused Mr. Lindsell to put down his razor, wipe the soap hurriedly from his face, and hasten to her.

"What's the matter, Caroline?"

"I feel—bad."

"You look green. I'll get you some brandy."

"No. Don't leave me, Adam."

Her words seemed to come from far.

She appeared to be going to faint. Mr. Lindsell put his arm about her shoulder. She sank back. She did not move. He raised her head on two pillows and went for brandy. He tried to pour it down her throat. She did not revive. He called his daughters, his voice cracked and old.

"Edith. May."

They came; looked at their mother with eyes that passed from uncomprehension to terror; ran to the bedside, crouching over her.

"Mother, mother!"

They rose presently. From one to the other the three pairs of eyes roved, and then back to the bed.

Kleinhans went to the Diamond Fields—Kimberley it was now called—for the nearest doctor. It took eight hours' quick driving to get there and back by Cape cart. When the doctor arrived, he could only tell them what they knew already, make enquiries about influenza and heart trouble, and write out a death certificate.

2

At first it hardly seemed as if anything were different. There were affairs to attend to. But afterwards a great emptiness settled down over the household. Now they began to realize, for the first time, that, for all the querulousness which the long farm years had bred in her, it was Mrs. Lindsell who had actually held the home together. It was Mrs. Lindsell who attended to their big comforts and their little comforts. . . . It was not that Mr. Lindsell, for instance, did not pay due attention to himself and his needs— but yet it was his wife's business to provide for those needs: to see that he got what he liked to eat, and that, at the same time, it suited his peculiar digestive fads; to have his socks ready for him when he got out of his bath, and arrange that they were nicely graduated to the seasons; to guard his woollens against moth in summer, and discuss with him the advisability of not taking them off too soon after winter; to stand as a buffer between him and the raw native servants; to listen to him when he wanted to talk; to be the butt of his irony, the repository of his complaints, and his scapegoat when things went wrong.

It had seemed to her, indeed, during the last years, that that was her chief function in life—to receive the blame of things. Not only her husband, but her daughters, turned to her in protest when fortune went against them. Mr. Lindsell told her it was her fault when the servants stole, and attributed it to her maternal deficiences that the girls were unattractive. The girls accused her of weakness in not having long ago persuaded their father to leave the farm, and held her responsible for their spinsterhood. When matters went awry, they grumbled at her, either for having advised them, or for not having advised them. . . .

The two girls, at least, if not their father, believed that they loved Mrs. Lindsell, but she seldom saw any proofs of it, because it had become the custom for them all to vent on her their ill-humour—and they were, very definitely, an ill-humoured rather than a good-humoured family. . . .

And so, in the end, she was rather tired of life; and although, if she had been asked, she would strenuously have objected to death, too, she did not sacrifice much by parting, as she religiously believed, soul and body from one another.

3

But now Edith and May, and even Mr. Lindsell, began to think that they had not always been kind to

her, and to feel that life was harder to bear without her.
Yet, as the months went by, they were able to console
themselves for any wrong *doing* on their part by recognizing that there had, at least, not been any wrong
intention; that, whatever they may have *said*, they had
still always *felt* the right way. They offered extenuating
circumstances to the tribunals of their souls, and gave
themselves a free pardon.

And life went on.

4

And then a thing more marvellous than death—which
was, after all, inevitable—occurred in the Lindsell
family. There came a neighbouring farmer to court
May. His name was Darrell Tibbitts.

May was now twenty-five years old, and Edith was
twenty-seven. But they were so alike in appearance,
in manner, and in history, that they were always
thought of and referred to in duplicate as the Lindsell
girls. As children they had been dressed alike; they
had gone to school at the same time, and, having begun
so, had always been in the same class and had finished
in company. They had returned to the farm together;
travelled to and from England together; still wore
clothes which were similar if not identical; got each
what the other got; and, in secret desolation, had
looked forward to a spinsterhood in each other's society.

And suddenly here came a man, a quite young and
not unpresentable man, a pleasant and jolly man, and
he differentiated between them! In May he found something to attract him that he did not find in Edith.
Where all the world saw merely two lanky sisters, with
pale eyes, rather dull, and very much alike, he saw one
as lanky, with pale eyes and uninteresting; but he saw

the other as slim and graceful, with eyes that were clear and tender, and a manner of sweet, soft complaisance such as he had always liked in a woman. Where Edith, in short, troubled his heart not at all, he discovered in May a thing which made him want to hold her, of all the world, against all the world—to share with him his home, his hopes, his life, his destiny, and his descendants.

And now, one man having made the distinction, others began to see it too. Perhaps it was that May really did change. She believed this man's judgment against that of everyone else; and, because he had found her attractive, she felt herself attractive, and even, with the confidence that she was so, became, if not attractive, at least more attractive than she had always been.

She had someone to please now, and, in making efforts to please him, became more pleasant also to the rest of her little world. She felt herself lucky and happy, and could afford to wish others luck and happiness too, where before only a grudging discontent had sat in her breast. Her spirit, freed from its load of bitterness, grew buoyant. She put on flesh, her sallow cheeks brightened, her mouth lifted itself to an upward curve. Her father suddenly discovered her as his favourite daughter, and addressed to her his criticisms and complaints. And everyone—that is, everyone in her restricted farm-life—now found her more interesting and liked her better.

Except Edith.

It was as if May had, vampire-like, sucked her added happiness from Edith; so much as May changed for the better, did Edith change for the worse.

Poor Edith, she was killing herself with envy!

Here she was, the older by two years, and May had
jumped ahead of her, had not only jumped ahead of her
—had run right away from her down the course of life,
and left her, Edith, alone, barely advanced from the
starting-point.

It was not as though she could expect to marry anyone also. May's affair had been sheer, unhoped-for,
unrepeatable good luck; and Edith, twenty-seven
years old, in the year 1888, knew as certainly as if she
had seen the tablets of her life written to the very end,
and signed by the word "Finis", that she was destined
to spend the rest of her life as what people called an
old maid. . . .

She saw May, loving, beloved, bustling about her
household, a wife, a mother, an employer . . . *my*
husband, *my* home, *my* babies, *my* servants, *my* cows
and horses and fowls and dogs and cats and plants. *I*
want this, shall do that, propose to buy the other. No,
still more beautifully, she would use the first person
plural pronoun instead of the first person singular. . . .
We. . . . And she, Edith, would spend her days not
living a life for herself at all, under the critical eyes of
an ageing and selfish father, despised and unwanted.

Lying in the dark, sleepless, her heart tight with pain,
she would clench her hands, the tears would run down
her hungry cheeks, in bitter, hopeless yearning.

And she would not confess even to herself that it was
only because there was no one to marry her. The very
pride that made her feel her position so fiercely, made
her also refuse to acknowledge her humiliation. She
believed that she was suffering, above all, because her
mother was dead.

"Only I," she thought. "Only I, mourn her."

CHAPTER V

I

AND so May married and became Mrs. Darrell Tibbitts, and went to live on a farm forty-five miles away from her old home. And Mr. Lindsell and Edith were left alone at Lindsell's Farm. And thrown so on one another's society, two selfish, unsympathetic people, they could not bear it. And there began to steal into Edith's mind an insidious thought that her father was getting on in years, and that he was rich, and that one day—one day, in the ordinary course of nature she would become independent. She settled down grimly to wait for that day.

It was to the household, thus changed within the last year, that Mr. Krell's letter was delivered.

Mr. Lindsell, reading it, had a vision of Elmira as he had seen her last holidays, a big, handsome girl, mature for her years, a golden provocative girl. Nearly seventeen, by Jove, and the fellows after her; and the father of one of these fellows very tactfully, but oh, so obviously, wanting to find out who her people were. An old friend!

Mr. Lindsell's lips came down cynically.

He went round in a strangely preoccupied way the next few days. When Edith addressed him, he seemed to be looking right past her. He hardly spoke. He would not eat or rest.

Finally he answered Mr. Krell's letter.

"MY DEAR KRELL" (he wrote), "I certainly remember you. And so the child has become a man, the inevitable problems have arisen, and the young lady in question is Miss Kleinhans.

"I am sorry to have to tell you, with regard to your enquiry about Kleinhans, her father (by the way, he differs from most people in having but one name to do duty for both Christian and surname), that I cannot give you the kind of information that I should like. The Kleinhanses are coloured people. Mrs. Kleinhans is a Cape girl, and used to be nurse to my own children before she married Kleinhans. Kleinhans, whom I employ, is the illegitimate son of a woman whose mother was a pure Hottentot. The other children are of varying shades of yellow and brown, but they are all darker than Elmira. I have nothing against these people personally, they are estimable in their class; but I think it my clear duty to tell you the truth, though I regret the painful necessity."

He added a few general remarks and concluded the letter.

His peculiar mood continued even after he had sent it away.

Mr. Krell, reading it, thought again of that expression his wife had used about black faces. . . .

At the end of that term Elmira returned home for good. She never heard from young Krell again.

2

It was a repetition of the time when, four years ago she had been sent back from the convent school. But it was worse now. Not only had she lost more, she had lost it irrevocably. She had lost her white status and her white hopes; and she was old enough in these days

163

to realize that, wherever she went, the past stalked her, panting close, audibly, at her heels, waiting its opportunity to leap at her, to hurl her to the ground and tear her flesh.

And it was not even, justly, her own past; it was the past of others.

She hoped, for a little while, that Henry Krell might find parting from her unbearable, no matter what the circumstances; she remembered the things he had said, his face as he had spoken to her that last time, and, sometimes, she almost found it unbelievable that, after all, he could give her up.

But the months went by and nothing happened. And now she knew that nothing could happen.

Of course, she had cared for him. Why not? Henry Krell was a handsome fellow, he lived in a good home, he said the most beautiful things to her, she knew her secret, she was young—it would have been contrary to nature if Elmira had not loved him.

And she did love him. But then she came back to Lindsell's Farm, and, looking round the table of brown Kleinhanses, shut in by the walls of the Kleinhans home, it seemed like a dream that fair-haired, blue-eyed Henry Krell, the son of an esteemed home, the associate of unimpeachable and popular young women, should ever have had any connection with her, Elmira Kleinhans. She put the whole affair behind her, hopelessly, as one of those things too good to have been capable of realization.

But she grew thin and yellow and careless of her appearance, she sank into the family rut—it was almost as if she had never been differentiated from them. Mr. Lindsell offered to have her in his dairy, and she agreed to try the work.

164

There was a thought running about Mr. Lindsell's head, not a new thought, it had sprung at him when Mr. Krell's letter came.

He was now sixty-three years old, and although at some times it seemed to him that he had hardly changed for—oh, thirty years (he could barely remember the time when, except that he was now quite bald, he had looked any different—less bony, less pallid, less hollow), at other times he felt that, if he did not take great care of himself, the years would begin to take advantage of him.

He had heard somewhere—was it in connection with some Biblical person, or just an old yarn he had come across?—about an aged man who had married a very young wife that he might draw, at the fountain of her youth, rejuvenation, and he could not get the idea out of his mind. It assailed him whenever he thought of Elmira. He would find himself looking at her in the dairy and wondering. He formed the habit of going to the dairy very often.

He considered the business thoroughly. Elmira, he could see, had reached even the end of desperation, that desperation which was, at least, still a struggling. She had gone beyond it to acceptance. She was without hope; in a mood where she did not care what she did, hardly, indeed, what happened.

That was Elmira's position. What was his own position?

Well, he saw no reason why he should consider any one but himself. Who considered him? May did not need him, had been only too thankful to get away. Edith remained with him because she had nowhere else to go; he had no illusions about her regard for him. Nor was she a pleasant person to live with. She attended to his wants, certainly, but with a perfunctoriness, a lack of interest, that got on his nerves. She spoke a few thin words to him during the day, they sat together through their meals . . . he narrowed his pale eyes in a sudden distaste of the life he was living. What sort of a life was it? And there was no reason why it should not go on for another twenty years—more; he believed himself to be a man who carried his years extra-ordinarily well.

Elmira! Young, tall, erect, delicate-featured, golden-brown eyes and golden-brown hair—a man might be happy merely to see her in his home. And for that little black blood—it had sounded coldly terrible when he had written about it to Mr. Krell; her mother had been their Cape nurse. Her father was the son of a woman who had been a pure-blooded Hottentot. But was it really as bad as it sounded? Kleinhans himself only carried a fourth of black blood, and Lena (he knew the type) was much further from the aboriginal than that. Elmira had for years passed as a possibly white girl. . . . Children? If they came at all, they could take their chance. As for Elmira's coloured family, he could, he was confident, keep them where they belonged, and Lindsell's Farm was not the only healthy place in South Africa where one might live.

There was, of course, the question of love. Well (his old lips curved in a downward smile), it amused the world to cherish the illusion that love was a spon-taneous impulse that came before reason. But, actually, did people very often love where it was not feasible for them to love? Most young men and women married suitably in their class and kind. First recognizing that the combination seemed sound, they then allowed themselves, or they persuaded themselves, to love. . . . And they loved; and they thought they were romantic. And they married, and they forgot about romance. And they shared, and they quarrelled, and they were friends, and they grew old, and life was done. . . .

Sometimes things did not immediately balance, and then there had to be a little manipulation with debits and credits. Thus, if he was—elderly (he would not use the word "old"), Elmira was coloured. If he was rich, she was beautiful. . . . He was prepared to recognize that she might not love him. Nevertheless, considering the lesson her affair with Henry Krell had been to her, considering his own advantages, he thought she should be satisfied to be his wife. It was enough.

The idea grew in his mind. It grew till it filled his mind so utterly that he could see nothing else. He cherished it as one of the most excellent and practicable ideas that ever, in his life, had come to him.

4

He began to give Elmira presents; a brooch, scent, a blouse. She took the things quite readily, but not very graciously. She wanted them, and yet she felt them to be useless to her. Who was there to admire her brooch, to be lured by her scent, to see how the blouse became her? Kleinhans, her father, remarked: "Mr. Lindsell has always been good to our family. He is a gentleman."

A faint smile raised the corners of Elmira's mouth.

But Edith said to her father: "I see you are beginning to take quite an interest in Elmira Kleinhans."

"I have always done so," answered Mr. Lindsell, his sunken cheeks faintly flushing.

"Yes, I remember——" Her father's flush was repeated on her own face. She closed her lips together suddenly, her sentence in the air.

"What?" asked her father.

She hesitated a moment longer. He kept his light, compelling eyes, unsoftened by lashes, on her.

"I remember it used to annoy mother."

Mr. Lindsell made no reply for a moment. Then he said calmly:

"Yes, she was always unreasonable about Elmira."

"I wonder what she would have thought of your giving her presents?"

"Are you really concerned with what might have been your mother's attitude, or is it that *you* have some objection to my behaviour?"

Edith looked at her father helplessly. He saw that her eyes were beginning to fill with tears. They flowed silently down her still, beaten face. All at once she ran to the wall, and, her head against it, her hands beating violently on it, she broke into a fury of fearful sobs.

Never—not even when her mother had died—had Mr. Lindsell seen her like that. Her abandonment frightened him, hurt him, softened him.

"My dear Edith——" he approached her.

"Don't! Don't! Don't touch me! Hate me! I am used to that. Don't touch me!"

"But, my dear girl——"

"No one has ever cared for me. No one has ever given me anything. You give presents—to a little coloured girl."

She turned round suddenly, ugly, accusing, her

light eyes hot, her lids red, her nose and lips swollen, her tears dry, her sobs ended. She pointed a shaking finger at her father.

"Don't think—I'm blind."

Mr. Lindsell's flicker of pity had died at her last words.

"No, you're not blind," he said with that smile she hated on his lips. "And what is it you see?"

"I see you are mad about that little girl," she said recklessly.

Mr. Lindsell did not answer at once. Then:

"That is something we must discuss later," he said, and left her.

5

And he had his cart inspanned, and drove over to the house of Kleinhans.

"There is something I want to tell you, Kleinhans," he said.

"Come in, Mijnheer," invited Kleinhans, and led the way to the sitting-room.

"It is private," said Mr. Lindsell.

Kleinhans waved his wife aside.

"See that the children do not trouble us," he said.

The two men sat down on the rickety "fancy" chairs, one a hearty, red-brown, middle-aged fellow, with huge limbs and great coarse hands, and the other a fleshless old man in whose veins ran thinly his superior blood.

"Well, Kleinhans, it is about Elmira," began Mr. Lindsell.

"Mijnheer is always kind to her," nodded Kleinhans gratefully.

L

169

Mr. Lindsell considered him with his customary calmness.

"Now I want to marry her," he said.

Kleinhans' eyelids drew apart in amazement, his lips forgot to meet.

"Well? . . ." suggested Mr. Lindsell.

"Mijnheer surprises me," stuttered Kleinhans.

"And what do you say to it?"

Kleinhans used his Dutch idiom.

"I must let my thoughts go. I don't know what to say."

"Is the idea unsatisfactory to you?"

"Elmira is a child."

"And you think I am old. Yes. But there are other things than years to be considered."

"Mijnheer means?"

"I mean, first, that I am white and Elmira is not."

"Yes, that is true. But perhaps one day a young fellow——"

"And I mean, second," continued Mr. Lindsell, "that it will be better for you on this farm if you and I get on well together."

Kleinhans looked at him nervously.

"It is hard for me to know what to say, Mijnheer," he pleaded. "Can Mijnheer not let me think it over?"

"By all means," said Mr. Lindsell, rising, "think it over. And think well. I want you on my side before I speak to Elmira."

He smiled his pale-lipped smile, and went back to his cart.

6

"It is not only the age," said Kleinhans in distress to his wife. "It is that he is not a man at all."

"You have always spoken highly of him before," said Lena.

"Yes, but not as someone for my daughter to marry. My Lord, no! when it comes to that, he is not a man, he is a tortoise."

And, indeed, with his wrinkled, lashless lids, his wizened neck, his bald, bony head, that was what Mr. Lindsell looked like—a tortoise.

Lena's mind flew backwards and forwards. She shuddered to think of her pretty child married to this hateful-looking old man. But, on the other hand, there flowed in her the blood of submissive slaves and acquiescent Eastern wives. There were women in her ancestry who had come young to the harems of old men, there were some who had been concubines casually taken up and casually cast off. While one side of her suffered at the idea of Elmira's marrying Mr. Lindsell, another side saw her the wife of a very rich man the most important man in the district—a white man. And not such a bad man either, as people said. Had he not been consistently good to all of them?

Now the status of the whole Kleinhans family would go up through Elmira. "My daughter, Mrs. Lindsell—at the Homestead."

Besides, it could not be for very long. Mr. Lindsell was old and sickly—he looked as if he might go any day. And then Elmira would remain, purgatory passed, in paradise—Mrs. Lindsell.

"Would you like it better if she married a poor young coloured fellow?" she asked.

"Young and young belong together," said Kleinhans. "And then who says he must be coloured?"

"See what happened in Cape Town."

"That one was too high for our sort, perhaps."

171

"You have spoken the truth. If a white man is satisfied to take Elmira, he will not be of a good class. Except just this one old man. I know. I have seen the thing."

"Still, it would be better," said Kleinhans.

"You forget Elmira is not like the rest of us. She has had the best schooling. She has been with the best people. It would be hard for her to settle down with perhaps, a bijwoner who can hardly write his name."

Kleinhans remembered how once he had vowed never to marry any but a white girl, how he had left Kokstad for that purpose, how he had hated the darkness of his mother. Did Elmira hate him in the same way? There came to his mind the picture of Elmira, sick in the convent, saying bitterly across the kneeling form of her mother, "Why did you come?" . . . On to his day at the diamond fields his thoughts ran. Well, that had cured him of white aspirations. And he had married Lena and been quite happy with her. He looked at Lena. Another idea had suddenly sprung at him. Who knew but that she had had her ambitions, the hope of marriage with a white man? . . . Unlucky people they were. She had said so, Lena, as they had stood there at the convent, waiting to be taken to Elmira. Unlucky. Unlucky.

And now his poor child, because of the black blight on her, had, as her best chance, this old man, this threatening old man.

"He says, Mijnheer says"—Kleinhans turned to his wife slowly—"that it will be better for us on this farm if he and I get on well together."

"Then he means if you don't help him to marry Elmira he will——?"

"He can do anything to us. The land is his."

"And he can force us?"

Kleinhans nodded. Suddenly he threw out his clenched fist. "Damn them—the white people," he cried.

CHAPTER VI

I

Now Edith Lindsell, too, began to go to the dairy. She would come there on some pretence or other and stand silently looking at Elmira, looking at her and looking at her, till Elmira could feel the top of her head throbbing. And then Edith would say a few words in a hard, painful voice, words of no intrinsic consequence, and yet, if one knew the mind of the speaker, charged with bitter possibilities. She would consider everything that Elmira wore with a suspicious eye. She would pretend to examine the milk or the churns, she would say something about the cows or the herds, and her little hating eyes would stare at Elmira with a significance that bore no relation to the words she was saying.

She would speak to Elmira about her people. She would ask her (and by this, if by nothing else, Elmira might have known what lay in her heart) how her grandmother, Deborah, was getting on.

"I suppose she will be coming to see you one day. She hasn't been now for a few years."

"Yes. I suppose so, Miss Lindsell."

"You must all be very fond of her?"

"Yes, Miss Lindsell."

"Isn't she getting too old now to live by herself?"

"I don't know, Miss Lindsell."

Whenever Elmira came back to the country she

found herself once more in the habit of never answering a white person without respectfully mentioning that person's name as often as possible.

"Would you be glad if she came to live with you always?"

Those fixed pale eyes frightened Elmira. She did not know what to say.

"Would you, Elmira?"

Would she be glad if her old half-Hottentot grandmother came to live with her always!

But she answered, as before:

"I don't know, Miss Lindsell."

"When did your grandfather die?" Edith would continue.

Elmira, facing her like a cornered animal, would struggle for safety. She knew all about Hans Kleinhans. Her brother Hans had found out and told her.

"I never heard, Miss Lindsell."

Edith would look at her clear, rounded face, her fine young body luxuriant with the promise of further growth, and lash her soul with comparisons.

But then she would, almost unconsciously, manage to put her thin white hand beside Elmira's vigorous dark one, and hold her head up again with the pride of race.

Back, back, back, over the years, Edith Lindsell's mind would run, bringing in to the present the material of which Elmira was made.

2

They hardly spoke to one another now, Mr. Lindsell and his daughter. And sometimes Edith felt that she must escape—even if the only place she had to run to was May's home. But then she would be afraid to go

175

away. She would be afraid of what might happen if she went away. She had a sort of feeling that her mere presence kept things from coming to a head. And yet, again, she knew definitely in her inmost being that destiny was laughing at her.

Mr. Lindsell had no thought but Elmira. He could not hold himself back from going to the dairy. He could not command himself when he was there. And suddenly one day he said to her:

"Elmira, I want to marry you. Wait. Listen to me. I know I am not young, but that is nothing. A man is not like a woman. The years make no difference to him. I don't ask you if you love me. I don't expect it. But you will be happy with me for all that. I will give you anything in the world you want. Nobody will ever come asking questions any more about whose daughter you are. You will be Adam Lindsell's wife. It won't happen to you again that you will be sent away from any place because you are not what people at first thought. You will be the most important woman for miles around. Your convent friends, who wouldn't have you go to school with them, will marry their little poor husbands and be honoured if a rich woman, such as you will be, will look at them. Yes, you shall have your very own money, Elmira, to use just as you please, without saying a word to me. You don't yet understand what money means. But I tell you, I tell you——" his voice rose for a reckless moment—— "it can make even black blood golden."

He heard the high-pitched note in his speech and checked himself suddenly. He must not get excited. His heart was beating too quickly. He embraced his left wrist with his right hand, feeling his pulse. Elmira regarded him motionlessly.

176

After a time he spoke again—quietly—words he did not believe.

"It may not be for very long, Elmira. . . . Make me happy these few years, and your whole life lies in front of you, a different thing to what it would otherwise have been."

("But I am good for another twenty years at least," he told himself.)

He watched her controlled face. It gave him no clue.

"With all your good looks and schooling, what can you hope for? What sort of a young man would be satisfied to have your father and mother in his family? It is just because I am not a young man that I am different. I can do as I choose. And if you marry me, it will be as you wish about staying here or going away. Just as you wish. I will always do just as you wish."

He came a step towards her. She looked at him calmly.

"Well, Elmira?" he asked.

She hated the tight, shiny, old skin on the back of his hands.

"Yes, Mr. Lindsell," she answered.

3

Mr. Lindsell handed his daughter a section of the fowl he had been carving. They seldom had beef on the farm, and not always mutton—it was more convenient to kill pigs or fowls; and, besides, the food that agreed with Mr. Lindsell best was boiled fowl. He would eat it readily day after day, and year after year. Whenever Edith visualized meal time at Lindsell's Farm, she always saw a dish with a boiled fowl on it.

Not that Mr. Lindsell despised food. On the contrary, he had a palate for good wine and cigars, and liked delicate puddings. It sometimes annoyed Edith, who was naturally ascetic, to see the gusto with which her father ate such things as his stomach approved of. He placated his digestion, as it were, with overtures of a simple meat course, and expected, in return, a little indulgence when it came to the more frivolous parts of the meal.

But sometimes at the end of it, he would look at Edith accusingly, and say:

"I've eaten too much again. You know I ought not to have second helpings of that stuff, and yet you offer it to me."

"You seemed to like it so much."

"Yes. But you should have reminded me that it didn't agree with me last time. In fact, you should never have had it on the table at all."

"I forgot."

"Naturally."

They would finish eating in silence, each thinking resentfully of the other's shortcomings.

To-night, as Mr. Lindsell handed Edith her plate, there was a little secret smile on his face that nauseated her. He cleared his throat, and said without embarrassment: "I have news for you, Edith."

Edith's heart seemed to turn over. She felt physically sick. The world was moving round her in slow throbs. She looked at her father, waiting for him to tell her what she knew already.

He told her. She went on cutting up her meat with hands that might have belonged to some one else.

"I don't quite expect you to congratulate me," said her father.

Edith put a morsel of fowl into her mouth, as if in a dream.

Suddenly she stood up. "I won't eat at this table again," she said, and walked out of the room.

CHAPTER VII

I

SHE stood in her bedroom gazing helplessly around her. She was glad she had spoken as she did—she had a streak of spiritedness in her, but what was she going to do now?

Her eyes fell on the little box on her chest of drawers where she kept her treasures. There were not many of them, and on top lay her mother's photograph. She took it out, put it on the bed, knelt beside the bed looking at it, and, in a flood, the tears came.

"Oh, mother," she wept. "Oh, mother. Oh, mother."

She had not been a very devoted daughter during her mother's lifetime, but now she felt that no one else in the world ever had cared for her, or thought her to be of any consequence—or ever would; she seemed to herself small and weak—like a little pathetic child; she wanted comfort ... there was the only kind of romance her starved heart could know in her action. Compounded with her own bitterness was this indignation on behalf of her dead, betrayed mother, which faintly raised her depressed heart towards sublimity. She believed herself at the moment capable of any sacrifice in defence of the family honour.

She did not hear steps coming down the passage. They were Mr. Lindsell's.

He was in a mellow mood, he felt amiably disposed

towards creation—he was, in fact, all but sentimental. And he had somehow been touched by the futile pride in the narrow, departing back of his daughter. He had sat over a glass of wine after she had gone, beaming fatuously into the future, and suddenly he had seen one aspect of it as it affected Edith. . . . Melodrama apart ("I won't eat at this table again." . . . Poor fool!), what was she going to do now?

For, whichever way one chose to put it, the conclusion was the same. Edith could not continue living at the homestead after her father brought his new bride home. Even in ordinary circumstances second marriages caused all sorts of difficulties among such relics of the first as children represented. And Mr. Lindsell was prepared to admit that here the position was just about as delicate as it conceivably could be. He had a momentary vision of Edith's pale, hating eyes following him about in his new role, following him and Elmira about as they went through their days together, and he shook his head.

Decidedly she would have to go.

But where to? Who wanted Edith? Not even May. She also would not be comfortable with Edith's pale eyes after her.

He poured himself another glass of wine.

And he had been—yes, it was true, he remembered it quite distinctly—he had once been glad at the thought of Edith's coming into the world. They had hung over the baby, he and Caroline, making plans for her. He had played about with her on the floor. . . . Ah, yes! But not for long. Too soon her teeth had begun to fall out, she had developed into one of those sallow, freckled children who are always meagre and ailing—not a child a man could be proud of.

181

He recalled Elmira's round and golden babyhood. Good Lord! She had attracted him from very infancy.

And now he was going to marry her! Well, he knew people would sneer disapprovingly at him. Let them. What did it matter what anyone thought? He was starting life over again. He felt ten years younger already. . . .

He took a cigar from the sideboard, lit it, and walked down the passage towards Edith's room.

She was kneeling before the bed, her head buried in it, her arms flung over it, her angular shoulders heaving.

"Edith!" said Mr. Lindsell.

She sprang up immediately, and faced him in her riot of misery. Her hair was hanging in odd strands over her tear-thickened face; she was shaking with passion. She snatched up her mother's portrait, and thrust it at him.

"Look!" she cried. "Look!"

"But my dear girl," murmured Mr. Lindsell.

She struggled for words, for scornful, bitter and pathetic words, but none came. And suddenly she ran towards her father, pushed him violently into the passage, and locked her door.

Mr. Lindsell stared at it in blank chagrin. He felt his heart beginning to beat too quickly, noticed the cigar shaking between his fingers, and leaned against the wall gathering his self-control.

Presently his anger smoothed itself down into a cynical smile.

"Well, she has more spirit than I gave her credit for," he told himself. "Much good may it do her," he added.

Much good did it do her. She spent the night packing together, by a feeble candle-light that shadowed her heart as it shadowed the room, all her possessions. And in the cold of dawn she went into the whitewashed, smoke-smeared kitchen, lit a few pieces of wood that she had collected in the yard outside, and made herself some coffee. Then she went towards the hut where the Kaffir boy slept and woke him.

He came out, smelling of the dirt he lived in and the old goat-skins between which he slept, in the tattered clothes that he never removed till they disintegrated of their own accord, and yawned at her sleepily.

"Yes, little Missis!"

"Span in the Cape cart, Klaas."

He stared at her.

"Does little Missis mean at once?"

"Yes, at once."

"And are we going far, little Missis?"

"We are going to Mrs. Tibbitts' place."

"But——"

"Did you hear me, Klaas?"

"But the old Baas wants the cart after breakfast, little Missis."

She looked at him with her pale, exhausted eyes.

"Span in the cart, Klaas," she said.

And Klaas went to the stable and brought out the two brown horses and the dirty harness.

"Take some forage," she ordered. "The horses will eat on the way. . . . We have no time now."

When the horses were inspanned, she made him hunt out a picannin to sit in the cart while she took him with her to fetch the boxes. The small things they put in the cart; her big box they tied on to the carrier. Then just as the sun was appearing from behind the far hills, they got into the cart, Klaas driving, Edith behind, and Klaas touched the horses with his whip and clicked his tongue. But the horses did not move. Klaas beat them with increasing violence, and they reared up on their hind legs.

He turned round to Edith and said:

"The horses are *steuks*, little Missis."

He had no need to tell her. Most of her recollections of driving were connected with horses bewitched into an immobility that was only varied by a plunging resistance to any forward impulse, while the native drivers plaintively remarked that the horses were *steuks* again. Occasionally the journey had even to be postponed—at the best of times it was a nuisance, but to-day Edith felt that she wanted to scream with nervous impatience. . .

Finally the picannin went to call some other natives, and they pushed the wheels forward while Klaas continued belabouring the horses . . . until suddenly they dashed away in a headlong gallop which Klaas dared not restrain for fear they might stop once more; and then gradually they settled down into an ordinary gait; and Edith relaxed her frightened hold on the seat and leaned back with closed eyes and shaking limbs.

It was early morning in July, and that meant a knife-like cold that cut through every garment Edith wore, and brought water to her eyes, and made her hold her breath till her lungs ached. She had not thought to take a rug. And she crouched into her seat, and felt that God had denied her.

In front, Klaas, unprotesting against Heaven or earth, held the reins in his frosted hands, and suffered patiently one more manifestation of the calamities that went to make up his existence.

At nine o'clock they drew up before a farmhouse, where they outspanned. The Boer, whose home it was, came forward, thrust his hand against Edith's thin, stiff one, and brought her into the living-room for breakfast. There all the family of wife, six sons, and two daughters, came forward, one after the other, offered her limp but friendly fingers, asked her how she was, and volunteered that with them it still went well, and then they all sat down to eat. They champed away for the most part in silence, but there was an intimate air about the homely, ugly room that seemed compounded of all those past welcomes extended, as a matter of course, to any white traveller who stopped at the farmhouse door, however he came, and whoever he was.

"You are tired, poor child," said the old *vrouw* at last. "Lie down after you have eaten."

Edith felt as if she could weep on that vast, unrestrained bosom.

"I must go on," she said.

Outside, Klaas, having fed and watered the horses, sat down in the sun and tried to thaw himself. He was not offered food; nor, indeed, was he accustomed to eat, except at evening, and then, as likely as not, only a lump of mealie-meal clogged together with a little fat. . . .

At Lindsell's Farm Adam Lindsell surveyed his daughter's abandoned room. Then he walked towards his stable.

Presently he came back to breakfast.

"Oh, well!" he said, and smiled his cynical smile.

M

185

CHAPTER VIII

I

It was evening before Edith arrived at her sister's home. Darrell Tibbitts and his wife were just sitting down to their meal when she walked in at the front door.

"Who can that be?" asked May, surprised. Her face was thickish-looking and blotched, her eyes had a startled look: she was very soon going to have a child.

Her husband looked at her with considerate affection, and said: "Don't you get up, darling. I'll go and see."

"Bless us, it's Edith," May heard him say. "My dear girl, why didn't you let us know you were coming?"

Uneasy at once, May hurried out to meet her sister. Edith was answering with stiff lips: "Wait, I'll tell you. Darrell, I——" She stood there swaying.

"Get her some brandy, May," cried Darrell, and led Edith into the lighted dining-room, and towards the sofa.

Edith took the brandy and lay there with her eyes closed. "Don't talk till you feel better," said Darrell.

"No," Edith answered. "I can't keep it in any longer." She sat up suddenly. "He's going to marry Elmira."

"He—Elmira?" stammered May, her eyelids quivering over her distended eyes.

"Father," said Edith. "Father's going to marry Elmira. I've left him."

"You don't know what you're saying," gasped May.

"Now, dear, don't you agitate yourself," said Darrell. "Take this chair. Who is Elmira?"

"The daughter of Kleinhans."

"Kleinhans, your father's *bijwoner!* But—Kleinhans. . . . Do you mean——?"

"Yes."

"Good God!" He looked from Edith to May, and suddenly restrained himself.

"I can't believe it," said May. "No, it can't be true."

"Why do you think I'm here?" cried Edith. "Go and see in the cart outside. Everything I have is on it."

She looked at May, her younger sister, a man's beloved, a wife, soon to be a mother. "I've come to you, now," she said, her voice hard.

Her brother-in-law put his arm across her shoulder. "And quite right," he said cordially. "Glad to have you. Cheer May up, too. Splendid!"

The two sisters looked at one another with pale, doubting eyes.

Then, surprisingly, May put her cheek against Edith's. She had lived with Darrell Tibbitts for nearly a year, and been warmed with his humanity.

"I've been wanting you, Edith," she said.

2

"Not another word about all this," said Darrell Tibbitts, "before we've put a little life back into Edith. Come and have a wash and brush-up. I'll have your things brought into the spare room. Don't you worry. We'll make you comfortable."

He ran to the kitchen and himself fetched her hot

water; he hovered round her unembarrassed and cheery while she re-arranged her thin hair; and he drew her cold, awkward hand protectingly through the crook of his elbow and led her back to the dining-room.

"Poor child," he said, patting it, and Edith's heart ached anew for the tender expression.

But May could not sit the meal out in patience.

"For Heaven's sake, Edith," she begged, "it can't be true. You are making a mistake."

"He told me himself."

"When?"

"Last night."

"Mad. He must be mad."

"He is no different from always. This has been going on for months now."

"But why did you never tell us?"

"I kept hoping nothing would come of it."

"You should have written to us, though. It wasn't right of you never to say a word. I can't understand you, Edith. Not to give us even an inkling."

"Well, well, my dear, he's not married to her yet. Don't upset yourself," said her husband. "Coffee, Edith?"

"Please." Her voice sounded choked. She turned to May.

"I watched him. I tried to stop it. I spoke to him about—about mother."

"As if that would help!" cried May.

She sprang up grotesquely from her chair.

"Do you understand what this means, Darrell?"

Darrell yielded to a momentary impatience.

"I think I do," he said with some dryness. "According to Edith, your father intends to provide you with a young coloured stepmother."

188

At this his wife ran to him, and grasped him fiercely by the shoulder.

"If you sit there quietly drinking your coffee like that, I'll go mad. Can't you *do* something?"

"What? Your father is his own master."

"But he must be out of his senses. He's sixty-three and Elmira—Elmira——"

"You'll make yourself ill," said Darrell. "Come now, sit down, and we'll talk it over quietly."

"Quietly!"

"Well, not quietly. Just as you please," said Darrell.

"Oh, treat me with contempt," cried May. "I expect it now. I'm entitled to it from anybody after what has happened in our family."

Darrell Tibbitts rose deliberately from his chair. "It's no use your going on like this, May. You must try to control yourself."

He put his arm across her shoulder, and forced her gently down into a chair.

"I'll do anything reasonable you suggest. I'll go to him to-morrow, if you like. Only we mustn't have scenes. We can't afford to let you get ill. And poor Edith is nearly dead with exhaustion, too."

Edith's pale lips quivered. "I didn't go to bed at all last night."

"And then you travelled the whole day!"

"I nearly died of cold this morning. I hadn't a rug."

Her weary eyes began to fill. Darrell looked at her with sympathy.

"Feeling better now, though, aren't you? . . Well, let us make an early night of it. I'll tell the girl to get your room ready and warm your bed. You must try and sleep, too, May. We'll be able to consider the whole thing better in the morning. I promise you I'll do my best. Be good girls now, both of you."

He piloted the two wretched sisters to their rooms, the one whom, by Heaven's mysterious dispensation, he loved, and the other to whom, for that reason, he felt a kindly duty, and himself returned to the dining-room. He took off his heavy boots and leggings and thrust his feet towards the fire.

"The old devil," he said. "The senile old toad. No wonder the poor girls——My God, what a bloody business!"

CHAPTER IX

I

WELL, of course, Darrell Tibbitts' visit had been fruitless. Mr. Lindsell had heard out what he had to say in an attentive, drooping-mouthed silence that had made him feel, not like a moral champion, but like a young fool. Mr. Lindsell's look had declared quite plainly: "My dear, silly ass, do you really think anything in this world matters to me except what I happen to want?"

But when Darrell had finished speaking, he answered him with smiling deliberation:

"Thank you," he said, "for putting the case before me so clearly. There are, as I see it, several points I have to consider. Some you mentioned to me, and some not. These latter are perhaps more directly important to you. To begin with, there is the inconvenience to you of keeping Edith. I admit Edith can be difficult. Still, I shall see that she is, at least, not materially burdensome to you. I intend to make Edith a respectable allowance. Then there is the question of a diminished inheritance for May. . . . No, please listen to me as I listened to you, without interruption. I take it you are about to say the conventional things. I know what they are, and there is no necessity for you to impress them on me. Such a thought never entered your mind. You married May for love alone. . . . Very well, consider your protest made. And here, by the way, we come to the word 'love' in connection with myself.

Strange as it may seem to you, I find Elmira quite as attractive as you find May." His wrinkled lids quivered ever so slightly. "And, from Elmira's point of view, she finds certain qualities in me that recommend me to her as a husband. There is no moral aspect in the matter of an elderly man marrying a young woman. The thing is simply personal."

He crossed one bony knee over the other, and a faint smile lifted the depressed corners of his thin mouth, and deepened the lines round his lashless eyes. He looked more senile than a much greater age than his own might have warranted.

"And now," he said, "we come to what you suggest is the most important factor in the whole affair—the social question, both in its narrow sense of family dignity and its wider sense of race purity. With regard to the first, I can only say that I have never noticed that children ordered their lives to please their parents, and I, for one, do not intend to order my life to please my children; and, with regard to the second, that—well, Darrell, that your assumption flatters me."

His hollow tones were charged with a cynical amusement.

Darrell had refused his offer of hospitality, and had ridden back to the nearest neighbour, the Boer who had welcomed Edith the morning before, to spend the night.

And two months later Adam Lindsell had travelled down to Cape Town with Elmira Kleinhans, and had there married her. He had been, financially, as generous as he had promised, and had settled on her, by ante-nuptial contract, £5,000 worth of stock, which he had deposited in her name with his Cape Town bank. "The dividends from these shares are your own pocket money to do with as you like," he told her. "So you see, I am as good as my word. Well, Elmira?"

She did not move as he approached her. "Yes, thank you, Mr. Lindsell," she said.

"You mustn't call me Mr. Lindsell now," he corrected her.

"I forgot."

He was in his sixty-fourth year, and she was not yet eighteen.

2

They spent their honeymoon largely in buying things for Elmira. She never made a demand herself, but she accepted whatever her old husband offered her in a spirit of calm acquiescence. It was as if she recognized that he was merely fulfilling his part of the contract in lavishing presents on her.

And the more he gave her, the more he wanted to give her. He threw his money over her in a frenzy of prodigality. He felt an urge to buy for her that raked him like a lust. Jewellery, clothes, ornaments for the house, he could see nothing which might be adapted to her use that he could resist. And he could not bear her out of his sight, and he could not restrain his delight in exhibiting her as his wife. He enjoyed being gazed at as he walked down the street with her, and he led her into shops, triumphant in his marital capacity.

Wherever they went they were stared at—the decrepit-looking old man and his tall, dark, beautiful child of a wife. People who would not otherwise have noticed her found her romantic and exciting in her peculiar matrimonial circumstances. All the men at the hotel where they were staying wanted to meet her;

and Adam Lindsell exulted the more in his possession of her when he saw the interest she aroused. If people thought she was rather dark-complexioned, they overlooked it as only another thrilling factor in the queer situation. It never entered Mr. Lindsell's mind to be jealous of her, and she behaved towards her admirers with an ease and grace, with a circumspection and dignity, that were not only beyond cavil, but really quite surprising. . . .

3

Until, suddenly, Mr. Lindsell got tired of it all. He had begun to notice that he looked more fleshless and hollow-eyed than ever; he had remarked that his digestion was more uncertain than usual, and that he wearied sooner; and he had gone and weighed himself and found that he had actually, from his already insubstantial enough body, lost five pounds in weight.

That had really frightened him, and he had told Elmira, that they must return at once to the farm.

Elmira had agreed without question or dispute. Although Mr. Lindsell had said to her at the time he offered her marriage that he would always do just as she wished, they both of them knew that promise to be merely a formula. It would never have occurred to either of them that Elmira might advance any opposition to her husband's suggestions or wishes; nor did she.

So now she went and packed up their things—his and hers together, his sober old man's clothes and the beautiful garments he had bought her, with the unquestioning composure that marked her whole association with him—as if she were fulfilling an inevitable arrangement of nature. As, without protest, the stars ran along their endless course, and woman went so many months with child, and seeds burst into life through the earth, and death came swishing along, so, with the same abandoned sense of fatality, Elmira accepted her function as Adam Lindsell's wife. . . .

It was springtime when they arrived back at Lindsell's Farm; and the air was invigorating to the point of intoxication; and the young grass (Mr. Lindsell said he had more varieties on his farm than the whole of the British Isles could show) was pushing towards daylight, and the animals were renewing life. . . . And Elmira unpacked her clothes and hung them in the wardrobe the first Mrs. Lindsell had used for nearly thirty years, and arranged her pretty new brushes and combs and mirrors on the dead wife's old dressing-table, and put the lace coverlet and curtains on the mahogany four-poster that had seen the birth of Edith and May nearly a decade before her own birth.

She did not ask herself whether she was happy or unhappy. She went on with life.

4

Old Deborah was visiting her son, and she seemed to be extending her visit in a way that suggested to Kleinhans and Lena that this time she had come to stay for good. But Kleinhans no longer hated her for her brownness. He had put aside his white aspirations many years ago.

Deborah was delighted with her grandchild's marriage. It satisfied her social sense. She had forgotten 'Kon'gap and Hans Kleinhans and the madness of young blood. Or, at least, she saw love now as a thing of little consequence in the scheme of things. What she did know was that in Kokstad, whence she had just come, white settlers had entered, pushing important coloured people like herself away into the background; and nothing, she felt, mattered except to be white. She was a year or two older than her granddaughter's husband.

She came, with Kleinhans and Lena, to the Lindsell homestead to visit Elmira. They were all dressed in their best clothes and they disposed themselves nervously in the dining-room, hardly daring to speak. Old Deborah was rather more at her ease than Kleinhans and Lena, but Mr. Lindsell sat examining them with his cynical pale eyes, and they were really in an agony to get away. They looked at Elmira, at the elegant clothes she had put on for the occasion, but they were almost afraid to kiss her a welcome, and she did not offer to show them her presents, nor go into many details about her sojourn in Cape Town. The Kaffirs in the kitchen were amused at the situation, and from where the visitors sat they could hear the sound of a talking and laughing that they hardly doubted involved them.

Kleinhans said: "How was the weather in Cape Town?"

And Elmira answered: "Sometimes it rained."

"Did you have good food at the hotel?" asked Lena.

"Yes, the food was very good," Elmira told her.

"Was the place full?" put in Deborah, and Elmira nodded assent.

Then Mr. Lindsell asked Kleinhans some questions about the cattle, which Kleinhans answered not as freely as usual, but still with relief. And Deborah spoke of farming conditions at Kokstad. And the Kaffir girl brought in some very cold and weak coffee. . . . And Elmira's brown relations rose decorously, shook hands one after the other, and departed.

196

Neither Mr. Lindsell nor Elmira made any comment on the visit. There was nothing much to say. The Kleinhanses would not be there very often.

The Kleinhanses drove home in the cart (which, through a sense of the family's new dignity, Kleinhans had recently bought to replace the broken-down old one) without speaking to one another.

But in the darkness of the night Kleinhans, turning restlessly about, accidentally touched his wife's face, and found it wet.

CHAPTER X

I

But Elmira's young brothers and sisters were not so shy.... They were always visiting her. At first they had come in clean clothes, and exhibiting their best manners. But, presently, they had begun to run in and out quite casually, brown and barefoot and grubby. And soon they were all over the place, using and breaking things; noisy; a ragamuffin nuisance.

Mr. Lindsell told them so without hesitation.

"I can't have this," he said to Hans. "You mustn't come here so often. I am getting tired of it."

Elmira offered no protest. She never offered protests.

But Hans, at a reasonable distance from the house, wrinkled up his nose and stuck out his tongue, shouting the vituperations that came to his mind. He was well-primed with them.

2

He was the least satisfactory of all the Kleinhans children—a very tall, dark boy, nearly seventeen, ignorant, lazy, disobedient, foul-mouthed and dishonest. He did no work at all, but he was a marvel with a gun, and it amused him occasionally to go out looking for the spoors of lost cattle. He had the predatory instincts of his aboriginal ancestors. And it was he who precipitated the departure of the Kleinhans family from Lindsell's Farm.

One day, out on the lonely veld with his brother

Adonis, fifteen months his junior, he challenged him to a shooting competition. He won so easily that it bored him, and he walked along boasting, telling Adonis that that sort of shooting was for babies, recalling the things he had done, and discussing the things he could do.

"That stone there—*there*—you see that stone right over there?—I could lift up my gun and hit it without looking. . . . That meerkat, the one running across the field to the right, I wouldn't waste the trouble to show you how easy I could get it. . . . The biggest range a gun can do—I am a man who doesn't miss at that range. . . . When did you see me miss anything last, Adonis?"

"You talk too much," said Adonis briefly. "I have seen you miss often."

"Now that is a lie," said Hans. "And you know it is a lie."

Adonis kicked along with his hard bare feet without disputing the matter any further.

But Hans had his blood up.

"And I'll prove to you it's a lie. Point me out any single thing within reach of a gun, and I'll hit it."

"Ach," shrugged Adonis. "You'll only boast the more if I do."

A maggot was working at Hans' brain, exciting him. . . .

And it chanced just then that a bow-legged Indian carrying in each hand a basket of the shoddy goods that he hawked about the country came into view, his fez bright red in the sun.

"Now I'll show you," said Hans. "Look at that Indian's cap. You see that Indian's cap? I'll show you if I can shoot or not."

"Don't talk madness," said Adonis. "You can't shoot at a man."

199

"I am not going to shoot at a man. Didn't you hear what I said? I am going to shoot at his red cap. The top of his red cap. Yes, God, the tassel on his red cap. See me do it."

He raised his gun. And "Don't you try to stop me, Adonis," he warned his brother, "because if you hinder me I might miss and kill the man."

Adonis stood by, frozen, not daring to offer any opposition, hoping humbly that Hans could achieve what he promised.

The bow-legged Indian came slowly and unsuspiciously along. In the distance he saw a man raise a gun, but did not connect the action with himself. Hans sighted and fired. The man who had worn the fez spun round and fell forward.

The brown face of Hans had suddenly turned a queer green colour.

"He got a fright," he grinned nervously at Adonis.

"You hit him," said Adonis.

"He fainted from fright," persisted Hans.

"A man doesn't go round like that before he falls through fainting."

"Adonis," whispered Hans, "let us get away. There may be trouble."

"We must go to the man. Perhaps he is only wounded."

Hans' face became greener still. "I am frightened, Adonis."

"Come," said Adonis.

Hans trailed after him.

"I am frightened. You should not have angered me, Adonis. It is your fault."

It did not require more than a look to know that the man was dead.

The two brothers stood facing one another.

"They will hang you," said Adonis.

"How will they know I did it?"

"They will know."

Hans dropped his gun and grasped his brother by the wrists.

"Will you tell them?"

"Let me go, Hans."

"Will you tell them?"

Adonis struggled. "I say, let me go. You are mad. Let me go."

"Will you tell them?"

Adonis was sobbing as he fought to get away.

"Yes, I will," he gasped. "Yes, I will."

"Then I'll shoot you, too," said Hans. He dropped his brother's wrists, and picked up his gun. "I swear it."

Adonis threw out his hands before his face. "I won't say anything. Let me go, Hans. Don't shoot me. I'll keep quiet. Don't shoot me."

They arrived home, the two brothers, ill with terror. A Kaffir who had watched the whole scene from behind a bush reported the deed. Hans was found guilty of culpable homicide, and sentenced to five years' imprisonment.

3

The scandal brought Mr. Lindsell's relationship with the Kleinhans family disagreeably into the limelight. It was all very well to exhibit Elmira—a detached Elmira—to the world as his wife. But it was another thing to have his relationship with the Kleinhans family made into reading matter for the newspapers. It angered him. "We'll make an end of this," he said to Elmira.

N

Elmira regarded him, as she generally did, with a look of silent inquiry.

"Your people will have to leave this place. I am sorry to lose Kleinhans. He has been a valuable overseer. But I can't allow my peace to be disturbed. It is not good for my health. Your family will have to go somewhere else."

He communicated his resolve to Kleinhans.

Kleinhans nervously fingered his greying, tawny beard.

"Mijnheer," he pleaded, "it is not my fault."

"I admit that," said Mr. Lindsell.

"I have worked well for Mijnheer."

"Yes. And I shall be sorry to lose you."

"Mijnheer said that if I helped Mijnheer to marry my child——"

"I meant it then. But things have changed. I can't have a half-Hottentot grandmother always about the place. There is this affair of Hans. It has made things very unpleasant for me. I have no complaint against you and Lena, Kleinhans. I must say you have known your place. But your children are not so well-behaved. No, it cannot go on."

"But, Mijnheer——"

Mr. Lindsell held up his hand.

"Mijnheer can't mean—after all these years——"

"There is no more to be said in the matter. I will act fairly by you. You know I have always treated you well. There are other places besides Lindsell's Farm. I have decided, Kleinhans."

And it was as he said.

Within three months the Kleinhans family, handsomely paid off, but bitter, had left Lindsell's Farm. And Elmira remained there, without friend and

without family, alone in the old homestead, with Adam
Lindsell.

4

From childhood she had realized that she was no
match for fate. Now she was as acquiescent as a dumb
animal; but she no longer knew what to do with her
days. Although she was not particularly devoted to
her relations, she had got into the habit, for something
to do, of visiting them almost daily. She walked there
or rode there or drove there. At first she had never gone
except by Cape cart. It had given her a faint satisfaction
to dress herself in her best, and to be seen by any passer-
by (even if it was only a Kaffir) being driven along,
looking like a lady. Then her husband had given her a
horse, and she had rather enjoyed riding over. But
latterly, to fill out the time, she had reduced herself to
walking backwards and forwards.

And here her principal activity was taken away from
her.

She was not given to reading. Adam Lindsell insisted
on several servants, and Elmira found that she had
nothing to do but sit all day long on the stoep watching
the grass grow.

Adam Lindsell himself began to be used to Elmira's
presence in the house, and to expect her to be more than
a mere delight to him. He thought she should attend
to his comfort, darn his socks, put out his clothes,
supervise his diet—take, in that way, the place of the
first Mrs. Lindsell.

She did obediently whatever he asked her, but
she was not very competent or enterprising, he
found.

The months went by.

Mr. Lindsell, angry one day because some cattle had disappeared, and his new overseer, so far from informing him of the fact, was not even himself aware of it, found all life distasteful. From bitterness over the loss of the cattle he ascended to bitterness because the loss of the cattle was, after all, of so little consequence to him. He felt old and tired. And what was he wearing himself out for? For the daughters who hated him? For the unresponsive coloured girl who did not even trouble to understand what, for the most part, he was talking about?

He looked back on his life, seeing himself as a man of intellect who had always done his duty; who had been liberal with his money; who had acted honestly towards the world—and what was his reward for it all?

He sat down palely to his dinner. The food was badly cooked, as often, recently. Elmira did not even satisfy his eye. He saw her suddenly to-night as much darker than he had always imagined, coarser featured, decidedly coloured. He thought her golden-brown eyes looked at him yellow and baleful as a tiger's.

"You are not so careful of your appearance as you used to be, Elmira," he said to her.

"I haven't got any winter clothes," she answered.

"I am not referring to clothes. I mean your hair and complexion. You ought to pay more attention to your complexion than other women."

He had never said anything like that to her before. The blood ran thickly to her cheeks. She may not have followed every remark he made, but she was trained to appreciate fully such an allusion.

Mr. Lindsell repented his criticism the moment it was

uttered. Now and then there did run a trickle of humanity through his meagre blood.

He leaned over from his chair (they sat at adjacent sides of the small square table), and put his arm across her shoulder. She moved away from him. He persisted. And all at once she grasped his long yellow hand, with the yellow finger nails and the shiny old skin, grasped it in her own young hand with a vicious strength that pained him, and flung it furiously away from her.

"I hate you," she said. "I hate you."

She sprang up from the table. "You ugly old man," she panted.

She had never shown him that she even possessed any feeling. He stared at her, unable to make any reply, his lips petrified into a faint grimace, utterly shocked. Presently his right hand mechanically approached the pulse on his left wrist.

Late that night as he was lying, sleepless, in bed, he heard her sobbing on the stoep outside.

6

After that they hardly spoke to one another for some days. At first he had thought that she might run away, as his daughter, Edith, had done, and he had strictly watched her. But he found soon that she was going as quietly and obediently about her small household tasks as ever and, strangely, she interested him more now than she had done when she seemed merely a creature of spiritless acquiescence. Now he knew that, at least, she had sensations of some kind. And although, naturally, it had hurt him to be called an ugly old man and to hear that she hated him, he took it that she did not mean these things literally, but had merely been outraged into saying the first virulent words that occurred to her. He was quite courteous during the next week or two, and she, although pale and heavy-eyed and withdrawn, seemed to be trying to fit herself again into her old scheme of existence.

And then, one Sunday, as they were sitting quietly on the stoep, she said to him:

"I want to go home."

"You would like to visit your father and mother?"

"Yes, I want to go home."

Her iteration of the word "home" as applied to where her parents lived annoyed Mr. Lindsell. But he tried to be playful:

"Don't you call this your home now?" he asked with a forced little smile.

She stared at him, at that smile on his old face, and lowered her eyes. Presently, as if with an effort, she looked up again.

"No," she answered him. "And I want to go home."

The smile remained a little stiffly on his lips.

"Why, suddenly like this?"

"It isn't suddenly. I have been thinking about it for a good while now."

"I see. And how long do you intend to remain away?"

Her eyes widened.

"I mean I am not coming back," she said simply.

Mr. Lindsell tried to control himself.

"Be careful what you say, Elmira," he warned her.

"Yes, I am," she accepted his reprimand. "I am careful. But that is what I mean all the same."

"Elmira," said Mr. Lindsell, very pale now, "don't make me angry."

"I can't help it if you are angry. I have to go.

You can't keep me if I've made up my mind about it."

Mr. Lindsell's hands on his knees were tightly gripped together that they might cease their angry trembling.

"You are my wife, Elmira," he said. "But if you behave like a child, you shall be treated as a child."

She got up from the chair and stood over him. "What will you do to me? I used to be frightened of you, but I am not frightened any more. All these months I thought I would die, shut up in one house with only you. Every time you touched me I wanted to scream. What good has it done me to be married to you? I am living on the veld the same as I did when I was with my father and mother. I have no friends. I don't go anywhere. What is the use of the clothes you buy me if no one sees them except the Kaffirs?"

She drew a hard breath.

"Why is it better to be Adam Lindsell's wife than Kleinhans' daughter? You said when you asked me to marry you that I should be the most important woman for miles around. Who thinks I am important. The sheep in the kraal and the meerkats on the veld? Who comes here? Who knows me?"

Her voice rose piercingly.

"And you said it would be as I wished about staying here or going away, and you would always do what I liked. But if I asked you to go away from here, you wouldn't go; and if I wanted you to do something, you wouldn't do it. And I live here like a servant to mend your clothes and cook your food."

Mr. Lindsell was unused to resistance.

"You never told me you were dissatisfied," he protested with a weakness that surprised even himself.

"Did you think all I needed to make me happy was to be married to a man that looks like a tortoise, and is old enough to be my grandfather?"

He got up, and gripped her wrists. She struggled to free herself, panting, her eyes dilated. And suddenly she fell to the ground in a dead faint.

7

She was lying on the bed in her own room when she came to herself, and Mr. Lindsell was sitting on a chair, looking at her. Her dazed eyes met his in a hate diminished only by her loss of strength, but he came and stood beside her, and said, with an expression on his face she had never seen before:

"Elmira, you have something to tell me."

And Elmira broke into bitter, helpless sobs:

"Yes, I am going to have a child. I hate you so much and I am going to have a child."

8

Now nothing Elmira could say or do had power to penetrate Mr. Lindsell's tenderness to her. She had effected a miracle. He treated her with an obsessed veneration.

And she lived on at the homestead in a lethargy, diversified only by bursts of fury against her husband. She was, as she had explained, no longer afraid of him; she did not care what she said to him, or how she expressed her unabating hatred.

He offered to have her mother visit them, sent her for a holiday to the seaside, suggested that he should engage a companion to help her pass the days of waiting. Every few mails there came some gift or other. His thought for her was ceaseless.

Elmira treated him and his homage with indifferent contempt. She realized her new power and his servitude.

And Mr. Lindsell—never had he been so happy. Here was his manhood vindicated; here was the wisdom of his marriage upheld; here was a routing of time and a very reinforcement of life.

He snapped his fingers at the sanctities of race.

PART IV

THE FOURTH GENERATION: BARRY
1890

CHAPTER I

I

THE son of Elmira and Adam Lindsell was born in the year 1890, and Mr. Lindsell called him after the family name of his mother, Barry. He was a small and weakly baby, wrinkled and hairless, and, sometimes, as Elmira held him, a sudden revulsion against him would come over her, and she would say bitterly: "He is his father. He is only that old man, his father."

But her mother, Lena, who was visiting her, would add: "Yes, he is a proper white child, Elmira. Yes. Thank God, he does not take after our family at all. He is really white."

And at this additional manifestation of his power of persistence—that the child should look like him and be so white—Mr. Lindsell's happiness was almost more than he might bear.

He could not tear himself away from the son of his old age. All day long he hovered over him beatifically, examining him, touching him, yearning over him. He had had children before, but that was three decades ago, when he was thirty-five and not sixty-five; when he had not thought it extraordinary to have children. And they had not been sons either, nor their mother forty-six years younger than he, and beautiful and contemptuous.

Barry had a peculiar impetus towards him too. Long before he learnt to recognize any one else he responded to his father. He cried eagerly when he heard his voice; nestled, content, against his lean body.

The first intelligible sounds that came from his mouth were "Da-da".

It made Elmira ill to see her son and his father together.

2

And when he learnt to crawl he was always crawling towards Mr. Lindsell. And Mr. Lindsell would get down on the floor and crawl about, stiff and ungainly, with him. All his bald head, with the tight, shiny yellow skin and the few white hairs just above his coat collar, could be seen by any one who chose to look down; and the back of his neck was criss-crossed with wrinkles. . . . And then he would rise creakingly, the knees of his trousers baggy and dusty about his thin legs, and look delightedly at Elmira, laughing on a high-pitched note of sheer exultation.

He was hardly ever without a smile these days, except when Barry's stomach was out of order, or he had a temperature, or he came out in heat spots.

It had taken them some trouble to find a food that would suit the baby—his mother's milk had not agreed with him at all—and they had had a trained nurse in the house, and they had tried one thing after the other, and every now and then, in desperation, Mr. Lindsell had sent for Lena, as the ex-nurse of the children he had had a generation ago and the experienced mother of a large family.

Kleinhans, on the stubborn piece of ground thirty miles away from Lindsell's Farm, which he had bought for his cattle, had resented Mr. Lindsell's demands.

"It is your own grandchild, Kleinhans," Lena had protested.

"Yes, I know that. But he sent us away as if we were nothing but a flock of sheep—for twenty years I worked for him, and then he sent us away."

"It is not the poor little thing's fault. Ach, Kleinhans, he is so sweet and white!"

The whole Kleinhans family, from Deborah downwards, revelled in the whiteness of Barry.

"But sickly," grumbled Kleinhans. "It is hard on a strong girl like Elmira to have such a sickly child."

"That is because her own heart is not in the baby," said Lena. "Sometimes she seems to me not to care for it at all. When Mijnheer holds him, she looks at the two of them together as if she hated them with one hate."

"I was against the marriage from the beginning," said Kleinhans.

But the weaker vessel replied: "The worst and the best are sometimes the same. It may be a bad thing to-day that Mijnheer is so old. But to-morrow it may be good. We must be patient, Kleinhans."

3

Mr. Lindsell was mellower now towards the whole Kleinhans family. Even old Deborah came to the homestead once to stay for two or three days. Her black fuzz of hair was grizzled at last (unless, perhaps, she lived to be a nonagenarian, it would never be really white) and she wore gold-rimmed spectacles, which lent her quite an air of distinction, and she was very, very fat . . . and she held on her knees her great-grandchild, begotten by the white man born in England

215

only a year or so later than she herself had been born in dark Africa of a white father and a Hottentot mother, the representative of the first mixed generation.

How strange to see them together, Mr. Lindsell and Deborah Flood, who called herself Mrs. Kleinhans—the wilted Englishman and the bloated half-Hottentot woman! Deborah spoke her English to him, which, during her long life in Kokstad, had become more Dutch than English, and they exulted together, these two people in the middle sixties, over the little baby who was their joint pride. "He is very white," Deborah would say, nodding her head with grave emphasis, "Yes, yes, he is very white."

"He is an extraordinary child," Mr. Lindsell would assert, fondling a little thin leg. "I'll tell you what he did yesterday. You wouldn't believe it. But it's a fact. . . ."

He would pour into Deborah's willing ears an enthusiastically exaggerated tale of childhood, and Deborah would go on sympathetically nodding her head, and saying, "T-t-t! . . . Fie! . . . Ach toch! . . . Sis toch! . . ." half in genuine delight and half in respectful flattery.

Mr. Lindsell had no shred of cynicism left in him when he was in the neighbourhood of his baby. He doddered over him with a blissful simplicity that was quite primitive. And his eyes watered with tenderness as Deborah bobbed Barry up and down, either to some hymn tune or else to the rhythm of the same old African songs with which she had, nineteen years ago, expressed her joy in Elmira's light skin, so that he could not resist snatching his son away from her and hugging him fast.

Elmira herself was not quite so pretty as she had been before she married Mr. Lindsell. She had grown stout, her skin had become darker and coarser, and even her hair had lost its suggestion of gold. She was no longer white as the baby Deborah remembered her to have been. Yet she was still, undoubtedly, handsome, and, however she looked, Mr. Lindsell would have been satisfied with her, since she was his son's mother.

For a time, too, she found life bearable at the Lindsell homestead. There was, at any rate, something to do. Barry needed all her attention, and, however much she resented his resemblance to his father and his evident preference for him, she could not fail him maternally.

And when Barry was two and a half years old they took him to the seaside for a holiday. He was stronger now, though he would never be exactly brawny, but they had a trained hospital nurse to attend to him. And all day, on the sands—or, at least, as long as the sun rested there—Mr. Lindsell would lie about playing with him, while the nurse (a middle-aged widow called Mrs. Gadd) sat comfortably at hand, crocheting or knitting. People used to stare when it was whispered to them that this old man was the father of that child, and they used to think it pathetic, too, how trustfully the little ·chap accepted the queer relationship. It really looked as unnatural as if Romulus and Remus had been seen there in the African blaze disporting themselves with their old foster-mother, the wolf.

They were staying, Adam Lindsell, his wife and child and nurse, at the same hotel where, just about four years ago, the honeymoon had been spent. And the
o

proprietor and his wife and the few regular residents of the hotel remembered them from that time. And, whereas it had then seemed to them exciting as well as sad that the old man and the young woman were husband and wife, now that the baby was there, it seemed, in a way, not only exciting and sad, but amusing, too. And Elmira was still the most interesting member of the group to every one. For, after all, a handsome young woman of twenty-one is bound to attract more attention than her husband of sixty-seven, or her son of two and a half.

If there was now very little doubt that she had black blood in her, it was yet not so clamorous but that one might ignore it if one chose.

There were young men at the hotel and elsewhere who thought it quite dashing to be friendly with Elmira.

5

And Elmira was no longer as circumspect as when last she had stayed at the hotel. She had been dazed then. She was reckless now.

Mr. Lindsell, absorbed in his boy, noticed very little what was happening to his wife. He used to go to bed almost directly after his evening meal. If Barry was still awake (he insisted on having him in his own room), he would play with him. If not, he would read a little, and then go to sleep. Elmira would come softly in hours later.

But one night Barry seemed to be very restless, and Mr. Lindsell, noticing that Elmira was not there, went to attend to him, and, his fingers on his little body, found that he was much too hot. He put on his slippers and dressing-gown, and went to fetch the nurse at the end of the passage. He had some trouble in waking her. But at last she called out sleepily: "Who's there?"

"Mr. Lindsell."

"Is anything the matter?"

"Barry is not well, I think."

"Just a moment. I'm coming."

He heard her strike a match, a little glow appeared under her door, and, presently, her hair in curlers, she joined him, and followed him to his room.

Her first exclamation as she entered it was: "But isn't Mrs. Lindsell——?" she stopped.

"She has not come in yet," said Mr. Lindsell.

Mrs. Gadd drew in her breath to stop herself from saying more, and bent over Barry. "He is a little feverish," she said. "But I don't think it is anything serious. Stomach, probably. You remember, Mr. Lindsell, I warned you not to let him have that cake."

"Was it the cake, do you think?" Mr. Lindsell asked anxiously. "I hoped he had got over that sort of trouble by this time. And I only gave him quite a small piece."

He looked at Mrs. Gadd very humbly.

She was a competent and not unkindly woman, but she could not help enjoying his subdued and frightened air, and she reprimanded him with malicious sternness.

"Yes. But he should have had none at all. As I told you at the time. However, you took no notice of what I said, and so this is the result."

"I'll be more careful in future," begged Mr. Lindsell.

And Mrs. Gadd, finding herself with the upper hand, and also rather annoyed at having been awakened like this, looked at his thin ankles and bony feet showing from under his night-gown, and used her advantage still further:

219

"You'd better give me the child. I don't know what time you are expecting Mrs. Lindsell back, but it was two o'clock by my watch when you woke me. I looked."

"Two o'clock!" exclaimed Mr. Lindsell, and hurrying to his bed pulled out from under the pillows his own large gold watch with the thick gold chain.

"Yes. Ten past two," he said. He gazed round the dim candle-lit room helplessly.

"I wonder where she can be," he said.

"I wonder," Mrs. Gadd repeated with sarcasm; and, taking the baby, returned to her room.

6

They were both still wondering next day, and so were other people in the hotel, too. For Elmira did not come back to her husband then, or ever again.

Mr. Lindsell, his eyes encircled in greenish-black shadows, his cheeks sunken, his beard unshaved, ran hither and thither, agitated himself extremely, communicated with the police. The police were able to find out nothing at all.

A few days later, however, there came a letter to the hotel. It was in Elmira's handwriting. And Mrs. Gadd opened it, for by that time Mr. Lindsell had had the stroke which, among other things, he had been dreading for over thirty years, and was in hospital.

Mrs. Gadd remained to look after the child, and when Mr. Lindsell finally came out of hospital, she took charge of him, too.

She duly returned with her two nurslings, the old man and the baby, in a position of complete autocracy, to Lindsell's Farm. She engaged a young girl to assist her, and became herself, in a small way, the matron of an institution.

Elmira's name was not mentioned in the house. No one knew where, as the years passed, she was living with the young commercial traveller with whom she had run away. But it was discovered that she had withdrawn from the bank the shares Mr. Lindsell had settled on her at the time of their marriage. At last she was, as Mr. Lindsell had promised her, doing as she liked with her money. Mr. Lindsell did not even trouble to divorce her.

And again, and (but for one abortive attempt) finally this time, were the Kleinhanses, her father and mother, her brothers and sisters, her grandmother, excluded from Lindsell's Farm.

CHAPTER II

I

AT the time of Mr. Lindsell's illness in Cape Town, Mrs. Gadd had thought it her duty to inform his daughters of the fact.

Mrs. Darrell Tibbitts now had two children, a son and a daughter, had put on a little flesh, and no longer looked exactly like her elder sister Edith, who was more desiccated in appearance than ever.

Poor Edith, they meant well by her, May and Darrell, and yet she was so obviously a superfluity in their home that her presence irked them. When they wanted to be by themselves, she was there. On their holidays they had to take her with them. If they had something to tell one another, they had to retire to secret corners. During their little marital disagreements there she sat all the time so obviously—so confoundedly obviously—with a "don't let me be drawn into this business" expression on her face. It made even the good-humoured Darrell feel that if only she would say something provocative that he might get openly angry with her, he would like her better.

And then May would afterwards complain: "You ought to be ashamed of yourself, Darrell, to behave like that to me in front of Edith."

"Oh, Edith be damned."

"That sort of remark doesn't improve matters."

"Well, what was it I said that was so bad then?"

"It isn't so much what you said as that Edith should think you don't respect me."

"Nonsense. She knows very well I respect you. But, in any case, what affair is it of hers?"

"She can't help noticing things if they go on under her very nose."

"No one keeps her nose where it is," said Darrell with rude gusto.

"Now you're speaking like a brute," May retorted.

Darrell was immediately contrite. "Yes, it's true. I am. But you know yourself, May. It does get on one's nerves always to have to consider a third person."

May sighed. "I must admit you're very good on the whole, Darrell. And I don't blame you altogether either for wanting your privacy."

"Still, you like to have her here, don't you? I mean, it's a lonely life, and she helps with the children, and you have some one to talk to while I'm out all day, and company when I have to leave you for a night or two."

"Yes, that is so," said May. "But it's just because it *is* a lonely life. You can't get away from each other."

"Still, what's the use of worrying about it? Poor old Edith has nowhere else to go, and we may as well bear with her."

He put his arm round May, and his ruddy, hearty face against her freckled one. "Come, sweetheart, let's make it up. I'll be terribly courteous and adoring towards you in front of Edith to-night, and let her see whether I respect you or not. Now give me a kiss. A good one. Love me again? That's right."

May's arm encircled his brown head. She thought suddenly how great was her fortune compared with Edith's, that this dear fellow should love her who was

223

no better than Edith, no better than any other woman and give himself to her, all he had and stood for.

She had a vision, her mind on Edith, of what her life would have been without him.

She was not an emotional woman, seldom demonstrative, and Darrell had to sue her for the affection he craved. But a fullness of gratitude flooded her heart now, and she whispered in his ear, as she returned his kiss, "Bless you, Darrell".

2

Darrell's love for May was something Edith positively could not understand. Why did Darrell love May? What did he see in her? She was not attractive, she was not clever, she was not competent, she was not even very amiable. Quite clearly Edith realized her sister's deficiencies. And she could not help believing that there was something in herself—something she could not define—still, *something* that made her superior to May. Yet May and not she had won a man's love. It seemed to Edith not only inexplicable but unfair.

And when Darrell praised May, as he often did, for something she had done or said. . . . "Now that's a good idea. You have got a sound little head, May. What on earth should I do without you?" or if he looked at her with admiration, and declared that the thing she wore suited her and she was really looking very nice, "Isn't she, Edith?" (as if Edith were just as enchanted with May's beauty as he was himself), Edith would feel herself sneering inwardly as she forced out her unwilling praises: "Yes, I quite like that dress. I wouldn't myself have put that trimming on it, but, of course, May has her own taste, and I certainly prefer it to the blue silk."

Darrell would be quite satisfied, but May would sense a secret hostility, and, with a heightened colour, would quickly change the conversation, thinking that Darrell, in his simplicity, was making her ridiculous, and that Edith despised them both for it.

3

A little happiness would have made all the difference to Edith. If only she were not eaten up with this jealousy. If only the servants did not call May, as the head of the household, "Missis", and herself, the elder sister, "*Klein* Missis"—"Little Missis". If only Darrell were not so grotesquely satisfied with May. If only the children did not so eagerly struggle away from their aunt towards their mother. If only May herself were not so complacent in all the circumstances of her life.

Ah, if only she had not to stay here with nothing to do but compare May's fate with her own.

In the dark of night she would stuff the sheet into her mouth that May, on the other side of the wall with her husband, should not hear her bitter sobbing.

4

"Bad news," said Darrell Tibbitts, coming in with Mrs. Gadd's telegram that had just arrived in the mail-bag which was sent from the nearest post-office.

The sisters did not think of connecting it with their father. Except for Edith's allowance, forwarded regularly from the bank (materially, at least, his family had never had any complaint to make against Mr. Lindsell), except for this one link, there had been no communication between Adam Lindsell and his daughters since the day Darrell had unavailingly gone to

225

argue with him about his marriage. They knew there was the child, Barry, they had managed to ascertain that his colouring was light, and there all the information they had ended. Even strangers had the delicacy not to mention their father's household to them. . . .

May ran to her husband. Edith sat watching.

"It's father, Edith," said May.

Edith's heart jumped. The emotion that agitated her was fright.

"Is he dead?" she asked at last.

May brought the telegram over to her.

"No. Look. Apoplexy."

"Is there danger?" And, although she never thought of her father except with hate, yet now, strangely, there was only a real filial anxiety in Edith's voice.

They both looked at Darrell as if he understood more about such things than they did.

"Oh, not necessarily. Oh no, I shouldn't think so," said Darrell, rising heartily to the occasion. "I am sure I have heard of people having apoplexy—what we call a stroke—and getting over it."

"But are they all right afterwards?" asked May.

"Why not?"

Yet May knew her husband well enough to recognize the uncertainty behind his cheery voice. He continued briskly:

"My dear girl, he'll last for years yet, a tough old customer like your father."

And he wondered, as he spoke, that these women, who for three years had hated and abused their father to the utmost, wishing him all evil to very death itself should now, when death actually faced him, be trembling at the prospect.

226

Well, people were like that, he supposed. . . .

"Do you think," said May, "one of us ought to go down."

"I couldn't," said Edith. And, suddenly, as she visualized him there at the seaside with his young coloured wife and child, all her bitter feelings against him returned.

And May, meditating on the situation, said, after a moment, "No, I couldn't either."

"And if the worst had happened?" suggested Darrell with some curiosity.

Edith shook her head. "I would rather die myself than meet Elmira with him."

But Darrell sent down daily telegrams, and received in return the information that Mr. Lindsell was going on as well as could be expected.

Finally Mrs. Gadd wrote to Mr. and Mrs. Tibbitts, telling them that Mrs. Lindsell had left Mr. Lindsell and the child, that Mr. Lindsell was not quite himself again, and asking them if she should continue in her present position. They answered, with such authority as was theirs, that they were satisfied with the arrangement.

And when Mrs. Gadd returned with her two charges to Lindsell's Farm, May and her husband went over to see the sick man. But Edith, her lips compressed, and her nostrils quivering, refused to accompany them.

She looked after them as they drove off, with a vision on her sharpened imagination of a suffering—a dying— father. She could not sleep that night for thinking of him with pity, yet she knew that if he were well she would hate him as much as ever, and she could not bear the thought of facing him.

May and Darrell found Mr. Lindsell sitting, after two months in bed, on a long chair on the stoep. They approached him with the difficult smiles characteristic of such occasions. The idea was to convey that they, for their parts, were not considering his illness seriously.

He acknowledged their greeting, speaking in a strange, thick voice that May did not recognize, and he got a little annoyed because she waited enquiringly for him to repeat his words. The left side of his face seemed, Darrell told himself, to have slipped. It no longer matched the right side. And those eyes, whose cynical regard had been one of the terrors of May's childhood, now looked at her in helpless disunion.

But he told them he was going on splendidly, was beginning to move about again, and expected in a short while to be perfectly well.

"I am not like the ord-ordinary man of my age. I can get over these things."

He spoke indistinctly. They had difficulty in following his words.

"Poor Barry misses his playmate," he went on. "Mrs. Gadd, will you go and fetch Barry. His—sister —has come to see him."

Mrs. Gadd, with an indefinably sarcastic expression on her face, went to look for Barry, who was generally now in charge of her assistant.

"Barry is an extra-ordinary child," said Mr. Lindsell after a pause. "A remark-able child."

May felt hot and cold and angry and contemptuous and pitiful and curious, all at the same time. But, chiefly, she felt curious. She wanted to see this child in whose veins mingled with her own blood the blood of savages and slaves. She had gathered, as one vaguely gathers such news, that Barry looked like any white child, and yet she could not believe it. The grandchild of Lena and Kleinhans! How could the grandchild of Lena and Kleinhans be white?

After a little time, spent, they were sure, in decorating him for the occasion, he appeared, led by Mrs. Gadd, in a brown velvet suit, the trousers of which hung too long over his knees, with a white lace collar, and black patent leather shoes. Mr. Lindsell's uncertain eyes, the quick eye and the poor slow eye, looked at his son with pride. Barry was a very small child for his age, his face was pale and tiny, but his grey eyes were large with a kind of pathetic intelligence, and his light brown hair was very straight and soft. He looked unquestionably like a white child. He came up to his paralysed old father, leaning against him with confident affection, and gravely considered the visitors.

"Shake hands with your sister," said Mr. Lindsell to him.

May flushed at the description.

Barry looked at his father with a small, knowing smile on his face, as if to say, "I appreciate the joke".

"Not my sister. My auntie," he said.

"You see," mumbled Mr. Lindsell proudly, "he under-under-stands you are too old to be his sister. . . . And only two years and nine months. Say good afternoon, Barry."

Barry approached May with his big, too-intelligent eyes on her, and held out his small, thin, newly-washed hand.

She thought of her own sturdy freckled children with their chubby, brown hands, with their little noses that wrinkled gleefully when they laughed, with their noisy rushing habits, and she gathered Barry to herself pitifully.

But then, as she held him, she suddenly remembered that he was Elmira's son, and she put him down, her heart painfully beating.

He stood where she had placed him for a moment, and then he went back to his father, pressing against him as before.

May and Darrell had, perforce, to remain a day at Lindsell's Farm. And early next morning there was a knock at their door, and the voice of Barry's little nursemaid said: "Mrs. Tibbitts?"

"Yes?" said May.

"Barry wants to know if he can come in and say good morning to you."

"Yes, let him come in," answered Darrell.

And Barry entered, and stood solemnly at the door examining them.

"Aren't you going to say good morning?" called Darrell.

Barry shook his head.

"No. I want to know where is my mammy," he said.

"Do you think all he really came in about was to ask us that?" May afterwards demanded of her husband.

"It seems so," agreed Darrell Tibbitts. "He is an uncanny child. But that is no wonder either."

6

"You must come again," said Mr. Lindsell to his daughter and son-in-law as they made ready to depart. "And I think I shall go with you to the gate. What, Mrs. Gadd?"

"Yes. But don't tire yourself," Mrs. Gadd warned him. "Here is your stick. Now take my arm."

She helped Mr. Lindsell up from his chair, and Mr. Lindsell, leaning towards his unaffected right side, shambled along beside May and Darrell, assisted by Mrs. Gadd. He dragged his left leg, scraping the side of his slipper on the ground as he slowly advanced, but he was quite proud of his achievement in managing to walk at all.

"Remember me to Edith," were Mr. Lindsell's last thick words as his guests sat in their cart, and May almost thought she heard through his laboured articulation something of her father's old ironic inflection.

CHAPTER III

I

ONLY once during Mr. Lindsell's remaining lifetime did any of the Kleinhanses venture to come to Lindsell's Farm. And that was when Lena insisted on going there.

"I must see my grandchild," she told Kleinhans. "His mother has left him. His father is sick. Only strangers are there to look after him. And they may be harming my poor baby."

"I hear he is well enough," said Kleinhans.

"Who knows?"

"There may be trouble if you go."

"It is *my* grandchild. And if they say much, I shall bring him back with me."

"Now you are talking nonsense," said Kleinhans to her, and she knew it herself. From all accounts the last thing that might happen was that Adam Lindsell should part with his son to any one. He could not even bear him out of his eyesight. He lived for nothing else.

Lena, who had wrinkled and thinned with middle age, opened the little wooden gate set in the loose stone wall that surrounded the garden made by the first Mrs. Lindsell and neglected by the second, so that all that remained of it now were a few degenerated blue gums and vines, and one or two almost exhausted rose bushes —she opened the gate and walked up the unraked gravel path to the house. Mrs. Gadd kept the house quite neat and clean, but it had adopted, with her presence, the rigid air of an institution.

On the stoep, in the sun, Mr. Lindsell was sitting on his long chair with a rug over his knees. Barry was solemnly occupying himself—one could never say of Barry that he played—with some blocks. He was near enough to his father to receive every now and then an affectionate little pat from him. And they were conversing, the old paralytic father in his thick voice that Barry seemed perfectly to understand, and his baby son in his little pipe.

Mr. Lindsell slowly moved his discordant face towards the crunching of steps on the gravel, and met the eyes of the coloured mother-in-law who was twenty years younger than himself and had once nursed his children.

His face flushed, and he rang the bell at his side. No one appeared. He rang again, a long and violent peal—urgent.

Mrs. Gadd came running out. Lena was already standing uncertainly on the stoep.

"Mrs. Gadd," said Mr. Lindsell more quickly and even more indistinctly than usual, "that person . . . send her away."

Mrs. Gadd, who had been engaged just before the Lindsells went to Cape Town, to look after Barry, had met Lena when she came to say good-bye to her daughter. She looked at Lena now, making a gesture with her eyes.

But Lena held her ground with a frightened obstinacy.

"I have come to see my grandchild," she said in a trembling but assertive voice.

"Go," shrieked Mr. Lindsell, half rising in his passion. "Go!"

Mrs. Gadd went to him and made him sit down again.

P

"You mustn't excite yourself, Mr. Lindsell. It's very bad for you. Of course, she won't stay. Now do try to keep calm."

Then she hurried to Lena and took her arm and led her away, whispering rapidly: "You remind him of your daughter. He can't stand seeing you. You must really not come here, Mrs. Kleinhans. You upset him badly. He might have another stroke."

Lena was whimpering now. "I have travelled thirty miles to be a little with my grandchild."

"Yes, but it's no use killing his father for it."

The tears ran rapidly down Lena's face. "I can't go back now, Mrs. Gadd. The horses are tired. What must I do?"

"Why not go along to the overseer's, and ask him to put you up till to-morrow morning?"

"He won't. He's a white man, and his family is white, too. He won't let me be there."

She was sobbing quite hopelessly and unrestrainedly by this time.

Mrs. Gadd glanced back at her patient.

"I can't stop to talk to you now," she said. "I have to see to Mr. Lindsell. You wait outside the gate for me. I'll come along as soon as I can."

Mr. Lindsell was lying back exhausted in his chair.

"Feeling all right?" asked Mrs. Gadd.

He nodded.

"It was very wicked of you to let yourself get excited," Mrs. Gadd admonished him.

He sighed profoundly. "Yes, I know. But that woman——"

"Yes, of course, of course," said Mrs. Gadd soothingly. "She shan't come here again. Don't you worry about it. You won't, will you?"

She spoke to him as if he were a child.

He shook his head, and put out his hand weakly towards Barry.

"Are you father's good boy?" he mumbled, and patted his straight, soft, brownish hair.

2

Later Mrs. Gadd went down to find Lena. She was sitting dolefully on a big stone, and tear marks showed on her dusty brown face.

"I am sorry about this, Mrs. Kleinhans," said Mrs. Gadd. "But you quite understand, don't you? that it's not good for him to see you. It makes him think about his wife."

"But the child?" asked Lena logically. "Doesn't the child make him think about her, too?"

"He's used to the child. It doesn't come as a shock to him to see the child. He feels as if Barry is only his."

She really felt quite sorry for this coloured woman who might not see her grandchild, and had nowhere to go.

"Poor little thing," said Lena. "Is he well, Mrs. Gadd?"

"Yes, well enough. But not very strong. . . . And now, what are you going to do?"

Lena began to cry again. "I don't know, Mrs. Gadd."

"I'll tell Minnie to keep an eye on Mr. Lindsell, and then I'll go along with you to the overseer."

They set off together. Lena recognized Mrs. Gadd's condescension in walking beside her. It was all very well for a white woman to stand talking to a coloured woman, but it was beyond a patronage—not, indeed, quite the thing—for a white woman to walk beside her.

Lena felt as if she ought to be following Mrs. Gadd instead of accompanying her. She spoke to her in a very meek and subservient voice, hardly ever saying anything without politely mentioning Mrs. Gadd's name, waiting, as a rule, to be addressed before making any remark herself.

At the overseer's home, which had for so many years been the home of Lena and Kleinhans, they found his wife, very fat, in a blouse without a skirt, and shoes without stockings, her heavy feet planted firmly apart, hanging up some washing.

"You know Mrs. Kleinhans, don't you?" said Mrs. Gadd.

The overseer's wife nodded indifferently.

"Mrs. Kleinhans has come to see her grandson, but Mr. Lindsell is not well, and I was wondering if you could let her stay with you till to-morrow morning."

The overseer's wife was Dutch, and followed Mrs. Gadd's remarks with difficulty. Mrs. Gadd repeated them.

"You would be doing Mrs. Kleinhans a great favour," she added. "There is nowhere else for her to go, as you know yourself."

The woman shook her head. "I don't like to keep brown people," she said bluntly in her slow and heavy English.

Lena shrank back.

"Oh, come," said Mrs. Gadd. "She'll pay you, won't you, Mrs. Kleinhans?"

Lena nodded her humbled head.

But the overseer's wife looked at her with contempt.

"My house is full," she said obstinately. "And I cannot find room for brown people."

Mrs. Gadd shrugged her shoulders.

"I told you, Mrs. Gadd," said Lena, in a choked voice.

They walked back in silence.

"There is the little room next to the stable that they gave my husband when Mr. Lindsell brought him to the farm," Lena remembered suddenly. "Perhaps I could stay there till the morning. Oh, Mrs. Gadd, he was so good to us then, and now——"

The nurse felt herself called upon to defend her employer.

"But you must blame your daughter for that."

"No. No. It was not Elmira's fault. The poor child. He was too much for her."

"Did you not think he might be, at the time?"

"I thought she could bear it, Mrs. Gadd," confessed Mrs. Kleinhans simply.

"I see. But she had no patience to wait long enough."

Lena heard the altered tone in Mrs. Gadd's voice, and became abruptly silent.

She slept in the little corrugated iron outhouse, where odds and ends of farm things were lying about: broken harness, a disused ladder, damaged pots and pans, an old pick and shovel, a lidless trunk, a few scraps of forage, some decayed and smelling potatoes— on a mattress in the same room in which nearly a quarter of a century ago she had first seen the man who was to be her husband. A swarm of bees hung from one corner of the unlined ceiling, there were dusty cobwebs everywhere, and, in the darkness, rats ran over her, and bats whirred about, hitting every now and then the walls.

Late next afternoon Lena returned to her husband.

"And how did it go?" he asked.

"Don't speak to me of it," she wept. "I can't tell you."

Yet for weeks she could tell him nothing else.

3

And that was the last visit any Kleinhans ever paid Mr. Lindsell. For the next four years—that is, till the end of Mr. Lindsell's life—he and Barry sufficed to one another for company. Mrs. Gadd was still there, very well paid, and managing competently. It was a lonely existence for her; but they went for two months every year to the seaside; she had had enough of hard, badly paid work in cities, and she was supporting a son at school in England with the money she earned. Except for this outlay, she was able to save practically all her money against such a time as she should be unable to work. And now and then she had hopes that Mr. Lindsell would not forget her in his will.

In the meantime she played piquet or bézique with him in the evening, took him for an occasional drive in the afternoon, hustled about her work the rest of the day, and read a little when, on rare occasions, she felt in the mood. There were worse ways of living. She had experienced them, and was not dissatisfied with her present lot.

When Barry was five she taught him his letters. He learnt them readily. At six he could read and write and even figure a little. He and his father used to spend enjoyable hours working laboriously on a slate. He was not able to compare his lot with that of many other children. He divided such children as he knew into three kinds: The Kaffir children, who ran about naked. The overseer's children, who ran about barefoot. And himself, who did very little running about and was always fully dressed.

He realized that he was very different from other children; that, for instance, he had no mother, and that his sister May, who sometimes came to see him, was old enough to be his auntie; and that his father, too, was much, much older than other children's fathers—than the overseer's children's father, or the fathers of little Boer boys who came on waggons that outspanned, in passing, at Lindsell's Farm. . . . Minnie, his nurse, had hinted to him, too, about strange relations not far away . . . but he accepted it that he had to be different, and was content.

4

It was of pneumonia, the same illness which had frightened him in his youth, that Mr. Lindsell finally and unresistingly died. But, as Mrs. Gadd said to the doctor who had travelled many miles to attend to him, anything would, by now, have done to finish him off.. He was just barely hanging on to the world. The wonder was that he had lasted so long. The thread of his life was perished, a line of dust—it scattered apart at the first direct breath.

Now they all came to see him. Mr. and Mrs. Kleinhans, with old Deborah, May and Darrell Tibbitts, and —at last—Edith.

Edith was thirty-six—thin, and stiff, and wrinkled, compressed spiritually as well as physically. All the time he was ill she had refused to see her father and his little boy, her half-brother, with that secret darkness in his blood. The things that May, through her greater happiness and the easier view of life it had brought her, could bear, Edith could not bear. She could not bear

239

to face her father with that relic of what she held to be his terrible sin. She grew harder and more rigid with the passing years.

"You have no principles," she would say to her sister.

"Because I visit father?"

"Because you have forgiven him."

"If you saw him," said May, "you wouldn't think of forgiveness or no forgiveness. You would only be sorry."

Edith spoke from tight lips that could hardly move.

"I don't want to be sorry. It wouldn't be right."

"You have no imagination," said May.

"*You* haven't," answered Edith.

"He has not much longer to live."

An uncalled-for ache asserted itself in Edith's heart, but she went on speaking in her hard voice.

"But long after he is dead, what he has done will live."

"You mean Barry?"

"Yes, I mean Barry—and the others."

"I know," said May. "And still"—she hesitated—"He is really white, Edith."

"And this is his ancestry," cried Edith harshly: "A mad white missionary who married a degraded Hottentot women, a thing like a beast. And his daughter who had an illegitimate son by a passing Boer. And a coloured nursemaid who married that son. And a woman who ran away with another man. That, on one side. And, on the other side, a bad old man who, when he was more than sixty, fell in love with a coloured child, and didn't care what happened as long as he got her. All this evil Barry has in his blood to hand on further. And he is my brother."

She had brooded over her thoughts until they had

grown vital, until they were ready to run like live things from her lips.

"And so," said May meditatively, "you would expect Barry to be bad?"

"Yes, I would," Edith asserted passionately. "He must be. They all must be—the children like Barry."

"And yet," said May, "as it happens, you are wrong. I know Barry. And I tell you I see no wickedness in him."

5

But now he was dead, Edith's father, and she felt she would never rest again if she did not see him this last time she might do so on earth. She was terrified by the irrevocability of that final departure. It seemed to her that if she did not *know* what he looked like, her imagination would never, in the years to come, be at peace, for she would not be able to find out. She was obsessed by a ghastly curiosity to see him once more, and also by the ceremonial aspect of such a visit.

They all found themselves in the house at the same time—Darrell and May and Edith; and Deborah and Kleinhans and Lena. And the white family and the coloured family exchanged cold greetings, asked each other how things were with them, mentioned the little boy, and then ceased communication.

Mrs. Gadd, on an uncertain footing now, but hoping that the Tibbitts family would recognize the loyalty of her service to Mr. Lindsell, and would acknowledge it if Mr. Lindsell himself had not done so, tried to make everyone comfortable. She was troubled about how she might provide meals for the two antagonistic parties, but Kleinhans settled her difficulties by telling her that they had brought their own food with them,

241

and would eat it sitting in the outspanned Cape cart they had come in. He had little spirit these days, Kleinhans, for it was the year of the rinderpest, and he had lost most of his cattle through that scourge and become a poor man.

But now they were all of them thinking of one thing besides Mr. Lindsell. They were thinking of Barry, of what was now to become of Barry.

6

"He is my child's child," said Lena, as she ate her bread and dripping, "and I am not going to let those Tibbittses have him."

"Perhaps they will not want to have him."

"Then——"

"And, at the same time, they may also not want him to come to us. . . . I have heard there are places where they keep orphans. They might send him to such a place."

"That I will not allow," cried Lena.

"It is hard for people like us to say one thing or another thing," said Kleinhans. "When I was young I had my big ideas, too, but I know better now."

"And when I was young," said Lena, "I let myself be thrown this way and that way, but I am not so soft any more."

"When I was young . . ." sighed Deborah, and stopped. She was seventy-three, and what was the use of talking about when she was young.

7

Barry sat at table with his white relations. He knew and accepted solemnly, but compliantly, the fact that his father was dead, and that his life was now to be

242

different. He was still, at the age of seven, a child who looked unquestionably white, with his pale face, grey eyes and soft brown hair. He was rather small for his years and very thin. Edith sat there, searching his little person for sinister traces. He answered politely when they spoke to him, but said nothing besides.

Presently Mrs. Gadd came to take him away. Instead of the quiet finality of death, there brooded over the old homestead the agitations of life.

May looked towards the door as he went out with the nurse.

"What about Barry?" she whispered.

"Shall we . . .?" asked Darrell.

She shook her head.

"Our own children. . . . I should hate to see them together."

"I've an idea that the Kleinhans family have their eye on him. There will be the money, too."

No one knew yet what was happening about Mr. Lindsell's money.

8

The Kleinhanses came back in the afternoon, and walked into the room where Darrell and May and Edith were sitting. Barry was with them.

Lena went straight to the point with the desperate defiance of forced courage.

"We have come to talk about the child," she said.

The white family made no reply.

She crossed over, her face set, to Barry and drew him towards her. He allowed himself to be handled without protest. "Come to your granny, my little heart," she crooned. She put her arm round him, and he stood there quietly, like a small waxen figure.

And Lena addressed them in a voice that trembled.
"He is our blood, and we are taking him."

"I am afraid that is impossible," said Darrell.

"Do *you* want him?" she demanded, and pressed the boy closer.

Darrell made no reply.

Edith sat rigidly, saying no word. The boy, looking helplessly round from the tight arm that gripped him, met her pale, burning eyes. Suddenly he wrenched himself free and ran to her as to a saviour. He flung himself against her unyielding body.

"Don't let the brown people take me!" he cried. "Don't let them! Don't let them!"

His baffling calm was broken at last. He was weeping wildly.

Edith's eyes were turned on him with a frightened look. It was the first time any human soul had ever needed her. Then, as if she hardly knew what she was about, her arms slowly crept up to encircle that small, racked form. It yielded itself to hers and melted into her being.

She spoke, and the words had to battle their way through her tight throat, past her frozen lips.

"*I'm* taking him," she said.

CHAPTER IV

I

AND, after all, Mr. Lindsell had left no will. He had
hated to consider his own death, and he had never been
able to bring himself to the point of making any
arrangements in connection with it. "Time enough,"
he had always told himself.

And so, in the absence of any will, the property of
Adam Lindsell was equally divided among his three
children, Edith and May and Barry. There was money
on fixed deposit in the bank, there were bonds and
shares, there was the farm and the stock it held—the
value of nearly sixty thousand pounds in all.

Edith said good-bye to her sister and brother-in-law,
and with her half-brother, whose guardian she had now
been legally appointed, she went to live in Cape Town.

2

It was, in a way, pathetic that here was this woman
of thirty-six with the child of seven that she told people
was her half-brother, and no one paid her the compli-
ment of believing for a moment that Barry might not
really be her brother. She had the look of the undesired.

She bought herself a house in the Gardens suburb of
Cape Town, and there for many years she remained
with Barry.

It was a quiet life. They were both unapproachable.
Edith had a natural hostility towards the world, and the
fact that the world cared little whether she had or not

further increased it. Barry was eaten up with a secret fear.

He feared his blood. The older he grew, the more was he obsessed with an instinctive sense of his own inferiority.

3

He was never comfortable with other children. He felt himself to be different. He had the contempt for black blood which is one of the nails in the cross that the black-blooded bear. No man so scornful of the native as the half-caste; no man so bitter against the half-caste as the native. "Nigger!" the coloured man calls the black. "Bastard!" the black man retaliates. No brotherhood in that blood so near the earth. Let the white man give his tolerance to whom he pleases, the degrees among the black blooded are viciously marked by themselves.

Never would Barry forget the horror of those brown people who had claimed him as their own—him, the Little Baas to all that was dark on Lindsell's Farm! Now there was not a day but he remembered the secret degradation under his skin.

Cape Town is as brown as it is white. Barry shuddered before the brown, and shivered before the white. One day, he was afraid, some Cape boy would come along and sense the hidden association between Barry and himself, claiming kinship. One day, he dreaded, some white person would feel that Barry was not as he was, and searching, would discover why. In his little childish arguments with other boys Barry always shrank back in anticipation that, sooner or later, the yell would break out that he was not white. When he saw boys or girls whispering or giggling together

and he did not know any other cause for the whispering
and giggling, he thought it must be that, at last, they
had found out the truth about him. If, as the years
passed, he ever got near enough to be friendly with a
school fellow, he could not rest in peace for fear that
the friendship would one day be disrupted by damaging
discoveries. Sometimes he even wanted to say right
out and have done with it: "Look here, I must tell you.
I am not really white."

But then he never altogether dared do it. As soon
as he had at last nerved himself to the confession, he
would begin to think that, as long as he *seemed* white,
he *was* white. For what was the whole affair, after all,
but a question of skin? And, certainly, his skin was as
white as anybody's. "But it isn't only the skin,"
some inner voice would whisper. . . . And "It must
be," he would argue against that inner voice. "See
if there are light and dark children in the same coloured
family, the light can go to white schools, but the dark
cannot. Which proves that if you look white, that is
all that matters."

And, in the end, not only did he not confess, but he
thrust his secret still deeper down, covering it with
layers of shame and hate and invective. Of all the
people he knew, no one spoke as passionately against
black and brown and yellow as did Barry Lindsell.

4

It was the tradition among the school boys, as it
was among their fathers, whose attitude they adopted,
as it had been among the school mates of Elmira, that
one preferred a real, straightforward black man to a
half-caste. Whatever else the black man might be, he
was, at least, pure. "It stands to reason," they would

247

tell one another earnestly—for South African children are bound to discuss question of colour as soon as they discuss anything—"that the white in them can't be good white."

"And the black can't either. They say the decent natives don't like to be mixed up any more than we do."

"So the coloured people must be worse than any one else."

That was always the conclusion reached.

And with that conclusion Barry would eagerly agree.

More white than the whitest Barry tried to prove himself in his hostility to colour.

5

It was a fact that he could not find much to be proud of among the half-castes of Cape Town, the Cape people as they called themselves.

They had become, by the time the twentieth century had thrust away the nineteenth, not only an accident, or even an association, a group, a clan, a tribe—but actually a nation, a people. They had intermarried through generations and had established a type. There were among them many who were meritorious— what might shortly have been described as decent folk; but too often they were small and vicious, and craven and degenerate.

In the Cape Colony they had political and industrial, if not social, opportunities, but they barely availed themselves of them. They achieved nothing of any consequence. Now and then (very seldom) it might happen that a real black man, the son of some African chief, rich in land and cattle (not so many of these left, either), would struggle as far as an English or Scottish university, and, through it, to a profession; and would come back to South Africa to practise that profession. But he would never really succeed at it. Putting aside all questions of prejudice, he could not hold his own against white competition. He had not the brain, the persistence, the temperament. Nor would his white colleagues greatly trouble their heads about him. They would hardly think him worth discussing. "Not much good," they would briefly say, and thus dismiss the subject.

6

And still this aboriginal would have done what practically no half-caste ever succeeded in doing.

As Barry grew into manhood and began jealously to look about him to see where the Cape people stood, he could find nowhere an obviously coloured man in a big commercial enterprise, in a learned profession or an artistic endeavour. They were many of them astonishingly capable with their hands, they made good masons, or carpenters, or mechanics; but there they ended. Either they had not the heart or they had not the head to strive for anything else. They often remained to the end of their days gamins by disposition, imitative and monkey like. And that was the far back Hottentot blood in them; as when, nearly a century ago, Barry's ancestor, the Rev. Andrew Flood, just come to Cape Town, had seen the little skin-clad, yellow folk, with their pepper-corn hair, and small mischievous eyes, capering behind their big white masters, over whom they held those tall umbrellas. . . .

Something of that blood there still lived in Barry. And he could not see past it.

And yet there *was* something else to see.

Q

For the brown people, the yellow people, might be as abandoned of hope as the inhabitants of Hell, but there were men and women all over South Africa, apparently white, but with an attenuated dark stain in them, and they were by no means hopeless. They were, on the contrary, not seldom among the best the land could show. However romantically South Africans might shudder at hidden drops of black blood; however Barry's school friends might tradition-ally assert that their flesh would crawl if they had to touch a person of colour, there were, nevertheless, people of whom literally dark things were said, and pure white folk were delighted to have the chance of shaking their hands. Nor did their flesh crawl, nor were they afraid to associate with them, or even marry them, forgetting the past and risking the future for the sake of the present. In spite of talk and talk and talk, if a man looked white, and had success enough, he was, in the fullest sense, accepted. That was the truth, and much of the shuddering and crawling was conventional hypocrisy.

Heaven knows through what generations of sorrow; through what daily bitterness of self-distrust; through what oceans of ostracism, the man with that fading, but never dying, darkness in him arrived at havens of social grace; but once arrived, his life was distinguished in no noticeable sense from the lives of those around him, and, as far as all outward appearances might indicate, the world held him to be as white as he looked.

7

But Barry, in his school-days, was far from being able to take a philosophic view of his position. Perhaps, indeed, however he might seem to be bold and unconscious, no man could really be at ease when there was something latent in his body which it was necessary for him and the world, in a kind of conspiracy, to ignore. It was really blackmail. As long as he paid the world in the coinage of success, the world would say nothing. But what if one day he ceased payment? No longer would his secret, which was no secret, be curiously whispered—it would be shouted in his face.

Yet, as far as Barry himself was concerned, it was not only the fear of discovery and contumely, that burdened his heart, it was, with advancing years, the fear that, being what he was, he could not maintain accepted white standards. He sometimes wondered whether he had the same instincts and feelings as the other boys. It was true, of course, that he did better at school-work than many of his fellows, but that, he fancied dimly, might not be the most important mental aspect. Without being able to express it to himself, he felt that the minds of pure-bred white boys might, nevertheless, be of different fibre—of superior quality—to his own. Whenever, in any small respect, he found himself not conforming to the general outlook and habits of those around him, he believed that that must be because there was something wrong within himself. He tried, in a panic-stricken way, to have the same points of view, to voice the same opinions, to act in the same manner as all the other fellows; and yet even when, as far as appearances went, there was no noticeable distinction between him and anybody else, he could not help worrying lest some essential, intangible difference might still not be *felt*.

He was always expecting slights, always self-conscious, never at peace.

He carried about with him a nervous atmosphere that would have been enough, without any secret reason, to bar him from the people around him.

His schoolmates called him a "funny chap", without meaning that he was in the least humorous.

For, although Barry laughed louder than any one else when there was laughter about, he had no humour in him.

CHAPTER V

I

THERE was only one person with whom Barry dared be absolutely honest, and that was Edith. He had known enough, even at the age of seven, when he had first come with her to Cape Town, not to mention his brown grandfather and grandmother to any one except her.

But she, speaking with distaste on the subject, had warned him, too.

"You must never say a word about them to anyone, Barry. Never. Never."

"I know," he had answered humbly. Yet how did he know? Who had told him it was shameful? Ah, but the sense of it was in the very air he breathed.

"What would people do to me if they found out?" he asked, however.

"They wouldn't care for you any more."

He nodded his small head.

"Yes, I know," he said again.

He looked up at her after a moment, shame-faced.

"But you are not like that, are you, Edith? You are not like me?"

She answered him in vigorous haste.

"No."

His pale face reddened. Pity for him, mingled with a little unbudging contempt, came to displace her pride. Poor baby, what had *he* done?

"But we are going to forget all about it. Be a good boy, Barry, and no one will ever know."

"*I* will know," he said in his grave premature way, and fell silent.

Then a few days later he said to her suddenly:

"Is it because we didn't have the same mother that you are not like me, Edith?"

"What do you mean, Barry? Oh——" she remembered the other conversation. He had been trying to work the thing out, apparently.

"Yes," she said.

"I don't remember my mother very much. Was she like those old brown people that wanted to have me?"

Edith shook her head.

"Was she white like me?"

"Nearly."

"Was she the same as cook?"

"No, lighter."

"Where is she, Edith?"

"I don't know," said Edith.

"She isn't dead, is she?"

"She went away."

"Why?"

And again, but not so honestly, Edith said:

"I don't know."

Barry remained thinking for a little while. Then he put another question.

"Could anybody tell she wasn't quite white?"

Edith sat puzzling for a moment.

"Could they Edith? . . . Could you?"

"Well, you see, I knew, Barry."

"But if you hadn't known?"

His persistency compelled an answer.

"Yes."

"If I had lived with her instead of you, would people think I wasn't white, either?"

"I suppose so."

He sat silent for a few moments.

"Edith," he said presently, "is it a wicked thing to be glad you haven't got your mother with you?"

He was repeating the attitude of every successive coloured generation, approaching white, towards its predecessors. As Elmira had been ashamed of her father, Kleinhans, as Kleinhans of his mother, Deborah, so was this child ashamed of Elmira.

Edith was conventional enough not to be able to reply.

"Because," he added, presently, "even if it is wicked I can't help it." He leaned his head against Edith's arm.

"Are you sorry I'm your brother, Edith?"

2

He had the same curious affinity for Edith as he had had for their common father. Although, young as he was, he realized the advantage to him of living with this altogether white woman, he really had a natural, affection for her also. And she, shut off from all love could not but respond. As time went on, too, she thought of his ancestry more seldom and more easily; and, presently, as he, growing older, needed her less, their attitudes were reversed, and it was Edith who sought love and Barry who yielded it.

3

But when Edith was forty-two and Barry thirteen, after the Boer War was over, and South Africa settling down again, a strange thing happened. Edith fell in love. Like a young, immature girl, she fell in love. And it was simply because no marriageable man had ever been kind to her before, and because she was terrified that Life should run away from her, without having given her womanhood a chance.

The man was the Rev. Michael Raill, the new minister. He was a bachelor, about the same age as herself, a big, good-looking follower of the school of liberal parsons. It was his hearty goodwill to all the world that had actually kept him unmarried. Just as he was prepared to put his arm across any man's shoulder and call him "old chap", so he found too many women pleasing to be able to choose from among them.

Edith could not realize that his agreeable manner towards herself was his natural manner towards every one. He was as friendly with her as he was with any human being, and because that was more friendly than had ever before been her experience, her heart, like a plant put in too late, its leaves already yellowing, sent out an unseasonable flower.

Edith in bloom! Poor Edith, so meagre and sapless, blossoming. She ran to shops, buying herself clothes; she altered the arrangement of her mouse-like, greying hair; she stood in front of looking-glasses examining herself, turning her head this way and that, posturing. And, sometimes, after she had done so, she would sit down forlornly on a chair, her heart tight, tears pricking her eyes. But at other times—particularly when she had just taken down her hair for the night, and it framed and softened her narrow hard face—it would seem to her that, really, she looked astonishingly young for her age, quite girlish and attractive.

"It is only a question of making the best of oneself," she would think. "There have been women——" and her bewitched heart would tell over a tale of middle-aged women for love of whom worlds had shaken.

Then she had a certain theory of her own. A woman of forty, destined to live to seventy, was as young as a woman of twenty destined to live only to fifty. Each had thirty more years to go. Surely the test of age was not how many years one had already lived, but how many years one still had in store in the future. At ten years a dog was old and a human being young, since the reckoning went by the years still before each. . . . The years spent were, of course, certain, and those unspent problematical. But why not assume a large number of years ahead, and choose to be young—as young as the world would grant?

There was one comfort she had—her figure was as slim as a young girl's, and she was fair rather than dark. Surely two aids to youth.

She went about trying to seem young. She had a vision of herself as young. Now and then she even conceived on her shoulders a head bearing only the most casual resemblance to her own. Written down, her mental catalogue would have described her not inaccurately: brownish hair, grey-blue eyes, narrow face, and so forth . . . but seen!—ah, when, walking along in an imaginative haze like this, she suddenly fronted a mirror and was forced to compare fact with fancy, it was as if the cloak of romance had fallen from her thin shoulders, leaving her naked to the world; and she would give one frightened look, and hurry wretchedly away.

4

She began to contrive reasons why Mr. Raill should come to see her; to manœuvre meetings with him; to waylay him in an accidental-seeming manner. She thought of nothing but him; with the greatest difficulty she kept herself from continually mentioning his name. She would go round in a kind of trance, a lovely, melting laziness of the flesh, and suddenly her heart would jump with a great shock and begin beating so furiously that her whole body seemed to vibrate. She would give a little excited laugh. And Barry would look at her in amazement. "She's getting very funny lately," he would think. And she would notice his stare and try to control herself. She would speak to him about matters of his own concern, but her voice would come out breathless and shaken.

Mr. Raill was used to female adoration, but so far was he from appreciating Edith's womanhood at all that he invariably thought of her as "that poor queer soul".

He pitied her in her unattractive loneliness, and always treated her, for that reason, with special consideration. "He finds something in me that he doesn't get in those silly, flighty girls," Edith thought. "Understanding and sympathy." She drew upon her reading. "Yes. Woman's chief charm."

And whenever he spoke to her, she would lower her head slightly, and look up at him with her pale eyes in a manner of absorbed attention. She saw herself, sitting like that, interested and interesting. It seemed to her to make a not unattractive picture.

Mr. Raill would go on labouring, like a dutiful Christian, to be pleasant to her.

5

Edith could not help sometimes thinking of her money in connection with Mr. Raill. She would not, of course, do either of them the injustice of assuming that it influenced his personal attitude towards her. And yet it must, she felt, give her some prestige, even in the eyes of a clergyman, that she was a person of substantial means. If one had money one was not considered with the derelict suggestion of something worn-out and useless, as an "old maid," one was regarded simply as an "unmarried woman". It made all the difference.

And then, to be frank, even in the eyes of the Church, money was money. Look how they went round collecting in dribs and drabs whenever something was needed for the church: the bazaars, the sales of work; the satisfaction that, after months of labour two or three dozen women had contrived to scrape together a few pounds that the husband of any one of them might, as it happened, have thrown carelessly on the table without noticing the loss. Besides, if there was any man who needed a rich wife, it was a clergyman. Edith's mother, the daughter of one, had told her enough about their penurious lives.

Really, her advantages in the eyes of Mr. Raill must be quite striking. Her rigidly moral character, so clerically suitable; her affinity with him so extraordinary that he had himself immediately recognized it; her interest in church work so providentially (yes, one might use that word) reinforced by her substantial bank balance—it was almost as if predestined.

They began to meet quite often. He always, she had noticed, walked down the Avenue into Adderley Street, towards evening. It was in the Avenue they generally chanced on one another: she, romantically, with a little book; he, rather abstracted, but, as always, very pleasant. There were various interesting matters occupying his mind these days; among them, not very importantly, the uncomfortable recognition that Miss Lindsell—Miss Lindsell. . . . Extraordinary. Well, but what could one do about it?

6

On Saturday afternoons she used to go and put flowers in the church. And on Sundays she went there three times during the day. Even in winter, when it rained, she did not neglect her early morning devotions. She used to wrap herself up well; but her thin nose would be red with cold, her hands blue, and her feet dead. Until, at home again, over breakfast, she thawed at last. Then her nose would get gradually warmer until all the fire in her body seemed to concentrate in it; presently it would glow redder with heat than it had before done with cold; and now she would feel as if it had swollen all over her face. . . .

When Edith went to church, Barry went with her.

CHAPTER VI

I

HE liked it. Barry liked going to church. He would sit there beside Edith, passionately interested in all the religious proceedings. He never found church a bore, as the other fellows said they did. And, recognizing the singularity of his devotional appreciation, it was a thing he never mentioned to them. They might think it was because—well, they might wonder how it happened that he was so different from every one else.

Above all, he loved Mr. Raill's sermons. They excited and inspired him. They made him feel good. They made him want to be, indeed, quite perfect. Would it not be glorious to be absolutely sure of getting into Heaven! He could not help thinking of the whole affair of human conduct and immortal award in the light of a school examination. If one got the requisite number of marks one was promoted to a higher form— if one scored enough good conduct points during one's term on earth one was admitted into Paradise. How terrible to think that one might fail to enter Heaven by just a single mark, and might, in consequence, have to remain for ever in Hell!

He would find his heart beating in terror. He would lie awake at night begging God to let him begin all over again, not to count against him the evil he had done when he knew no better. If one studied the Bible there were so many sins one might commit without even being aware of sinfulness. And the disproportion between mortal commission and eternal consequence was so startling. According to whether one was good or bad for a few insignificant earthly years all eternity lay in the balance for bliss or suffering.

Barry could not understand how, considering such tremendous issues, people had the heart to think of any other thing but religion.

He went about praying, being meek and kind and obedient, doing things for people, trying to bring himself to give away whatever he possessed; and his sister, her nerves unsteady with the strain of her feelings for Mr. Raill, told him that she did not know whatever had come over him lately, that he seemed to her to be going mad.

2

Coming into the world a hundred years after his ancestor, the Rev. Andrew Flood, Barry Lindsell had had deposited in him the same religious germ that had made his great-great-grandfather want to give the boots from his feet to a beggar and walk barefoot; suffer a great misunderstanding in silence; pray in fasting isolation. With adolescence that germ had wakened into life; and now that his features, too, were forming themselves to the mould of manhood, there was something even in Barry's physical appearance that resembled the Rev. Andrew Flood. His eyes had exactly that wistful and fervent look, the bones of his face were becoming equally prominent, the same religious emotions gave him also the air of embarrassed ardour that had characterized the missionary. If Deborah had seen him she might have been startled at the resemblance, but there was no one else alive to wonder at the strangeness of the physical and spiritual recapitulation. No picture of the Rev. Andrew Flood existed anywhere in the world; his eldest child, Isaac, was probably dead by this time; Deborah was nearly eighty now, and just barely remembered him as a prematurely aged man whose senses had taken leave of him.

He had a few score black descendants through Isaac in Canaan; he had descendants brown and yellow and almost white in the Cape Colony; he had this one great-great-grandchild recalling from the dead his very features and emotions; yet he himself was so utterly gone that barely a thought of him remained.

And even after Edith left off going to church so regularly—so assiduously—Barry himself did not relax his religious observances.

Edith's devotion faded when the Rev. Michael Raill passed beyond her hopes.

3

It happened this way.

"I saw Mr. Raill this afternoon in Adderley Street," said Barry one day at dusk.

"Did you?" said Edith, her heart jumping as always at the mention of his name. A little flush crept up her face towards her eyes. "Did you speak to him?"

"Yes. I was walking past, and he stopped me himself. He asked me how I was getting on, and how you were, and——" Barry was nearly fourteen. Something in his sister's face made him hesitate.

"Yes? And what did you say?"

"I said we were both all right."

"And was that all?"

"No."

"Really? Did he talk quite a lot to you?"

"A fair amount."

Barry was feeling very uncomfortable now. He wished he had not so unthinkingly spoken of his meeting with Mr. Raill. He reached for his hat. "Well, I must be going."

"Are you in a hurry?" demanded Edith sharply.

Barry was not the man to make himself guilty of an untruth these days.

"No," he admitted.

"It's nearly supper-time. Don't go," said Edith, and there was a little pleading note in her voice. "Tell me, what else did Mr. Raill say to you? Was it anything about me?"

"No, I don't think he said any more about you."

"Was it anything interesting?" She tried to conceal the thrill in her tones that always came when Michael Raill was in her mind. She tried, unfortunate soul, to smile playfully. "I haven't been out all day. I'd like to hear some news. Sit down, Barry."

The words dragged themselves from Barry.

"Well, you see, he was with a girl——"

"Oh? Who was she? Some one we know?"

Barry shook his head.

"A young girl?"

"About eighteen. Her name is Miss Brown. He introduced me to her. He said I should be the first person to hear the great news——"

"The great news!" breathed Edith.

"About his engagement," said Barry.

The little flush ran down again from Edith's face. She hardly seemed like a living thing. Barry watched her curiously.

After a time she spoke in a flat voice.

"What was that you said, Barry?"

"I said," repeated Barry obediently, "Mr. Raill

264

told me I'd be the first to hear the great news of his engagement."

"To Miss Brown," remarked Edith with lips that hardly moved.

"Yes, to Miss Brown, the girl who was with him."

They had their supper together, Edith talking to Barry in a voice as dry as the crackling of dead twigs underfoot.

She said good night to him shortly afterwards.

As Barry turned away, she called him back suddenly.

"About eighteen, you said, Barry."

He knew well enough what was in her mind.

"Yes. About that."

"And pretty, I suppose?"

Barry nodded.

"Very pretty?"

"I thought she was very pretty," said Barry with simple candour.

4

He lay in bed thinking of Edith. He knew about love. Lots of the chaps at school had girls. And in nearly all the books he had ever read, people fell in love and got married. But they had always been young, the lovers of his experience. And to associate his own middle-aged sister with such an emotion had seemed to him really not quite decent. Edith's feeling for Mr. Raill was no secret to him. Nor, indeed, was it, in general, a secret. Those of his school-fellows who knew the Lindsell home were greatly amused over the whole affair. They used to tease Barry about it. "Has he proposed yet?" they would bawl at him . . . "When is it coming off?" . . . "Is he going to ask you for your consent?" . . . "Invite us to the wedding."

R

They liked to tease Barry about something or other. He was so different from themselves.

He wondered what they would say when they heard about Mr. Raill's engagement to Miss Brown. He felt he couldn't stand it if they said anything about his sister now. He wished he had not always, so coward-like, received their teasing in silence.

Her drawn face, saying good night, passed across his mind. Her love might be ridiculous or not, but she certainly was unhappy. He determined to spend his whole life caring for her. He wondered if it would do her any good if he prayed. . . . He prayed. . . . In the middle of praying, he fell asleep.

But Edith who, for nearly a year, had begged heavenwards like a child: "Oh, God, let him love me," was lying awake in the next room, blasphemously discounting Barry's prayers. God had failed her, and she felt she had no further need of Him.

Things did not seem so desperate to Barry when he woke next morning. Edith appeared to be going about her household duties as always. Perhaps he had exaggerated the whole affair in the night.

Nevertheless he wished he had the courage to tell her that, whatever happened, she would always have him, Barry. He hovered around her after breakfast.

"Go to school, Barry," she said in a harsh, distant voice.

He went to school. He never, in all his life, told her how he had determined to devote himself wholly to her.

5

But what Edith heard that day about Miss Brown did not make matters pleasanter for her. Not that there was anything exactly wrong about Miss Brown. Only she was poor. She worked for her living. She wasn't of any social consequence. Edith had a feeling that if Mr. Raill had at least chosen to marry some one a little more distinguished; some one whose father was important; some one who was, perhaps, an accepted local belle: a woman, in short, whose superior claims on his heart she could readily acknowledge, she would not have found the loss of him so unbearable.

But to know that he had succumbed, like any green youth, to the mere charms of immaturity, to precisely that which she herself did not possess—to realize how far she was from being the kind of woman who attracted him—in this recognition lay her chief bitterness.

She saw herself trying to allure him (forty-two, and he had chosen eighteen—oh, the fool she had been!) and she despised herself utterly. But now and then a little sneering smile would come to her lips when she remembered that she was not the only one to whom Mr. Raill had preferred Miss Brown.

6

She taunted herself with deliberate recollections. She remembered how she had exercised herself to meet him on his habitual afternoon walk through the avenue into Adderley Street; how she had so carefully dressed herself to look younger and better in his eyes . . . and he on his way, she understood at last, to meet Miss Brown after office hours! Miss Brown, who might be nothing and nobody, but who, at least, did not need to labour in pretence of that which she simply was. Whatever Miss Brown possessed lay on the outside for any one to see, and it was enough.

From girlhood Edith had envied the women who had

but to exist and Life came kneeling at their feet, offering them bouquets. She herself respected such women— she could not help it. She gave them homage, felt humble in their presence, scorned herself for the feeble competition she offered against them. She knew that, however she might strive for spiritual and intellectual achievement, an accidental shaping of a contour here, a haphazard deepening of a pigmentation there, were, by comparison, enough to stamp the womanhood out of her. Yet she was but a mundane person, swayed by earthly views; a minister of God, she had hoped, might look for other excellencies than fleshly ones.

But he had been no better than any callow youngster, the Rev. Michael Raill, in the desires of his heart. A little ignorant girl, because her eyes were a bright brown and her cheeks freshly flushed, had satisfied him for a mate.

His parishioners discussed the affair with an indignation the more exuberant for Miss Lindsell's presence. She sat there tightly, being very just about Miss Brown's merits, saying the little amiable things about her that were not meant to influence any one favourably, very careful, abnormally indifferent and impartial —Miss Brown's only advocate.

They said she was very plucky about it. She deceived nobody.

CHAPTER VII

I

EDITH's disappointment reacted curiously on Barry. He became a need to her so intense that it coloured their association with bitterness. If she had not Barry, she would be cut off from the human world, she felt. She followed him about hungrily. She not only loved him; most extraordinarily, she hated him at the same time. And she hated him because she was afraid he might not love her as she loved him; might love some one else better; might want something else more. She was jealous of his friends, his occupations, even his religion. All day long she went round dreading the possible girl who might come into his life.

She felt that it was a kind of mania with her, and tried to control herself; but by the time he was sixteen or seventeen she was always talking to him about girls —about how silly they were, how affected and selfish, how mercenary, how ruinous to a man's endeavour. The man, she said, who could live his life free of women was the only man who might fulfil his destiny unhampered. The news of an unhappy love affair or marriage released from her an excited flow of triumphant exposition.

Barry would listen, frightened. She herself would be frightened too. "I am going mad," she would tell her denied and aching heart. "Why do I say these things? I must be going mad."

She would keep off the subject for a few days. And

then, irresistibly, she would begin again, sneering and violent—a crusader against love.

2

One day she produced her ultimate argument.

"Barry," she said in a gentle voice that she knew herself was as false as it was gentle—and she suffered as she spoke because she was so wicked—"Barry, do you realize that you are different from other people?"

He looked at her silently. And she felt that not only was he different; she was different too.

"Poor Barry!" she said. And she meant "Poor Edith!"

"What's the use of talking about it?" he mumbled.

"But it's my duty to talk about it, to explain to you."

"I know everything there is to know."

"Yes. You know the past. But do you know the future?"

"I don't understand what you mean."

She gathered her forces.

"Don't you, Barry? Must I tell you?"

Her light eyes were steadily on him. She hated herself for her cruelty, but it would have outraged all her natural forces not to speak.

"You are not a baby any more. You are seventeen. I suppose you have sometimes thought about—your heritage."

He felt as if she were advancing upon him physically, pushing him against a wall. A thrill of desperation mounted in him.

"You mean—— Yes, I have. Yes, I have. Edith, leave me alone about it. Why can't you leave me alone about it?"

270

It was as if she were being driven to battle, the urge she now had on her to strip his heart.

"I won't leave you alone. Things have been left alone too long. They should have been stopped hundreds of years ago—hundreds of years ago. It should never have been allowed to happen in South Africa that—that white children should have come into the world with shame and sorrow in their blood."

She told herself that she was speaking right and just words, but in her inmost soul she was well aware that she was not speaking them because they were right and just, but because she loved and hated this boy both at the same time.

His face was very pale.

"You mean me," he said in a voice almost inaudible.

"And your mother, and your mother's father, and his mother. All, all like you."

"It wasn't the fault of any of us that we got born."

"No, not that you got born." She paused a moment. "That you allowed others to get born."

He struggled up from his chair.

"I don't know why you are telling me these things. What can I do? Do you want me to go out and kill myself!" His voice rose. "My God, you make me feel like doing it, too. . . . Not because—Not because . . ." he was trembling as he spoke, his very forehead was burning now . . . "of what you said about the shame and sorrow in my blood, but because it's enough to make any one wish he were dead to have to live in the same house with a woman like you."

She tried to interrupt him. He went on. "I don't know why I do it, either. I'd be better off anywhere else. All day long you're at me about one thing or another thing. . . . Now it's my blood. Now you'll

271

never leave off about my blood. Edith, I tell you—I tell you——"

He sat down again in his chair, and began suddenly to sob.

She came over to him, in her senses again, genuinely sorry that she had so hurt him.

"I didn't mean to do this, Barry. You know I only want you to be happy."

She made an attempt to put her arm round his shoulder. He shook her off.

"Go away."

"I thought it my duty——"

"Leave me."

"I wasn't blaming you. I only wanted to warn you about the future—to explain to you why you will never have the right to—marry. To—have children. I thought it was time you understood that you ought not to allow yourself ever to care for a girl. Because it would be unjust to her—and to the race."

There she was again. She couldn't keep the words from her tongue. He hardened himself to control his tears. There was a look of his father, Adam Lindsell, on him as he answered her. She remembered the look.

"I suppose you think I don't know why you're going on like this," he said, with a slow venom she had never heard in his tones before, and that was yet familiar to her. "Every one in Cape Town knows about you, Edith. Every one. Even the boys at school used to laugh at you."

"Yes?" said Edith in a hard voice. "Yes? Go on."

"They all know you wanted Mr. Raill to marry you and he wouldn't."

"Yes?" said Edith again.

"I used to be sorry for you about it." He stood up, finished with tears. "But I'm not any more. I'm beginning to understand why you're always at me not to care about girls and that sort of thing. It isn't the right or wrong of it. It's only that you can't bear any one to be happy because you've been disappointed yourself."

He was very near a truth which she had never disguised from her own mind. And yet he did her an injustice, too. It was not the right or wrong of it—not altogether—so far he understood. But, on the other hand, it was also not pure malice that influenced her. She would have given up much to see him happy, despite her own misery. She would have given up everything, indeed, except one thing—himself. . . .

They had both done their utmost and were staring at one another with the same look of forlorn hate on each face. There was a strong resemblance between them now.

"I'll live as I please," said Barry at last. "The black blood in me has never done anybody harm. But if you don't like it, I'll take it away from here."

Her lips smiled faintly in response.

"Do," she said. "Take it to church, where your praying has taught you gratitude for all I have done for you. Go on being holy, Barry."

3

For the first few hours after their quarrel all Edith could think of were Barry's words: "Every one in Cape Town knows about you, Edith. Every one. Even the boys at school used to laugh at you."

She had had her moments of suffering, but never before had anything so lacerated her heart as this

273

knowledge that she was an object of contempt to Barry. Her love for Mr. Raill was long since dead. She had sent him a wedding present. His wife had, after all been accepted in Cape Town. She was a pleasant and modest girl, Mrs. Michael Raill. Edith did not find it difficult to speak to her, or to ask her how the promptly-arrived baby was getting on. When she thought of that year of excitement and exaltation through which she had gone, hoping for the Rev. Michael Raill, it seemed to her like a period disconnected from the rest of her rigid life—a time of fever or intoxication. She was forgetting about it now, except to wonder how it could have happened at all.

And suddenly to have it thrown in her face by Barry; to realize that she was not to him a superior being to be trusted and admired, but a foolish old maid who had, under his comprehending eyes, fatuously and unsuccessfully pursued a man in marriage—to know that there was not in all the world a single thing of flesh and blood to whom she had any value—oh, she could not bear it.

She had a vision of herself, all dressed up, smirking after Mr. Raill, with Barry's friends laughing at her. She saw herself standing there, as in a picture, fronting a row of amused young eyes. And worse than anything was the fact that Barry had been, not amused, but (as he had just told her) sorry. So contemptible was she that she had put the little coloured boy she had fostered in the position of pitying her. . . . Yes, better that they should part—better that Barry should go away than remain on despising her. . . .

And why had he flung himself at her like that? Simply because she had done her duty. Was it not her duty to warn him against himself? Had she ever, in duty, failed Barry?

There ran through her mind an inexhaustible list of her goodnesses towards him. Who else would have done for Barry what she had done? She had been more than a sister to him, more even than a mother. She had nursed him through his delicate childhood. She had helped him with his lessons. She had played games with him when, nervous of his fellows, he had spent lonely hours at home. She had been his friend and protectress. She was prepared to devote her life to him. And yet now, on the threshold of manhood, he thought of her not, according to her due, as a creature next to God, but as a being to despise and reject.

She looked after him, quivering, as without having addressed her, he went to school next day. He would be a middle-sized man, but he looked small because of his slenderness. His legs were particularly thin. He stooped slightly. There was an expression on his face as of waiting. His grey eyes were very patient, and yet they had an exalted, fervent look too. His light brown hair was still soft as a child's. There was habitually something pathetic about him that made her feel that she wanted to do things for him. Never had he reminded her of their father until yesterday. Never, indeed, had she seen him roused to passion. . . . Watching him now, she could hardly connect the baleful expression she had met on his face then with the Barry she knew. The Barry she knew was the too-gentle boy walking down the street there.

Irresistibly the yearning she habitually had towards him came over her. Why could she not have left him in peace? Why must she dig at him and dig at him? Why had she to drag that into daylight which was his dark secret?

And even as she asked herself the rhetorical questions she smiled ironically. Too well she could give the answer. Even if he despised her it was not, as she had told herself yesterday, better that he should leave her. She would do anything rather than lose Barry. If only by the bonds of his own unhappiness, she wanted him tied fast to her.

4

He came back from school in the afternoon, continuing the silence of the morning. Edith hovered around him waiting for an opening to establish contact again. He allowed none. He went straight to his room and locked himself in. He did not appear for their evening meal.

At half-past eight Edith stood outside his door calling his name.

He did not answer.

"Barry!" she said. "Aren't you coming to dinner?"

She waited a few seconds before speaking again.

"I haven't had anything myself yet, Barry."

There was a trembling in her tones as she spoke. It did not move him to any response.

"Shall I wait for you?" she tried again.

She leaned against his door, hoping for his voice. It did not come.

Then she said: "You can't go without eating. I'll send your food in to you," and went back in despair to her solitary meal.

5

Barry was standing in the middle of his room fronting the door outside which Edith had been calling. "Your heritage," she had said to him yesterday. "The shame and sorrow in your blood."

It had maddened him. He had tried the best he could to insult her. "The boys at school used to laugh at you. You can't bear any one to be happy because you've been disappointed yourself." (He could hardly recognize his own voice for anger.) . . . And then her final words: "Go on being holy, Barry."

For years she had not left him in peace, and when finally she had provoked him beyond endurance, she must needs taunt him with his holiness. . . .

Now she stood outside his door asking him to come and eat with her—her hypocritical voice so mournful. After all that to come and eat with her! He could not bring himself to answer.

He heard her dejected footsteps going away down the passage, and began to tell himself anew the evil she had done him. But even as he counted out the evil, there came stealing up thoughts of the good too.

He sat down on his bed, torn this way and that. What right had he, after all, to resent her warning about his blood? Was not what she said just?

He had heard about heredity—he had been told stories of black children born to apparently white parents. It was true that, living all his young life in a mixed population, he had not come across such cases himself, but he did know of families where some children might pass as white, and some as coloured; and on account of these things, and what they involved, Edith had thought it her duty to speak to him as she had done. . . .

Yet, on the other hand, how were the white-skinned people whom rumour credited with black blood different from other people? How was he different, except in that he was afraid he was different; Why should Edith say to him that he must never allow himself to care for any girl?

Of course, it was an unspeakable thing for a white man to cut off his own children from the civilization that was their due, to throw life backwards to the inferiority that black blood meant; but what noticeable effect on future generations could his own drop of black blood have? Why should Edith come and speak to him, at his age, of such things as love, and marriage and children?

His thoughts ran painfully backwards and forwards. She had sneered at him: "Go on being holy, Barry," yet she wanted him to live celibate like a priest.

His heart jumped. And why should he not do so? Why should he not go into the church, cast aside earthly hopes, and give his life to God? It would be some recompense for what his ancestors had done.

For a moment he sat there, in a state of dazed sublimity. And then a warm and shining peace flowed over him.

He sprang up from his bed, and ran towards the dining-room. Edith was not there. He went to her bedroom. It was in darkness, except for the light of a thin new moon. But he could see her stretched on the bed.

He came and knelt beside her. "Forgive me, Edith," he said, and rested his head beside hers on the pillow. "Will you forgive me?"

"Oh, Barry," she moaned.

There was a little silence.

"I see now you were right," he said then. "I must give up everything."

"Not everything," she whispered against his cheek. "Only one thing."

"Yes, only one thing," he repeated.

"Only woman's love," she said, and her heart beat luxuriously now that he was hers for ever.

"Only woman's love," he echoed.

CHAPTER VIII

I

BARRY took his degree at the South African College in Cape Town, and then, at the age of twenty-one, he sailed for England. He was going to Oxford, and it was definitely decided that he was entering the church. He had never wavered in the resolution he had taken four years ago to dedicate himself to Christ.

Edith was now fifty. Except for her devotion to Barry, her life had settled down into a stiff routine of little things. Her days were so mapped out that they seemed very full. And she really found it necessary to get up quite early in order to encompass all her activities. At seven she had coffee. Then she went into her garden and did some work there. Then breakfast with her *Cape Times*. Then orders for the day. Then sewing or shopping. Then lunch. Then a little rest. Then croquet or a call. Then dinner. Then a game of cards, perhaps; or a theatre or concert in company with some other isolated woman. Then bed with the devoted fox terrier on the mat beside her. The next day the same. The next day the same.

Only on mail-days there was news from Barry. And the moment she had finished reading his letter, she began already waiting for next mail-day and another letter. As her small occupations filled her days, so her thoughts of Barry linked them together, and linked also week to week, and month to month.

She saw him coming back to South Africa, and herself keeping house for him; visiting his parishioners as his representative; proudly facing him in church. It was as if he were making a career for her as well as for himself, working there at Oxford.

He came out to spend one vacation with her; and the anticipation, his presence, the retrospection, passed a whole year.

She was not unhappy. Not only had she Barry, she was, among all her friends, the only one who had money that might be called *money*. She was able to do little things for them, to patronize them. She had been a few times to visit May, still on the farm, which Darrell refused ever to leave—a fat and dowdy woman now, and it gave Edith some pleasure to appear to her country sister as a city woman, a worldly person. She taught them bridge, spoke about Barry, described her social festivities to them; and May quite pathetically asked her if she couldn't do something for her eldest girl (actually twenty-two already!), who was making her life a misery by complaining of the dullness of farm life.

What, in the end, was May, whom she had so envied, getting out of life more than she was getting?

2

When Barry had been away in England three years, the war came, and inevitably the time arrived when he wrote to Edith that he was going over to France as a Chaplain to the Forces. At least, he would go over when his regiment went. At present he was still training in England.

Now Edith had a share in the war as other women had, and she sat among the sewing and knitting, and

s

281

talking blood-thirstily, full of secret apprehension. Barry was safer than other men. He was, indeed, at the moment, quite safe there in England. Even when, at last, he should be in France, he would not face exactly the ordinary risks. . . . And yet stories were coming through of chaplains acting as stretcher-bearers, going under fire, as open to the chance of death as the wounded they carried. . . .

It was not till the end of 1915 that Barry crossed over to France. He was back within three months. Shell shock. In the middle of 1916 he went out again. And in even a shorter time than before he was once more in England. Shell shock. He knew it now. It was no use. He couldn't stand it. His spirit would not uphold his cringing flesh. His flesh shrivelled back upon his fainting spirit. He had tried telling himself to be white, he had besought God for strength—nothing helped. They might give it any name they liked. Barry suffered from fear.

He remained in England, taking the place of another man more able to withstand terror.

He did not come back to South Africa until the year 1920.

He brought a wife with him.

3

He had simply written to Edith a week before he was due to sail telling her he was married. "You will love her, Edith. She is as good as she is beautiful—everything a man could desire. She looks forward eagerly to our return home. She calls it 'Home' herself already, and longs for our South African sun as much as I do. I have told her about you—about all you have been to me and done for me. In less than a month your new

282

little sister will be in Cape Town. May I bring her straight to my old home?"

Not a word about that secret thing in him. Not an allusion to his boyhood's vow. Nothing, nothing, but a lover's exultation in his love—the usual talk of goodness and beauty—the inevitable fatuous expectation that she must be as delightful to every one as she was to him. "Your little sister!" Sister! Edith was a year from sixty, old enough to be the girl's grandmother!

But she understood how it was. Barry had been away from Africa nine years. He had lived in a land where colour was no crime. He had met brown men at Oxford who were not despised as brown men were despised in Africa. He had seen white women walking around in England with what they themselves called niggers.

And even then, on a general survey, colour was so rare a thing that it was only a matter of casual consequence: the ordinary person did not think of it, or brood over it, or consider it, or understand it. Barry had gradually learnt to forget himself that he was not altogether as his fellows. And even if he had not forgotten, he would no longer hold the meagre differentiation as of any importance; he would be amused now rather than otherwise at the romantic—the tragic—aspect the subject had worn for him in childhood.

Edith told herself that she was trembling with indignation for the sin Barry had committed in marrying a white girl, but she knew in her heart that she was suffering for more personal reasons. For nine years she had dreamt of Barry's return. And now every moment of his return would, she foresaw, be stabbed with jealousy for her.

She wished he had remained with his wife in England, that her eyes need not rest on him as the possession of another woman. She wished—sometimes, for the flash of a moment, she even wished he had died in France. She could have borne better to have owned him in death than to know that, alive, he was yet not hers.

Gone were her dreams of a peaceful old age, hallowed by his need of her and by her pride in him. In neither sense was he any more hers.

4

Yet she met him and his bride at the docks, and she said—she actually said—"Welcome home, children." And the girl, Nora, kissed her on her thin lips with their radiation of little wrinkles—she kissed her heartily with a soft, amiable, red-lipped, smiling mouth.

Barry had told Nora that her eyes were blue as the African sky, her hair golden as the African sun, her skin pure as the African air; and, putting aside comparisons with natural phenomena, her eyes were certainly blue, her hair fair, and her skin fresh. She was a pretty girl. Even Edith had to admit it. Hardly interesting—Nora had no need to comfort herself with what any girl might assume as a virtue if she had no other—too definitely pretty to be interesting.

She chattered away to Edith without any shyness. She believed pleasantly that Edith was charmed to have her there, that Edith complacently recognized her ownership of Barry. "Barry must do this," she said. "I want Barry to arrange that," she said.

She held Edith's thin, unresponsive hand in her happy one as they drove home in a taxi. She made herself at home at once. She described Edith as she had never been described before.

"Your sister's a dear," she said to Barry, as she let down her coil of luxurious hair in the bedroom Edith had bitterly furnished for two.

CHAPTER IX

I

IT was not as bad—not the Hell—Edith had expected it to be. She no longer wished Barry had been taken from her altogether rather than returned in this wise. Once she could bring herself to the point of realizing that Barry was not hers any more, she could also begin to take a mild satisfaction in the happy youthfulness that now possessed the quiet house. And then she tried to tell herself, as mothers tell themselves when the time comes: "She fills one need for him. I shall fill another. He will turn to me again for the deeper things."

It was a fiction, of course. The son seldom, in the past, had turned to his mother for the deeper things. He never would now. But the expectation persisted and gave consolation. . . .

And there were even times when Edith felt that Barry was so cut off from her that she could almost consider him as if he were a stranger. She saw very clearly now his weaknesses and faults—his general spinelessness. "Strange," she told herself, "that a pretty girl like Nora should not have wanted a more manly man for a husband." Panic, probably, she mused. The War. So many potential husbands gone. The girls in Europe were frightened, took what they could get. And then, of course, Barry had money.

But, again, that flaw in his blood. She wondered if he had told Nora. For weeks she wondered, and dared not ask. There had been a time when there were no hesitations between her and Barry. Now her heart began to beat with nervous excitement at the mere idea of putting him an intimate question—any intimate question.

But she did it at last. Suddenly, one evening, while Nora was playing about the garden with Edith's old fox terrier, she opened her mouth and the significant words rushed out. She had not definitely formulated them, had not even consciously known she was going to say them, yet her face was flushed, and her voice breathless even before she spoke . . . as if her crafty inner self, having secretly laid the plan, had wrought compulsion on her innocent outer self to execute it.

"Have you told her?" she said.

Barry looked at his wife for a moment before answering his sister. Then he shook his head. Here, back in South Africa, all the old fears had returned to him. He felt his blood once more.

"Did you not think it necessary?"

"She loved me. It would have made no difference."

"How do you know?"

"England isn't Africa."

"But it might make a difference—one day."

"I was not going to distress her for the sake of remote contingencies," said Barry stiffly.

"But children?" said Edith. "Do you regard children as remote contingencies?"

Barry got up from his seat, walked the length of the stoep, and back again.

"Do you mind," he said, standing in front of Edith and trying, but without success, to meet her eyes steadily, "if I don't discuss the matter with you?"

"Yes, I do mind," said Edith, and made a little formal speech on that which lay uppermost in her heart.

"Considering many things, I do mind your not answering what I believe to be an essential question. On the other hand, I quite realize that now you are married I have no longer any claim on your confidence. You have made it quite clear ever since you came back."

She would never have believed that she could so give herself away, could so humiliate herself as to let Barry know that she resented his defection—cared for him, in short, more than he cared for her.

"But, Edith——" he protested.

Edith had stood up, too, now, and was facing him.

"That will do, Barry. Don't apologize. I shall not interfere again."

She spoke with cold dignity, but she could not keep her voice from trembling.

"I didn't mean——" said Barry.

She saw that he was beginning to waver. It stiffened her.

"You know your business best, of course."

"But you don't understand——" the prominent bones in his face seemed to be moving with agitation. "You don't understand."

She shrugged her thin shoulders very slightly. Her tight face gave him no help.

"I know I should have told her before we married," he said desperately at last. "But now it is too late. Too late, Edith."

"Too late to tell her at all, do you mean?"

"Too late to matter any more. Whatever there is to find out she will find out for herself."

"How?" Edith's face had flushed suddenly as she put her mechanical, unnecessary question.

"When our child is born," said Barry.

Edith's face reddened more deeply still. The idea of birth always violated her virginal seclusions. That gestation should be going on under her own roof offended her deepest sanctities. That her brother (a clergyman, too—it seemed to accentuate the matter) should be anticipating paternity really struck her as not decent. She had begun almost to like Nora. She looked at her now, so falsely girlish, playing with the dog, and found her, all at once, unpleasant.

She could say nothing to Barry.

"So you see," said Barry helplessly.

Now other thoughts began to assail Edith. There was a child to be born in relationship to her, whom all the world might know to be a child not white. Barry, and even his mother, had been lucky accidents. His maternal grandparents had both been coloured people. Not one of his uncles or aunts she knew could have passed as pure Europeans. Barry's child might be—anything.

And even that was only from the simple point of view of pigmentation. Down the future generations would run that black blood mingled with her father's. And Barry spoke as if the colour of his child's skin was all that need trouble Nora. It was, according to him, only a question of waiting to see whether the child would turn out to be brown or white.

She said so to him in stiff words.

"Nothing else *need* matter," said Barry. "The rest is only sentiment.

"*You* ought to know," said Edith with simple bitterness, and walked into the house.

289

Nora, coming in dishevelled from her romp, found him standing there alone, and pulled him into the living-room after Edith. But there was an uneasiness in the attitude of brother and sister towards one another that even Nora, for all her amiable obtuseness, could not quite help blundering upon.

"What is the matter with you two?" she demanded pleasantly.

Barry smiled palely. Edith did not trouble to make any reassuring gestures.

"Funny people," commented Nora. "How can you look so glum with all that lovely sunshine about? You South Africans don't deserve your luck."

She bent suddenly towards Barry, and gave his hair a cheerful rumpling.

"What's wrong with my little husband?" she asked.

Barry took her mischievous hands from his head and held them between his. But his eyes were on Edith's face. Its sternness terrified him. For a moment Edith looked at husband and wife with her pale, steady eyes, and then she said slowly, as if speaking from under a spell: "Barry has something to tell you, Nora."

"Really, have you?" exclaimed Nora, with a little thrill in her voice.

Barry shook his head. "Not now. Not immediately."

"Oh, but you have. Edith has just said so. He mustn't keep it from me, must he, Edith?"

"Barry knows what he ought to do," said Edith.

Nora bent down and whispered something in his ear. She looked up at Edith, laughing and blushing. "I've just been telling him I ought to be humoured—now. You've heard why, haven't you? I saw you both talking very seriously on the verandah while I was playing with Jock."

"It is in connection with that," said Edith, and left the room.

She did not know what had made her force the position like this. Walking about in the garden outside, she visualized the two of them together facing their problem, their lives disrupted perhaps; and a pang of pity for them went through her heart. Although it had hurt her to see them happy, although the jealousy in her had made her force this ruinous crisis, no sooner had she done so, than she would have given, she felt, anything in the world to make them happy again. She could not understand herself. Now, suddenly, she thought of Nora's pretty affectionateness; she remembered how Barry had run to her, in his frightened childhood, as to a saviour. The tears started to her pale old eyes. "Oh God, why am I like that?" she cried in her heart. "What is this twistedness in me that won't let me be good? Why do I have to make suffering for others, even if it causes me to suffer myself?"

It struck her all at once with an irony that dried the tears in her eyes that God would be able to answer that question. He, too, had created suffering for which He must suffer.

4

The smile had left Nora's face.

"Well, Barry?" she said.

He made a gesture of helplessness.

"What is it, Barry?"

291

"I can't tell you."

"But ought I not to know?"

"Yes. And you ought to have known before ever we were married."

"Then why didn't you tell me?"

"I was afraid."

"Of what?"

"I was afraid you might not marry me."

He remembered he had explained to Edith that his confession would have made no difference to Nora. But it was not true that he had believed so at the time.

"Then it is something terrible. And we have been so happy. But what can it be? What could you have told me that would have prevented our marrying? Why, Barry, you can't—a clergyman—you can't have done anything so very bad."

"It's not altogether what I have done myself," said Barry, smiling miserably. "It is what was done to me, and what I shall do to—others."

"Oh!" She looked at him. "I understand. It's something hereditary."

He nodded.

"What? Lunacy? Sickness?"

"No."

"What, Barry, what? Why don't you *tell* me?"
She was crying now.

He sat rigidly beside her.

"There is black blood in me," he said at last.

She gazed at him curiously through her tears. He could not meet her eyes. He felt them searching his body.

Presently she said: "But you are quite fair, Barry!"

The agitation seemed to have left her voice. The

292

exclamation was but an amiably-surprised commentary.
He turned to meet her innocent face.

"Is that all?" she asked.

5

Barry's first feeling at her words was one of shock.
That she should regard this awful thing that had
haunted his whole existence so lightly seemed to him
almost immoral. He felt that he had to make her
realize what his words meant.

"I am not dark," he said. "Nor was my mother.
But her father and mother and brothers and sisters
were like some of the Cape people you see here in Cape
Town."

"Really?" she said. "As brown as all that? What
did your grandfather do for a living?"

She was taking quite an amiable social interest in the
phenomenon of Barry's ancestry. He felt that she was
like the boy in Grimm's fairy tale who could not shudder.

He answered her abruptly.

"Farmed."

"Well, that's not so bad. Quite good people farm,
don't they?"

He regarded her speechlessly.

"I suppose your father made what might be called a
mésalliance when he married your mother. Still, as
you've told me, he was very old, and she was young and
pretty; and I suppose that sort of thing has happened
in nearly every family some time or other."

Tragedy had gone from the situation. It had become
a silly banality.

"But colour, Nora," Barry protested feebly.
"Colour! Don't you understand? Your own child will
have it in his blood."

He could not enjoy the feelings he ought to have had of relief and gratitude, for the irritation that possessed him because he was addressing an uncomprehending mind.

"I don't see what difference it can make," said Nora. "We're all awfully light on my side, and you're not dark yourself. The chances are we'll have quite a fair baby."

"And if we don't?" said Barry in a low voice.

"I love dark children myself," said Nora cheerfully.

"But, Nora——" he began, and, rising from his chair abruptly, crossed the room to the window. He saw Edith walking agitatedly up and down among her flower-beds. He had argued with her as Nora was arguing with him, as if it were simply a question of skin. Yet he had known better within him. He felt suddenly at one with his embittered sister, and far away from his easy-minded wife.

She came and stood comfortingly beside him.

"Poor old Barry," she said. "Don't worry. It will be a white child."

They were a repetition of words spoken seventy years ago by Deborah to her father, the Rev. Andrew Flood, when she had come back from Kadesh carrying within her body the burden of future generations. And, across time, the Rev. Barry Lindsell echoed his ancestor:

"There can be no white children, Nora. No white children to us."

CHAPTER X

I

AND yet, as the days passed, he began to feel that Nora's attitude towards him was changing. She was still as pleasant and cheerful as ever, but every now and then he caught, or he fancied he caught, an abstracted look on her face that was new to him. "She is thinking about it," he told himself. "She is wondering. She is getting nervous."

He could not walk beside her down the streets of Cape Town seeing all the half-castes about—the Cape people—without feeling that the sight of them must affect her distressfully. He had heard of Europeans who could hardly regard these brown and black folk as quite human. How must it seem to Nora to know suddenly that there was that growing within her hitherto pure body that was akin—however distantly—to these *unnatural* creatures? She had seemed not to care when he told her, but perhaps she had not then grasped the significance of his confession. Perhaps she had thought in her English way: "Fair or dark, what is the difference?" Perhaps it needed the constant sight of these Cape people to make her understand. Perhaps— oh, perhaps, she did at last understand.

He became afraid to mention to her the words Kaffir or half-caste. He scanned the daily papers before giving them to her, lest they might contain any references to misdemeanours of coloured folk, any slighting allusions to them, or talk of what were known as "Black Peril" cases.

Unexpectedly, in his unhappiness, Edith gave him the sympathy she had never extended to him when he had been happy. It was as if she felt she could afford to be kind only to people less lucky than herself.

2

It was while Barry was still waiting for his call that the letter came. This was the letter:

"DOORNKRAAL,
"*January* 28*th*, 1921.
"MY DEAREST NEPHEW, BARRY,—Just to let you know we are still in the hands of God, hoping to hear the same from you, and I drop you this few lines to-day to tell you bad news; your dear mother came back last week very sick, and if you can be hear soon we will be very glad. We did tried our best but life is heavy for us hear, and if the Lord is against a person what can a person do; we can only pray and remain yours dear aunt,

"CHRISTINA KLEINHANS.
"*P.S.*—It is the will of God. We all sent best greeting to Miss Edith."

"Who's that letter from?" asked Nora, as Barry sat staring at it.

She picked up the envelope which had dropped to the ground. "What a funny scrawl!"

She tossed it with her knitting on the table, and came and stood beside him. "May I see?"

He looked up at her uncomfortably. "Please, Nora!

I don't quite understand myself yet what it's all about."
He put the thin sheet face downwards on his knee.

Nora walked back to her seat, a little constrained.
"I don't know why you should make such a mystery of
it. I never hesitate to show you my letters."

"I haven't refused to do so," said Barry. "Only—
it comes as a shock. Do, Nora, let me think it over
before I explain to you."

Nora returned to her knitting. Her needles made an
impatient sound in Barry's ears. He moved about
uneasily in his chair for a few minutes, and then he got
up abruptly, and, without a word, went out of the
room.

Nora put down her knitting, and stared after him
angrily, with a flushed face. When Edith came in
shortly after, Nora's hands were still idle, and her face
disturbed.

"Has Barry gone away?" said Edith.

"I don't know," Nora answered abruptly.

"He hasn't left the house, has he? I have just got
tea ready for the three of us."

"He may be somewhere about."

"Well, I suppose he would have told you if he
intended going to town. We'll wait a moment or two,
shall we?"

Nora shook her head.

"Barry's in a peculiar mood. He got a letter which
seemed to upset him, and when I asked him to show
it to me, he didn't exactly refuse, but he said he had to
think it over first."

Edith raised her faint eyebrows in comment.

"So I said no more about it, and went back to my
knitting. But he jumped up from his chair, and
rushed out of the room, and simply left me sitting here."

T

Edith glanced at the envelope on the table.

"Did the letter come in this?"

"Yes. And look at the handwriting."

Edith examined the envelope.

"I know the postmark," she said. "This comes from our part of the world. I mean from somewhere in the neighbourhood of Lindsell's Farm. We used to have to send our letters in a bag to this very post office."

"Then do you think the people who have Lindsell's Farm now are writing to him about something?"

Edith drew her lips together. "What can they have to tell him? We left Lindsell's Farm twenty-four years ago. No, that's not likely. But, of course, the Kleinhanses——"

"Who?"

"Barry's mother was Elmira Kleinhans."

"Oh . . . I don't think he ever mentioned the name to me. It never struck me before."

"I see. Well, I should imagine the Kleinhanses would write through the same post office. They were neighbours of ours as distances go in South Africa."

"That will be it then," said Nora, heavily. "Those people."

She put her knitting together with fingers that trembled, and stood up.

"Do you mind if I don't have any tea, Edith? I don't really feel I want anything."

"Oh, but you must," Edith protested, her heart wakening to pity at distress as it never experienced sympathy with joy. "Come. It may be nothing to worry about. We need not wait for Barry. Let's just have our tea together at once. You keep me company."

"Edith—I—Please!" Nora made a gesture with

her hand, unable to speak. After a time she continued in a tone almost inaudible: "I didn't understand these things at first. I do now. Barry should never have brought me to South Africa."

"But why should this letter trouble you particularly?"

"If it's from his people. If it means we have to have anything to do with them. Sometimes now when I think about it all—Edith, if Barry wants me ever for a moment to be easy in my mind again, he must take me away from here—back to England, where I need not see these brown creatures, and think how they came into the world, or be made to remember all the time that my own little baby. . . ."

Her voice failed her again.

"The baby will be all right," said Edith as heartily as she could. "Any number of well-known people are like that, and nobody thinks anything of it. Why, if a woman were to begin considering all the evils from generations back that may lie in her child's blood, she would never dare to bring it into the world at all."

She was arguing against her own tradition, and yet, as she spoke, she thought suddenly how true her words were. But then, again, it came to her that the evil in Barry's blood represented, in a way, just those other evils of mind and body as well.

But Nora was easily swayed. "You are so clever," she said. "I am glad you put it to me like that. There are always some chances one has to take, of course." She smiled a little. "You're really a dear, Edith . . . I think, perhaps. . . . Shall I help you get the tea?"

"Do," said Edith, and, having cheered her, despised her a little because she had been able to do so.

"Only," said Nora, as she followed Edith, "it would

299

be better if we settled in England, don't you think so?
And you'll come with us, of course. I should hate to
leave you here by yourself. It will be rather jolly to
live in England, after all."

Immediately Edith grew cold to have it brought back
to her that Nora had the power to allow her Barry's
company or not, as she chose. She could not even be
grateful for the girl's easy consideration for her
("patronage" was the word she used to herself), and it
really annoyed her to find Nora already quite confident
again.

"I wonder what that letter was about," she said,
deliberately stabbing her back to recollection.

3

They did not see Barry until dinner-time that
evening.   He came in, looking paler than usual, and
said:

"I have to go away. I got a letter this morning,
Edith—did Nora tell you?"

Edith nodded.

"Here it is. Do you mind if I show it to Edith
before I explain it to you, Nora? It is something Edith
knows even more about than I do, and you don't know
about at all."

He gave it to Edith.

"She told me this afternoon," said Nora.

"What?"

"She judged from the postmark on the envelope that
it must come from your mother's people."

"Then you know. Well, read the letter if you like."

He spoke in tones whose flatness sounded like
indifference.

Edith handed the letter without comment, to Nora.

They all sat very silent while Nora, with a flushed face, deciphered the elaborate flourishes.

"I see," she said in a hard voice when she had finished. "And who is this Christina Kleinhans?"

"I don't know her," said Barry. "Presumably a relation of my mother's. A sister or a sister-in-law."

"I can't remember any Christina," said Etdih. "But there were a good many Kleinhanses—eight or ten. And, as you say, it may be a wife of one of the sons. When are you going?"

"To-morrow."

They all sat down to dinner without saying any more about the letter until, as they were having coffee, Barry remarked in the same flat voice:

"She must be dying, I suppose. She never sent for me before."

"We did not even know whether she was still alive," commented Edith. "I wonder——"

She had been going on to some speculation about Elmira's life during the twenty-eight years that had passed since she had left Adam Lindsell.

Nora, her hostility aroused once more by her reading of the uneducated, pious letter, said good night shortly, and, without looking at Barry's suffering face, went to her room.

"Aren't you going to her?" said Edith.

"Would she want me?" answered Barry. "And what is there I can say to her?"

For the first time that evening there was a note of passion in his voice.

CHAPTER XI

I

He left next morning after a farewell to Nora that was the merest perfunctory gesture. He felt she hated him, and he dared not appeal to her. While he still stood on the verandah with his luggage, waiting for the taxi that was to take him to the station, she left him and walked back into the house. He kept his eyes fixed on the road and did not turn to look after her. Edith came out and joined him. "Would you like me to see you off?" she asked.

"Thank you," he said. "But. . . . No, please don't!"

Edith felt towards him again as at that first time when he had come running to her for protection.

"Barry," she whispered, "I have not been a good sister to you."

He pressed her hand in denial.

"But perhaps, one day—if you should ever need me——"

Long after the taxi had turned the corner Edith's tear-dimmed, unseeing eyes were still staring in the direction of its going.

Barry sent a telegram from the station: "Leaving this morning. Meet me."

He was travelling the greater part of the journey by train, but the last stage of it would still, as when Mr. Lindsell had first gone to settle there over half a century ago, be made by Cape cart. It was not likely

302

that any of the Kleinhanses had risen, as had most
prosperous farmers, to a motor car. It was not likely
that the Kleinhanses had risen at all. They never did,
he reflected bitterly, these half-castes.

Barry tried to remember the Kleinhanses he had
known. The most distinct in his mind was Lena, his
mother's mother, who had wanted to take him to her
when his father had died. He wondered if she were
still alive. Then there was Kleinhans, his grandfather,
who returned to him dimly as a big, dark, burly shape,
standing in that little group which represented the
coloured side of his family at the ceremonial of his
father's death-bed, and who had never, so he understood, had any other name but Kleinhans on account
of the accidental character of his birth. . . . Kleinhans
he signed himself simply. . . . Like an English peer.
Barry smiled ironically.

And there had also been present, he recalled vaguely,
that old woman, Deborah, the mother of Kleinhans;
she, of course, must be long since dead. Why, she was
of the very first generation of mixed blood in the
family! Edith had told him about her. She was the
daughter of that mad missionary, the Rev. Andrew
Flood, who had married a Hottentot woman nearly a
hundred years ago. And that was all any one knew
to-day of the Rev. Andrew Flood. . . .

Well, those were the three whom he remembered
since they had come to claim him at his father's death;
but he knew that his mother had had a number of
brothers and sisters—one, Edith said, had been sent
to gaol for shooting in sport an Indian hawker—and
these brothers and sisters were, with their wives and
husbands and children, by this time, probably the
only relations, on his mother's side, he had left. The

Christina Kleinhans who had written the letter was, no doubt, one of them. . . .

As the train traversed the empty vastness of the land, the thoughts of Barry ran ceaselessly backwards and forwards from the past to the future. His ancestor, the Rev. Andrew Flood, had thrown away his white heritage, and for a hundred years at least one branch of his descendants had struggled to reach it again. They had ever diluted the blackness of their blood with whiteness until it was more white than black, until the whiteness was just barely tinted with black, until it was almost indistinguishably white, until there had resulted, in short, himself.

And he, again, had followed the family tradition and had married upwards, and his child. . . . A spasm of terror passed over Barry Lindsell's face. His child. Nora's child. The vagaries of heredity. Who knew but that he, Barry, had made poor innocent Nora the vehicle of the vengeance of the Lord for the sins of the fathers? Who knew but that his child might be the sacrifice. His mind stood still for a moment, then began feverishly grinding out thoughts again. And yet it did not happen. And yet it might happen. And yet. . . . Ah, what was God going to do with them all?

2

He remembered his mother suddenly whom he was travelling over six hundred miles to see. She had left his father, so Edith had told him, when he himself was only about three years old. She had taken the money that had been settled on her at marriage, and she had run off with a young commercial traveller, and that was the last any of the Lindsells had ever heard of her.

And his father had had a stroke, and, four years later, had died. Barry recalled him very clearly, and, even now, with affection.

But he was able to understand these days how it was possible that his mother might not have been able to bear this marriage with a man forty-six years older than she was. . . . He tried to think of her in terms of Nora. The same age as Nora she must have been when she ran away, and pretty too, as even Edith, in her grudging but honest way, was compelled to admit, very pretty.

He wondered what she looked like now, how she had passed all these years, what sickness it was that this Christina Kleinhans had so vaguely described in her letter. But he could not think of her as if she were really his mother. He was going to see her because he felt it to be his duty, but it was a duty he hated. It appalled him to realize that he, the Rev. Barry Lindsell a white man to all the world, was on his way now to identify himself filially with this coloured woman who had returned to die in the bosom of her coloured family—his coloured family!

3

He got off at the railway siding, and the train moved on again. He had been the only passenger to alight, and, except for a solitary official, there was only one other person in sight—a tall, thin, coloured boy of about twenty, in a rather dirty, open shirt, a pair of corduroys, and on his feet, without any socks, the rough shoes that are called veld-schoenen. He came directly to Barry.

"I am Gert Kleinhans," he said, "the son of your mother's second brother, Adonis Kleinhans. Are you Mr. Lindsell?

He held out his hand and Barry took it. It struck Barry that it was the first time he had ever shaken hands with an obviously coloured person (it would have been difficult, indeed, to find many South Africans, except clergymen, who would do such a thing) . . . and this coloured person was his cousin!

"I have brought the cart for you," said Gert Klein-hans.

He spoke English with a strong kitchen-Dutch accent, and with, now and then, a word of the Dutch, if he could not think of the appropriate English expression—for Dutch was the home language; and there was an air of gay impudence about his quite handsome face. He had straight black hair, fine dark eyes, regular features and magnificent teeth, but he looked, somehow, a shifty customer. He treated his white relative who wore the cloth without any particular deference.

He indicated an old Cape cart standing under a *waacht-een-bietje* tree. On either side of the shaft drooped a dejected looking brown horse. A little Kaffir boy was holding the reins. A group of other Kaffir children were standing near by, among them one child whose lighter skin and rusty-coloured, fuzzy hair proclaimed that a white man had passed that way. As soon as they saw Barry they ran towards him shrilling: "Penny, Baas. Penny. . . . Bread, Baas. . . . Bread. . . . Penny. . . ." He put his hand into his pocket. All along the railway line little naked Kaffir children had appeared, as it seemed, from nowhere, running alongside the train and begging passionately for bread and pennies. They had need, very obviously, of both; but, in fact, their begging was a recently developed form of sport.

They crowded around him now as they noted the favourable movement of his hand. "Me, Baas," they yelled. "I asked first, Baas. . . . No, me, Baas. Me, Baas. Penny, Baas. . . ."

He left them scrambling for the pennies, and climbed on the cart with Gert, who was carrying his suit-case.

"Have we far to go?" he said to Gert.

"About twenty miles. It will take us three hours or three and a half. We don't outspan."

Barry wanted to ask Gert how Elmira was, but he could not bring himself to speak of her to this half-caste boy as "mother". Instead he said:

"And who is there at home now?"

"All of us," answered Gert.

"Who?"

"Me and my brother and sister and father and mother and Kleinhans and old Deborah and——"

Barry stopped him.

"What? Old Deborah? Is old Deborah alive still?"

Gert laughed. "Yes. But she is nearly finished now."

"Why, she must be nearly a hundred?"

"My grandfather, Kleinhans, says she is ninety-six or ninety-seven. He is nearly eighty years old himself."

"And how is he?"

"He is still strong. He even helps a little on the farm. It was when grandma died——"

"Lena," said Barry, and remembered that she was his grandmother as well as this coloured boy's.

"Yes, her name was Lena. It was when she died that we went to live there to look after the old people. That was ten years ago."

"And who is Christina?" asked Barry.

"My mother."

"She wrote to me."

"Yes. She comes from Kimberley. She is learned. My father never went to school because when he was young there was no school here except for Kaffirs, and so he isn't learned, and she writes the letters."

They had spoken about everything except Elmira, and her son could not bridge his pride to say the word "mother". He hoped the boy might mention her, but he, having seen a springbok in the distance, had begun to talk about game-shooting now.

Barry tried to bring him back to personal topics. "And how are they all at home?" he asked.

Gert looked at him puzzled.

"Didn't I say?"

Barry flushed.

"You told me only about Deborah and Kleinhans and Christina, but not about—any one else."

"Your mother, you mean," said Gert directly.

Barry nodded.

"She is sick," said Gert. "We do not think," he continued with simple bluntness, "that she will live."

They drove along silently for some time. Then Barry said: "When did she come?"

"Last week."

"And—you don't know?—how things have been going with her?"

"Not too good," said Gert. "No. Not good at all. No. Very bad, I can say." He flicked his whip at the horses. "She walked some of the way from the train to our place."

"She had no money?" said her son.

Gert shook his head.

"And you did not know she was coming?"

"No. Wednesday, a week ago, in the evening we see an old woman——"

"An old woman?"

"An old woman—yes, she looks very old—before our gate. She can hardly stand. We all go out to look. We don't know who it is. 'Who are you?' grandpa says to her. And pa looks at her, too, and wonders who can it be. 'I am Elmira,' she says. And grandpa and pa look again. And grandpa says 'My ears are not very good any more, but it seems to me I know the voice. The face I cannot say I know.' And he begins to cry. And then we bring her in, and we see it really is Elmira, and we put her in the bed. And we write to you. And that is the whole thing."

Barry's voice was unsteady as he spoke again.

"And what is her illness?"

"It is not certain."

"Did you not call a doctor?"

"Yes. He thought it is something growing inside her, a cancer, he thought, and he wanted to cut it out. But she wouldn't. She said no, let her better die. And the doctor was not sure either."

Miles passed and they did not speak.

Then Barry said: "Did she ask about me?"

And Gert answered: "I can't say. It was not talked of in the family that she asked about you."

Presently Gert took out a cigarette, lit it, and began to tell Barry about the affairs of the Kleinhans family.

"They say," he began, "that at one time my grandpa Kleinhans was a rich man. He was rich even in the old Kokstad days; but he was most rich, he always tells us, when he was living on the farm of your father, and had many sheep and cattle and horses there. But that was before Mr. Lindsell married Aunt Elmira. Afterwards the troubles began to happen. Your father sent Kleinhans away, and he trekked to Doornkraal where we still are, and that land was not so good for beasts, there were many sicknesses there. . . . Then came the rinderpest——"

"In ninety-six."

"Yes, in ninety-six."

"That was just before my father died and I went to Cape Town."

"I hear so. He talks always of those days, my grandpa Kleinhans. . . . Well, he says it was the rinderpest that took nearly all his cattle, and the Boer War that finished him altogether."

"How?"

"It was told of him that he was keeping Boers in his house. He says it was not true; but still the house was burnt down, and everything he had was taken away from him."

"And he never found his feet again?"

Gert looked puzzled by the expression.

"I mean, he stayed poor after that?"

"Yes. Since then he is poor."

"And now?" asked Barry.

"Now my father works on the farm and the old man helps a little, but it is only a small living for all of us."

"And what do you do yourself?"

"I help, too. But I would like to go to a town and learn to drive a motor car. If I had a little money to make a start that is what I would like to do. It is no life here for a young person."

The same plaint throughout the world, thought

Barry. How had the friends of his adolescence craved for "life"!

Gert took out another cigarette.

"I hear," he said slowly, and paused to light his cigarette, "I hear you are very rich."

And he sighed with envious significance.

CHAPTER XII

I

IT was dusk when they arrived at a small house of corrugated iron, surrounded by a tumbled-down wall of loose stones. A few hundred yards away from the house there was another loose-stone wall in the shape of a rough circle. That was the cattle kraal, said Gert. And the smaller one next to it was the sheep kraal. Even now, he explained, they must be milking the cows.

About half a mile away there were a few Kaffir huts; black they looked against the setting sun, and like big hives of wasps. These huts were, Barry knew, made of bits of sacking and tin over a foundation of mud and reeds—windowless and airless, and with a small opening, through which nothing larger than a dog could enter without crouching.

Here a whole family would live together, eat and sleep and suffer sickness together, and, however hot it was, they would fasten down the flap of the entrance and inhale and exhale as one the poisonous air. In winter they would make a fire of sticks and cow-dung in a tin, and they would cook their mealie meal on it, chatter loudly with each other through the blinding, stifling smoke, and go to bed with their heads under their skins or blankets. . . . And sometimes, if they forgot to remove the fire or extinguish it, they would be found dead in their huts in the morning.

They lived without happiness, without hope, and

without question, working for the farmers, or going to Kimberley or Johannesburg to the mines. In other parts of South Africa, among the Zulus, the Pondos, the Swazis, the Damaras, and other such tribes, the people were big, and black and vigorous—they had their joys and chances; but here, round about Griqualand West, they were nothing but an untidiness on God's earth—a mixture of degenerate brown peoples, rotten with sickness, an affront against Nature.

And in these people, Barry thought suddenly, there was something of that blood which was also in him.

"They are all waiting for us on the verandah," said Gert, as he stopped the horses.

2

And, as he spoke, there detached themselves from the shadows of the narrow verandah that completes even the meanest South African home, a group of people, who came slowly towards the cart, preceded in a rush by two excited, barking, leaping mongrels. Barry knew well enough who these people were: Old Kleinhans, Adonis and his wife and their other two children, the sister and brother of Gert.

They met the visitors at the broken wooden gate, and old Kleinhans, his hand not so steady these days, but still maintaining its habit of fingering his beard, whitened now from the tawny pride of his youth, old Kleinhans said with formality, but in the hushed voice that is the concomitant of deafness: "Mijnheer is welcome." He waited for Barry to offer a hand before advancing his own, and inclined his head one-sidedly towards him to hear his speaking.

And now, the ceremony of hand-shaking between
U

Barry and his brown relations having been established as a convention, they all came forward, one after the other, with hands extended, and gave him greeting.

But they none of them, the younger ones, as Kleinhans had done, called Barry "Mijnheer". They were of a newer and less respectful school.

Christina, as the learned member of the family, was the most prominent of them all, and she ushered him volubly forward into the sitting-room. She was a buxom Cape woman of the class Barry knew well in Cape Town, who spoke Dutch in private and English in public, and she had been in service in Kimberley when Adonis, at that time working there as a bricklayer, had married her. As she walked beside Barry, she whispered in his ear, more for the purpose of establishing a special intimacy between them than for any other reason, what Barry could not have avoided immediately noticing for himself, that "the old gintleman was a little deaf".

She forced Barry into one of her rickety chairs and offered him coffee.

"But—my mother?" said Barry, bringing himself at last to the painful word.

Christina shook her head. "Bad," she said.

Barry made to rise.

"No, no." Christina stopped him. "Have the coffee first. It is ready. You will feel better when you have had the coffee. You look finished now. It is far from Cape Town to come here."

She bustled off into the kitchen, the girl, Susie, at a gesture, accompanying her to help with the preparations, and left the others to entertain Barry in the sitting-room with its unsteady odds and ends of furniture, its torn lace curtains, its dozens of chipped and damaged ornaments, its characteristic stuffy smell.

But with her going an awkwardness fell on the room. The only other bold and loquacious member of the family was Gert, and he was occupied in outspanning the horses. All Barry's remaining hosts could do was to sit gazing at him in embarrassed silence—at the lightness of his skin, at his clerical clothes. . . .

Yet, finally, old Kleinhans made a remark.

"It is strange how white you are," he said.

The silence that followed gave his words the full flavour of their tactlessness. And then Adonis began desperately to talk about the drought.

"Yes, yes," he said. "The poor beasts. There is no water for them. If we only had a good dam it would not be so bad. Yes, yes. If we only had the money to build a good dam."

He had not meant to speak of money to Barry so soon, but there it was. His embarrassment had led him to offload the thing uppermost in his mind.

They all looked anxiously towards the kitchen door, and saw with relief that Christina and her daughter were at last bringing the coffee—the coffee, and the cakes, and the watermelon preserve—the konfijt.

The coffee was good and put a little heart into Barry.

"Now," said Christina, "if you are ready——" and she motioned with her head towards the door opposite the other door through which she had gone to the kitchen.

Barry followed her as if he were not himself at all.

3

He entered a room, dim in the light of one candle—a small and hot room, the window closed upon its smell of sickness. There were two beds in the room, both

315

occupied. "That is old Deborah," whispered Christina, but led him to the other bed.

A long, thin woman was lying on it, covered with a counterpane made of odd rags, frayed, faded with washing, her face turned in his direction. The single candle was standing on an upturned box beside the bed, and over the box was spread a newspaper, its edge snipped in an elaborate design. The light of the candle fell on her face and blackened the hollows of it. The rough grey hair lay in a plait on each side of her face. Her large sunken eyes looked at him with a heavy steadiness, as if she were too exhausted to move them. Her mouth was a little open, her nose sharply outlined by the candle-light, her skin a greenish-yellow. She said no word to him, nor did the expression of her face alter. He came to her side and could not think that this was one who concerned him. He brushed his lips across her forehead, horror in his heart. He stood there looking at her, trying to smile. Her eyes—he could see now they were a yellowish-brown—travelled slowly upwards to his face.

"You are not like your father any more," she whispered.

Christina brought him a chair, and he sat down on it while she took up her station at the foot of the bed.

"How are you feeling?" he said to his mother.

She closed her eyes in a gesture of pain.

He found one of her thin hands and held it between his. He did not know what to say. His mind jumped about from one thing to another, but they were none of them things he could speak of. He saw himself at Oxford—a large, happy life—he could not believe it was he who had been there and had come back to sit here. He thought of Nora—they had loved under Eng-

316

lish trees—Nora, gold, and roses, and laughter . . . and this was his mother. He remembered God and tried to pray.

"Why did you never," he said at last, "let me know where you were?"

A spasm of a smile changed for a moment the contour of her lips.

"I was in Cape Town most of the time," she answered, her voice, with an effort, a little louder. And now he could hear that its accents were not those of the other people in this house, and trace in it her gentler upbringing.

"I saw Edith there once or twice," she added. "But she did not know me."

"You should have come to me," said Barry.

She moved her head in negation. It was useless to protest much. They both knew it was better that she had not come to him.

She was silent for a little while, and then she asked him to tell her about his life. And he told her the bare facts: how Edith had taken him with her, and how they had lived together——

"Was she good to you?" Elmira interrupted.

"Very good."

"But she hated me."

"Perhaps you didn't understand one another."

He spoke to her about his life at Oxford.

"And the war?" she asked.

"Yes," he said shortly, and remembered how he had failed there.

"I am married," he finished.

He thought she shook her head slightly.

After a time she whispered, her voice faint again: "Have you children?"

"Not yet," said Barry, and could not bring himself to mention the one that was coming.

"It is better for people like us not to be born," said Elmira, and closed her eyes that he might know her strength could bear no more.

The figure in the other bed had not moved at all.

"Perhaps she is sleeping, or perhaps not," said Christina, as she accompanied him out of the room. "We never know now. She lies like that."

4

They made him a bed in the sitting-room, and how he fell asleep there he did not know, but when he awoke the world was full of sunshine. It had seemed to him the night before as if the sun were dead for ever.

There was a knock at the door, and Christina, brown and buxom, brought him a big cup of her good coffee.

"Are you rested?" she asked.

"Quite, thank you," he said. "I was very tired last night."

She sighed her sympathy. "We are in God's hands," she said, repeating the consolation of her letter.

Then she brightened again. "And what will you have for breakfast? There is some mincemeat."

"Anything will do, thank you," he told her. "At home I have just a soft-boiled egg."

"Only an egg?"

"Please. . . . About washing. . . ." he added.

"I can bring you some water in here. Or, if you like——" she hesitated.

He encouraged her with a smile.

"The house is small," she said. "But there is a bath we use in the forage room. If you wouldn't mind——"

"That will be admirable," he said, and began to drink his coffee.

5

When he had dressed he took a short walk about the farm. It was an arid place; many of its trees, in times of money-difficulty, had been cut down and taken by ox-waggon to Kimberley for firewood. But the air was so fine and clear that he was not surprised it had kept Deborah alive to nearly the age of a hundred. There were bushes of various kinds here and there, and even in the sand little meagre flowers were growing. But the effect was not one of greenness. The scanty grass lay yellow and withered with drought. He wondered what the cattle found to eat at all.

After breakfast, when the men had gone off to their work, Christina gave herself a little leisure to entertain her guest, and told him something of the history of the Kleinhans family. "Except one," she said, "who is just living with a Griqua woman, we are all married. Some have married our own kind, and a few have married white and keep themselves proud with us. There is Hans who went to gaol for shooting an Indian. When he came out he started diamond digging on the River Diggings, and he found a big diamond, and married the daughter of a white *bijwoner*. And they bought a piano and made as if they were too good for us. Hans, mind you. Now I hear they are poor again, but we never see them."

"Adonis was telling me," said Barry, "that you have a struggle here on the farm."

"Yes," sighed Christina. "It is the way of life. The good ones have the worst time. Adonis and I and the children came to live here for the sake of the old people, and from that day to this it has not gone well with us. The farm does not pay; it is hard for me to look after my father-in-law and his old mother; the children grumble because on the land there are no chances for them, and no pleasures. Often we have thought of selling the place and going to a town. But first there is the trouble with the old ones. What could we do with them in a town? And then, since the war, times are bad, and people do not want to buy farms. . . . Well, Adonis and I are no longer young; we must make the best of it. If we only had a little money" (she looked delicately away from her rich relative, and, through the window, at the veld) "we could improve the place, and then it would not be so bad; but the children, I know, will not stand it much longer."

There was a little silence while Christina gave Barry time duly to appreciate her words.

"The worst is old Deborah," she said finally.

"Yes. She must be a great trial to you," Barry endorsed. "Is she . . . has she the use of all her senses still? I mean, can she see and hear, and so forth?"

Christina made a long-drawn-out "no" while she shook her head. "Old Deborah isn't a person any more. But till two or three years ago she was still all right. It was really wonderful how she kept herself. She could walk about with a stick, and she could see to read the Bible a little (Deborah, perhaps you have heard, is a learned woman—she was a teacher, yes, at Kadesh, eighty years ago); only her hearing was not too good. . . . But lately she just lies there, and sometimes we hardly know is she awake, is she sleeping, is she dead. Up to this summer we used to bring her out on the verandah every day to get the sun. But now

she cries if we move her. So we leave her there in
the room. . . . No. It is not too nice with old
Deborah."

"It must make it worse for you since my—mother
came," said Barry in the hesitating voice in which he
always spoke of Elmira. "I appreciate your goodness
to her."

"Yes," said Christina, with effective simplicity,
"We have been thinking it would please you."

"When shall I be able to see her?"

"Susie is doing the room now. As soon as she is
finished. Wait, let me go and see."

6

She came back, nodding her head.

"Yes, go in," she said.

This time he saw Deborah more distinctly. The
sunlight coming through the blue-gum tree beside the
window was dancing about on her old face and mock-
ing it. The brown, wrinkled flesh was shrunken back
upon the sharp Hottentot cheek-bones. There were still
a few stumps of teeth in the high mouth, and some
white fuzzy hairs on the brown head. Her eyes were
like little liquid slips between her half-closed lids—the
colour of them could not be identified, they were only
a narrow shine. Barry did not know whether she
saw him or not, and he did not address her, but went
directly to his mother, and again, as the night before,
put his lips to her forehead.

"Had you a little sleep?" he asked.

"Perhaps—I don't know," she said. "My head goes
round, and I can hardly tell if I am sleeping or dreaming. But I feel a little better to-day."

He sat down beside her, and could not think of

anything to say to her.   Presently she smiled a little.

"If you knew my life, perhaps you would not be here."

"I am your son, and a minister of God," he said.

"When I left your father I went with another man."

"I know that."

"When he spent my money and left me, I went with another."

Barry made no motion.

"Then he also left me.   But he was the last. . . ." She stopped for a moment. "The child I had with the first one," she added presently, "died. But the second man's child is alive still. The man was fair, and the child is lighter than you even. He has red hair. He must be twenty-three now."

"Where is he?" asked Barry, and it ran like a shock through his heart that somewhere in the world he had a brother.

"I don't know," said Elmira. "He was ashamed of me because he was so fair, and by that time I was not young and fresh-looking any more, and people could tell about me. He went away when he was eighteen, and I have not heard from him since. I was a good mother to him, and a bad mother to you; I worked hard for him, and I ran away from you; but he has forgotten me, and you are here."

He felt a sudden sense of holiness, as if, by sacrifice, he might expiate the sins of his life: his weakness before danger, and his weakness before love. A kind of peace he had never known fell on him.

"It will soon be over now," said Elmira, and stared away from him.

Then, from the other side of the room, there fell an

odd, cracked noise on the silence. Deborah was making it.

she sang.

"She used to sing that to all the babies," said Elmira. "It belongs to the time when she was a girl in Canaan."

CHAPTER XIII

I

OLD Deborah was singing the same song again when, five days later, Elmira died. When they were all gathered together there in her little room of corrugated iron—the four representatives of the four generations that had sprung from the Rev. Andrew Flood's sacrifice to God: Deborah, and Kleinhans, and Elmira, and Barry. And, as he stood looking at the brown faces around him, through the ceremony of his prayer for the dead, Barry made a vow. . . .

They buried Elmira in the little farm graveyard, and Barry said good-bye to his coloured relations, and Gert drove him back to the station:

"We thought you might help us a little with money," he said to Barry. "But we did not expect so much as you have done. And you have not kept yourself proud with us either."

2

Barry was not looking out of the window when Edith and Nora came to welcome him at the station; and, as Nora ran up to him with all her affectionateness (her doubts and fears apparently quite forgotten again) he did not meet her inviting lips. He took her hand, and turned his eyes away.

He had said in his telegram: "Mother died to-day. Returning immediately," and Nora, associating his reticence now with the tradition of filial grief, pressed his fingers, and walked beside him in decorous silence to the waiting taxi. Edith, understanding him better, was more perturbed.

He told them little on the way home, and, even when he arrived there, it was as if he could not speak.

But after dinner, in the evening, Nora said:

"Have you been thinking at all about settling in England, Barry? Edith and I were talking it over while you were away, and she believes, too——"

"Yes," said Barry.

Nora found herself puzzled by the tone of his voice.

"And what have you decided?" she asked.

"The child would be happier if it never saw Africa."

Nora leaned in happy satisfaction against his shoulder.

"I thought you would see it that way in the end," she murmured contentedly. "When can we go?"

Barry did not answer her at once. Then he said:

"There are some things I have to explain to you."

She waited for him to speak again. He moved a little from her. "Whatever I have is yours," he said. "But I am not going with you, Nora."

She sat erect, staring at him.

"What do you mean? Are you taking that silly difference we had over that letter seriously?"

He almost smiled.

"Poor Nora. How impossible it is for you to understand. If you could harm me as I have harmed you, I should welcome it. It would balance things a little."

"You mean . . . . Oh, that again . . . . But if we went to England we'd never think of it. It's being in Africa makes one morbid and hysterical."

"It's being in Africa makes one realize the truth. . . . Nora, I have just come back from where I found

325

myself at my beginnings. There at Doornkraal, I saw my whole story. The natives in their huts. My great-grandmother, old Deborah. Her son, Kleinhans. My mother. Myself. I saw what had come down to me, and what I was handing on to others. . . . Don't stop me, Nora. Let me tell you everything. . . . And, standing there among my brown people, I made a vow." His voice was rising. He was trembling as he spoke.

Nora sprang up from her seat.

"I won't hear it," she interrupted him.

"I made a vow," he repeated.

"Oh, you are mad, Barry!" she cried.

"Edith used to call my ancestor, the Rev. Andrew Flood, the mad missionary," said Barry, calmer now. "Perhaps I owe him other things besides my black blood."

He seemed to be sending his mind back. Nora looked at him, frightened.

"This is my vow," he said at last. "For my sin in begetting him, I am not to see my child. And, for the sorrow I share with them, I am to go among my brown people to help them. . . ."

"I thought," he added after a moment, "of settling down in those very parts around Canaan where the Rev. Andrew Flood had his mission. In no other place, I hear, are things so bad."

He stood up. She had never seen strength in his face before.

"It seems to me right that I should go there," he said.